PENGUIN CANADA

VINYL CAFE DIARIES

STUART MCLEAN writes and hosts the popular CBC Radio show *The Vinyl Cafe*. He is the author of many bestselling books, including five collections of Vinyl Cafe stories. Stuart has won awards from the Canadian Authors Association for both fiction and non-fiction, and is a three-time winner of the Stephen Leacock Award for Humour. He has sold over one million books in Canada, and is also published in the United States and the United Kingdom.

Also by Stuart McLean

The Morningside World of Stuart McLean

Welcome Home: Travels in Smalltown Canada

Stories from the Vinyl Cafe

Home from the Vinyl Cafe

Vinyl Cafe Unplugged

Dave Cooks the Turkey

Secrets from the Vinyl Cafe

STUART McLEAN

Vinyl Cafe Diaries

PENGUIN
CANADA

PENGUIN CANADA

Published by the Penguin Group

Penguin Group (Canada), 90 Eglinton Avenue East, Suite 700, Toronto, Ontario, Canada M4P 2Y3
(a division of Pearson Canada Inc.)

Penguin Group (USA) Inc., 375 Hudson Street, New York, New York 10014, U.S.A.
Penguin Books Ltd, 80 Strand, London WC2R 0RL, England
Penguin Ireland, 25 St Stephen's Green, Dublin 2, Ireland (a division of Penguin Books Ltd)
Penguin Group (Australia), 250 Camberwell Road, Camberwell, Victoria 3124, Australia
(a division of Pearson Australia Group Pty Ltd)
Penguin Books India Pvt Ltd, 11 Community Centre, Panchsheel Park, New Delhi – 110 017, India
Penguin Group (NZ), 67 Apollo Drive, Rosedale, North Shore 0632, Auckland, New Zealand
(a division of Pearson New Zealand Ltd)
Penguin Books (South Africa) (Pty) Ltd, 24 Sturdee Avenue, Rosebank, Johannesburg 2196,
South Africa

Penguin Books Ltd, Registered Offices: 80 Strand, London WC2R 0RL, England

First published in a Viking Canada hardcover by Penguin Group (Canada),
a division of Pearson Canada Inc., 2003
Published in Penguin Canada paperback by Penguin Group (Canada),
a division of Pearson Canada Inc., 2004
Published in this edition, 2007

2 3 4 5 6 7 8 9 10 (OPM)

Manufactured in the U.S.A.

Library and Archives Canada Cataloguing in Publication data available upon request

ISBN-13: 978-0-14-305510-5
ISBN-10: 0-14-305510-0

This one is for Dave and Morley

The job of the artist is always to deepen the mystery.

FRANCIS BACON, 1909–92

CONTENTS

Sam

Dave

Dave's Thoughts

It is Thursday afternoon—3:30. There is a courier scheduled to arrive in half an hour. If we are going to be precise, in twenty-nine minutes. They phoned me an hour ago and told me the book is at the printer and they have *to have my contribution this afternoon. Or else. Actually, they didn't use the words "or else," but they might as well have said "or else."*

I am supposed to be describing how I feel about being in this book. Well, that is a complicated question. Good, of course. I have always enjoyed Stuart's work. But you can understand that things have changed since he began writing these stories ten years ago, and to give a thoughtful answer requires some thought, and I don't understand what the panic is. The book isn't coming out for at least another four months.

When I was on the road with bands, there were lots of times when I used to get things like programs or posters printed overnight, or even at the very last minute. Lots of times. I remember once when I was the front man for a band called Mace, I got into town—Skokie, I think, or maybe Gary, Indiana. Somewhere in the Midwest at any rate. But not Wisconsin. I'm sure of that. Anyhow, when I got to town, I found out that the guy handling the advertising had come down with chicken pox but was too embarrassed to tell anyone, so there were no posters for the band anywhere. I phoned the first print shop in the Yellow Pages—AAA Quikky Print—and had a thousand handbills in the back of the car two hours later (and okay, the band's name appeared as "Mice" but you have to expect a few typos with that kind of turnaround).

Well, there are plenty of little print shops like AAA Quikky Print all over the place (not only in the Midwest) just aching for business, and you would think that a publisher like Penguin would take advantage of this kind of opportunity to come up with a more reasonable schedule.

I understand that getting programs printed is one thing and a book is something else—well, so is putting down exactly what you think about something as complicated as having your life written about in a book that the entire country can read. It takes some thought. Actually, it takes more than thought. It requires talking to others. Because I don't know how it is for you, but I have found that often other people know more about what you think and feel than you do yourself. And I have been meaning to talk to some people about this for a few weeks now, but here I am with half an hour left—nineteen minutes, actually—and what am I supposed to do with that?

I know what you're thinking. You're thinking, If he has known this for a few weeks (well, okay, a few months), why is he sitting there, at a typewriter of all things, at the back of his record store at the last minute? *Well, the thing is, it's not my fault.*

I tried to get going last week. I thought, Okay, if I am going to do this I should do it right. *So at lunchtime I went to Lawlor's to get a legal pad, which I seem to remember some author saying is what he liked to write on. I know I didn't need a legal pad, but I was trying to treat this thing seriously, and I thought I should start off right, like whoever that author was who always wrote on a legal pad—who might, come to think of it, have been Richard Nixon, but I hope not.*

The thing is that I don't have a chance to do something like this every day and I was trying to get into the spirit, and I thought the best way to do that would be to write the first draft by hand. Well, then

I got back to the store and there were no pens. Please understand me, I am not trying to make excuses. There were pencils, and I could easily have got going with a pencil. I'm just saying that I thought I should go and get a really nice pen.

So the next day at lunch I found a pen at the stationery store down by the pizza place, and I loved the pen. It had a padded part and wrote almost like a fountain pen, very smooth, and I felt with a pen like this I could write anything—especially with all those long yellow pages beckoning me. And this was a week ago, so I didn't exactly wait until the last moment, which I know is what you are thinking. And I don't blame you, because it might seem that way.

Then, on the way back to the store, I realized that I had spent my last few dollars on that pen, so I went to the bank. And like always when you are in a rush, the machine ate my card. I was going to go into the bank to get a teller to help, but then I thought, what if someone comes in to use the machine while I'm inside the bank and the machine decides to spit out my card and give it to a stranger? Or worse yet, what if that stranger tries to get money out of the machine and it takes the withdrawal out of my account because my card is still in there? That's when I stuck my new pen up the slot to try to get the card out. Of course, then there was the whole thing with the security guard.

The good news is that they are not going to be charging me, but they certainly weren't interested in refunding the cost of the pen. And to be perfectly candid, I was feeling a little discouraged at that point so I left the essay for the weekend.

And then on Monday after lunch I was trying to get back to the store in a hurry, thinking I could work on the introduction in the afternoon, and I got this cramp in my left foot. Not exactly a cramp. It was one of those funny pains that shoot up the side of your foot, from the tip of your toes to the heel. Does anyone else get those? Have you any idea what causes them? And I was thinking maybe I should go for an X-ray or something, which in the end I didn't have to do. Because I was going by Alex's place—Alex is the veterinarian who opened up a few doors along from Kenny Wong's—and I went in and asked him about my foot and he agreed to put some ultrasound on it and said as far as he could tell everything looked fine. Alex is a great vet. I don't think my dog, Arthur, trusts him entirely, but I can highly recommend him. After I left Alex's I went back to the store and iced my foot like he suggested, which worked out but didn't leave a lot of time for writing.

Speaking of which, I only have about ten minutes left, and some guy has just walked into the store with a slice of pizza, and now all I can think of is pizza. I know when I finish this I could go for a slice myself, but what I really feel like is thin-crust pizza, and ever since that place from Quebec closed up there are no real thin-crust places around. I mean paper thin, the way that place used to make them, and I never understood why they didn't make a go of it here. I mean, when you go to Montreal the places like that are booming. And those pizzas are so good, especially with anchovies, olives and garlic. Does anyone know where you can get a slice like that? Anyhow, I'll probably end up settling for a sub.

The point of this all being that I didn't exactly leave it to the last moment, and I don't think it is fair that I have to wrap it up right now just because some courier guy says he can't wait any longer. He has been pacing around for the last few minutes making it almost impossible to concentrate, and now he has his hand on the page and says he is going to tear it out of the typewriter if I don't stop. Which is outrageous, if you ask me.

They said this was my opportunity to say a few words about how I feel about having my life on display (I don't mind—not many people have made the connection, and so much about so many of the stories seems to change that by the time it gets on the radio it all feels like it happened to someone else); and whether Stuart McLean is as nice as he seems on the radio (sometimes yes, sometimes no); and whether the stories are true (see above); and where is the record store and why can't people find it? (they aren't looking hard enough). And I realize that it is also my chance to tell you . . . Oh, geez . . . the guy has his hands on the paper. I guess that's all.

Walking Man

DAVE BEGAN SMOKING CIGARETTES when he was twelve years old. So, by the winter he turned twenty-six, he'd had fourteen years' experience and he was pretty darn good at it. That was the winter he quit smoking—for the first time. Dave was living in Edmonton then, sharing a place with a bunch of musicians while he waited for the summer rock tours to begin.

You need some sort of significant moment if you are going to do something as momentous as giving up the weed. After Dave sailed through both New Year's Eve and his birthday in a cloud of smoke, he began to get twitchy, because there weren't that many days of consequence left between where he was and where the summer began. And he knew he didn't have a hope of quitting smoking while he was on the road.

The best he could come up with was Groundhog Day. He stayed up most of the night before, reading Dostoyevsky's *The Idiot* and smoking his brains out.

One of Dave's flatmates that winter was a sax player from Prague who claimed to be a friend of Václav Havel's. The sax player had fled to Canada after being beaten and arrested when his band played at one of the now famous Second Culture Music Festivals in Soviet-controlled Czechoslovakia. The sax player smoked nasty little cigarettes from Turkey that came in a white package with a red moon and a red star and a bunch of snakes squirming around.

Everyone else thought he was a nice enough guy, but as far as Dave was concerned the sax player was the Antichrist. He only smoked at home and only in the kitchen. So that's where he left his cigarettes—in the kitchen, for convenience, in full view, on a small table by the phone where everyone wrote down phone messages. Which, of course, was the first place Dave looked whenever he walked into the apartment.

Dave managed to go four weeks without a cigarette, which was about four weeks longer than he should have lasted. He missed smoking so much he was surprised he lasted a day. Dave said giving up cigarettes was like losing his best friend. He didn't just miss the act of smoking. He missed everything about it. He missed going down to the store to buy cigarettes. He missed opening cigarette packages. He even missed the act of lighting his smokes.

Dave was never great at sports—he is not a natural athlete—but lighting a cigarette was a piece of business he could do well. When it came to lighting a cigarette, Dave's hand-eye coordination was as good as anyone's. He could open a package of cigarettes and get a smoke out and into his mouth and close the packet and put it away all in one fluid movement. Without missing a beat, he could take out his matches and strike the match against the striking surface (which is something in itself). Striking a wooden match along sandpaper was one of Dave's favourite things. So much happens in that moment. There is that little explosion, the match flares and the smell of sulphur fills the air. You have to wait for the flame to subside, so it's perfect when you bring it up to your face to light your cigarette. And it's not over then, because you still have to extinguish the match, which Dave believed he did as gracefully as a symphony conductor waving a baton, shaking his arm in the air rhythmically before he dropped the match in an ashtray. As someone once said, smoking can be as graceful as ballet. And lighting a cigarette can be performance art.

So when you're trying to give up cigarettes, there is much more than nicotine to miss.

Dave missed it all. He even missed the dirty ashtrays. Most people look at an ashtray full of old filters and grey ash with disgust. Not Dave. Dave knew if you dumped those butts into a garbage can there was burned stuff underneath. Black and sticky stuff. Most people hate that stuff. Not Dave. He loved that stuff. He loved it because it represented all the cigarettes he had smoked. And smoking was what he was about. Cleaning out an ashtray was part of the ritual. Not because the ashtray was revolting and cleaning it was a necessary penance, but because rinsing all the tarry residue down the drain was an act of profound promise, of unmitigated hope. Once you cleaned an ashtray you were free to begin anew, to make a fresh start, to fill it again.

Quitting smoking meant giving up a lot more than a few hits of nicotine. And it was especially hard because you didn't just do it once. Once would be hard enough, but Dave soon learned he had to quit over and over and over. He would forget he had quit. He would go to sleep and he would wake up and he would look outside and think, *What a glorious day—I think I'll have a cigarette*. And then he would remember he was not supposed to have cigarettes any more, and he would have to weigh the matter in his mind and quit again. During the day he would sometimes get completely absorbed in a task, something like looking up a number in the phone book. He would get so absorbed he wouldn't think of cigarettes for long periods of time—sometimes as long as a minute. And then he would find the number he was looking for in the phone book and he would think, *I did that rather well—I should have a cigarette*. And then he would have to quit again. Quitting smoking every minute or so for four weeks can wear a man down.

One night, Dave was sitting in the kitchen and the sax player from Czechoslovakia was smoking his Turkish cigarettes, and Dave was watching him the way a cat watches a bird, thinking, *What is this mom and apple pie stuff? Smoking is what I do. I smoke. Therefore I am.*

He said, "Give me one of those."

The Czech sax player said, "It's about time."

Dave said, "Damn right."

He snatched one of the nasty brown smokes out of the white package with the red moon and star and the snakes writhing about, and he lit a match and brought the match towards his mouth.

He thought it was going to be the greatest hit of tobacco he had ever had in his life. He thought pulling that sweet nicotine into his lungs was going to be like sipping from a glass of the finest burgundy. But it wasn't. It tasted just like all the other cigarettes he had ever smoked. The only difference was he didn't have to worry any more. He had his friend back.

Dave quit twice more between 1976 and 1978, the most memorable time being at the end of the summer of '77. He was road-managing the Canadian leg of a Doctor Hook tour when he met a promoter in Thunder Bay who earnestly explained how he had stopped smoking. They were standing in the penalty box in the Fort William Gardens while Rooster Head, a heavy metal band that was opening the show every night, went through their disturbingly loud sound check.

"Walking," said the promoter, for about the tenth time. "Start walking." The promoter kept rubbing his head obsessively above his right ear. When he stopped, Dave could make out a bald spot the size of a silver dollar.

They were doing a show in the Sault the next night. After that it would be Sudbury and North Bay. Then they'd be finished. After North Bay they would have two weeks off in Toronto, and Dave was going to see Morley. He was trying to find the courage to ask her to marry him. He was desperate to stop smoking before he did that, before he got to Toronto. He couldn't stop thinking about what the promoter had said.

It was ten o'clock in the morning when the tour bus pulled into the little diner on the edge of Highway 17. They were somewhere around Blind River. All morning it had been rocks and trees and not much else. They had seen only the occasional town. Everyone jumped off the bus and went inside to get coffee. They stood around the parking lot in pairs, smoking and stretching their legs.

It was when they were filing back onto the bus that Dave was filled by a sense of moment. He looked at the soundman and said, "I'm going to walk from here. Will you deal with tonight's show?" The soundman, a taciturn kid from the Rock who was still half asleep, said, "Whatever." And that was that.

Once in their life, everyone has probably thought of not getting back into the vehicle that has brought them to some lonely gas stop on some lonely highway. Once in their life, everyone has wondered what would happen if they had the nerve to walk away.

This is what happened to Dave. He walked out to the highway and stood on the shoulder and watched the bus roar off down the road. The last person he saw was Rooster Head's bewildered drummer, his face pressed doubtfully against the back window. Dave lifted his arm in a sort of salute and shrugged. Then they were gone. And he was standing all alone on the shoulder, the summer sun hot on his neck.

The first thing Dave noticed was the silence, then the gravel at his feet and the grasshopper that whizzed by his face. He turned and walked back into the restaurant, stopped at the cash register and bought himself a package of cigarettes. Belvederes. He sat down at the counter and ordered a cup of coffee. He opened the package of cigarettes slowly and looked at the neat rows of smokes inside. First he pulled out the one on the bottom row, left. Then he pushed it back and took the one on the top right instead. He lit it and smoked it right down to the filter. Then he stood up, put a two-dollar bill on the counter beside the nearly full package of cigarettes—and he walked away. He wasn't just quitting smoking. He was quitting that pack of Belvederes. That pack he left on the counter at the diner outside of Blind River.

He walked out of the gas station and he started walking down the highway, heading east, the sun in his eyes. He had his wallet in his back pocket, and nothing else.

The road at his feet was white-grey and hot when he bent to touch it—as if he had been shrunk, as if he had become impossibly small and was walking along the never-ending ash at the end of a giant cigarette. *Easy,* he told himself, *one step at a time*.

Nothing much happened for the first hour. The occasional car passed him. He startled a porcupine that was drinking from a puddle in the ditch. He gave wide berth to a snake that was sunning itself on the shoulder. Mostly it was quiet. Dave felt an overwhelming sense of freedom descend upon him. The smell of the sun on his arms reminded him of boyhood summers. He felt loose and lighthearted. No one knew where he was. No one. *He* didn't even know where he was.

He looked up at the sky as he walked. It was something he hadn't done for years. As he watched the clouds change form, he felt an inexpressible sensation bubbling up from his gut. He had walked about four miles before he recognized what it was. It was happiness. He was happy. He was happier than he had been for . . . for so long he couldn't remember. He couldn't remember the last time he had felt so happy. It was a perfect moment. A moment so perfect it called for—a cigarette.

Dave stopped and reached for his smokes. When he realized he didn't have any, he looked around in a panic. He saw a butt on the ground that someone must have flipped out a car window. And it was at that moment, standing over that butt on the edge of the highway, that Dave understood that he had to keep walking. He couldn't stop. If he stopped walking he was doomed. As long as he kept moving he wouldn't smoke. Couldn't smoke.

So he started moving again, with his jaw screwed tight, swinging his arms back and forth. He was a man in a hurry, and not a happy man at all. He was a man with worry bubbling around inside him. He was The Walking Man.

That's how he went through the town of Blind River. It was lunchtime and he was hungry but he marched right through the town with his eyes on the road. He didn't look at the stores or the offices. He didn't look at the houses. He just stared at the road at his feet. The highway that was taking him out of town and away from temptation. The highway of despair.

Two hot hours later he came to a sign that said "Welcome to Algoma Mills." Dave knew he had to stop and get something to drink or he was going to be in trouble. There was a general store up on the right. A bunch of kids on bicycles were hanging around in front.

As he turned into the parking lot, a kid who looked to be about fourteen appeared from behind a pickup truck and started walking beside him.

"Mister," he said, "will you do me a favour?"

Dave was a little dehydrated, and he was suffering from a touch of heatstroke, but he didn't stop moving. He kept walking. The kid had to struggle to keep up.

Then the kid looked around and lowered his voice.

"Will you buy me a pack of smokes, mister?"

Dave turned and looked at the boy beside him, but he didn't stop moving towards the store.

The boy was holding out a handful of money. "Please, mister. Come on."

Dave frowned and sighed and changed direction—wheeling away from the store, heading back to the highway.

The kid stopped for a moment and then ran after him. "Please, mister. You can keep the change."

Dave stopped. He stopped and stood stock-still

but he didn't turn around. It was the first time he had stopped moving in over four hours. His body began to vibrate. He felt dizzy.

The kid stopped in his tracks. He was about five yards behind Dave. He was staring at Dave's back.

"Is there a beer store in this town?" asked Dave. He still didn't turn around.

The kid looked puzzled. "Yes," he said.

Dave said, "You want a beer?"

The kid, who was starting to look a little worried, shook his head. "No," he said a moment later, realizing Dave couldn't see him.

Dave said, "If you want beer, I'll buy you beer. I'll buy you a bottle of rum if you want." His fists were clenched by his thighs.

The kid started to back away. Dave turned around and started to walk towards him.

"I'll buy you booze," said Dave. "I'll buy you any kind of booze you want. But I'm not buying you cigarettes."

Then he turned and started walking down the highway again.

After he had gone about twenty-five yards the kid called out after him. "Jerk," he yelled.

There was a doughnut store on the edge of town. There was no way he could go into a doughnut store, but they had a drive-up window. Dave lined up behind a family from Saskatchewan in a station wagon packed with vacation equipment. Behind him was a van that belonged to “Bonkers the Clown . . . Quality Clowning for Half the Price.”

“Coffee,” said Dave when it was his turn, bending over to shout his order through the half-opened window. “Coffee, and two tuna sandwiches.”

He took the sandwiches and the coffee and kept moving. If he stopped moving he was sure he would start smoking.

He had eaten one sandwich by the time he was fifty yards down the road. He shoved the other one in his pocket. He opened the coffee and immediately splashed half the cup down his pants. It was impossible to drink and walk at the same time.

The clown van passed him, and the middle-aged lady who was driving it slowed down and waved. Dave lifted his arm. On the back doors in red script was painted: “Bonkers! A clown. Not a clone.”

Another hour of walking and Dave was back in the middle of nowhere. Back with the trees and the rocks. A green Hydro truck lumbered past him and then slowed down, pulled over and reversed back along the shoulder. When Dave was standing beside the cab, the driver opened the passenger-side door. Smoke billowed out of the cab.

“Hi,” said the driver, waving his cigarette at Dave. “You need a ride?”

“No,” said Dave. “A cigarette. Give me a cigarette.”

“What?” said the driver.

“Give me a cigarette,” said Dave, “or I’ll kill you.”

The driver stared at Dave for a moment, trying to size him up, then he slammed the door. "Jerk," he said, and peeled off down the highway.

That was in the middle of the afternoon.

Dave had passed the turnoff to Elliot Lake and gone through the town of Spragge when the dog joined him. The dog, which looked like a cross between a German shepherd and a wolf, appeared on a stretch of road devoid of evidence of any place a dog might belong. A stretch of highway barren of dog owners. The dog had appeared out of nowhere and had begun to pad along about ten yards behind him.

After a while Dave stopped and turned around. The dog stopped too. Ten yards back.

They stared at each other, Dave and the dog—neither of them blinked.

Dave took a step forward. The dog took a step back.

Dave crouched. The dog sat.

Dave pulled the second tuna sandwich out of his pocket. He held out half of it and said, "You got any cigarettes?"

The dog didn't budge.

Dave put the sandwich down on the road, stood up and walked away.

Three minutes later the dog was walking by his side.

Dave looked down at him and ran his hand lightly along his head.

"I'm Dave," he said.

The dog kept walking.

"I bet your name is . . . let me see," said Dave. "Filter Tip."

At dusk, between Spragge and Spanish, Dave spotted a man fishing over the edge of a bridge. When he got close, the man turned out to be a woman.

"Name's Jen," she said.

Jen was wearing jeans and a jean jacket. She was probably thirty-five or forty years old, a little heavy and rough around the edges, but she was a motherly type nevertheless. Her green pickup was parked at the far side of the bridge.

"Any luck?" asked Dave as he stopped and leaned on the railing.

"Plenty of luck," said Jen, "but no fish." And she spat into the water.

"Me too," said Dave.

They both watched the dog—the dog Dave now thought of as *his* dog—watched as it picked its way down the bank of the river and stepped tentatively into the water. Before long the dog was standing in the river up to his belly, drinking enthusiastically.

"What's your dog's name?" asked Jen.

"Tobacco," said Dave.

The dog was climbing back onto the riverbank now, shaking himself dry, rolling in the tall grass.

"You have a cigarette?" she asked.

"No," said Dave. "I was about to ask you the same thing."

"I quit," said Jen. "I don't smoke no more except for what I bum. You chew?"

"Pardon?" said Dave

"You want a chew?"

She was holding out a blue tin disc the size of a hockey puck. Dave looked in. It looked like coffee grounds.

"Go ahead," she said. "It does the job."

Dave took a pinch of tobacco between his fingers.

"Got to take more than that," she said.

Dave took more.

He stared at the tobacco he was holding. He wasn't sure what he was supposed to do with it. He didn't know if he was supposed to put it up his nose or in his mouth.

"Under your tongue," said Jen, taking the tin back and slipping it in her pocket.

Dave slipped the plug of tobacco under his tongue. His eyes widened. *So this is what it's like,* he thought. *It's like having a mouthful of gasoline.* His mouth was quickly filling up with saliva.

He looked at Jen for help.

"They say you get a better hit if you don't spit," she said. "They say you get a better hit if you swallow."

What was he going to do? Dave swallowed.

It was a mistake.

His throat felt as if it were on fire.

He began to cough violently—so violently that he inhaled the soggy plug of tobacco that was resting under his tongue.

His face turned red. His eyes bulged. He couldn't catch his breath.

Jen watched him with academic interest. He was doubled over, his left hand clawing at his throat, his right hand pawing the air in front of him. Jen took the right hand and rested it on the railing of the bridge.

"Me," she said, "I spit, myself." And she spat in the river.

Jen was a taxidermist. She and her husband had moved north so he could open the business. Six months after they arrived, he took off with another woman. She taught herself the business and kept going. What else could she do?

Dave walked through the night, stopping to spit every few minutes.

Dawn came around five—first grey, like ash, then streaks of pink, until the horizon caught fire and the whole sky began to glow like the tips of a thousand cigarettes.

Dave stopped for breakfast at six at a diner in McKerrow. He had to go in, but he didn't have to sit down. He gave his order at the cash register and then said, "I'll wait outside." He sat on the wooden steps and watched an ant struggle to carry a huge crumb across the sandy pavement.

The lady who had taken his order opened the door and handed him a brown paper bag. He had a bacon sandwich for the dog, and a coffee and an order of toast with cheese for himself. He had been walking for nineteen hours. He was tired and worn out, but he kept walking, into the morning sun. This time he spilled the coffee down his shirt.

At nine he came across a country graveyard. The trees were tall and straight around the perimeter. The grass between the gravestones was dark and inviting. He walked through the open metal gate and wandered around, reading the stories carved into the stones.

There was a man with a power mower working in the far corner. When he saw Dave, he turned the mower off and walked over.

He was wearing tan pants, a soft plaid shirt and a worn fishing hat. He looked about as relaxed as an old chamois.

Dave figured he was—what? Sixty-five, seventy?

"Nice morning," said the man.

Dave nodded.

"You're not from around here," said the man.

Dave wasn't sure where he *was* from just then. He had a few boxes in a basement in Edmonton and some stuff at his parents' house in The Narrows. And there were the two suitcases on the bus.

"Name is Alf Murphy," said the man, holding out his hand. "I cut the grass every Thursday morning. My wife's buried here. Do you want to see her?"

Dave followed Alf Murphy around a stand of birch. The ground below the trees was brown and spongy with dead leaves. The men were heading for the far corner of the little graveyard.

Alf stopped and pointed at a large red granite stone. It read:

Barb Murphy
Beloved wife of Alf
Mother of Sarah and René.
November 12, 1910–November 11, 1972

There was a matching red stone beside it.

On it Dave read:

Alf Murphy
March 12, 1904

Then there was a line and a blank space.

"This is where I go," said Alf.

He was digging something out of his pocket. It was a small camera. A Kodak Brownie.

"Would you do me a favour?" he said, holding the camera out. "I'd like to have a picture of myself beside my stone. I'd like to send it to my sister. She lives in Saskatchewan."

Dave took the camera.

Alf stood beside his stone, his hands awkwardly at his sides the way people stand when they are having their picture taken.

"Cheese," said Dave.

"Cheese," said Alf.

Dave handed the camera back.

"Much obliged," said Alf. "Well, I guess I'll finish the lawn."

As he walked away he said, "Too bad about Elvis."

"What?" said Dave.

"You didn't hear?" said Alf, stopping and turning. "Elvis Presley died last night."

The drone of Alf's lawn mower hung in the air for a good ten minutes as Dave walked down the highway—away from the graveyard and Alf Murphy.

As the first three cars passed him, he stuck his thumb out. He wanted to get to the next town and see a newspaper. Listen to a radio.

He wanted to know what had happened.

His mind kept jumping.

He thought about the graveyard, about the flu epidemic of 1917, coming so hard after the war. They must have felt the world was ending. He thought of the MacPherson family whose stone he had stood in front of twenty minutes ago. In six months they lost a two-year-old daughter, a four-year-old son and his nine-year-old brother. How did they keep going?

He thought about Alf Murphy standing beside his tombstone. That was something. What if it had been Dave's camera? What if he'd promised to mail Alf the photo and then, when the film was developed, Alf wasn't in the picture? What if the picture just showed a tombstone with all the dates there and everything? Rod Serling would like that one.

And, of course, he thought about Elvis.

There was nothing in Nairn when he got there. And by the time he reached Naughton he didn't want to know. He just kept walking.

He's never been sure where he actually gave up. Somewhere on the Toronto side of Sudbury. He walked right through the Big Nickel without stopping. Then, south of Sudbury, he found himself sitting on a bench at a gas stop—pretty well baked—and a bus that said "Toronto" stopped right in front of him. He figured it was an omen, and he got on. It was the middle of the night. He had been walking for maybe forty hours; he had covered over 150 miles.

There was a twenty-minute stop in Barrie.

He had a coffee and a cigarette.

He got to Toronto at dawn.

He got a hotel room and slept till supper. He phoned Morley and they went out for dinner to an Indian place on the Danforth. After they had ordered, he came right to the point and said, "Do you want to get married?"

She didn't say anything. Not a word. She stared at him, and then at the floor.

After about a minute he said, "Well?"

And Morley said, "Have you got a cigarette?"

Dave said, "You don't smoke."

She said, "Just give me a cigarette."

"I'm out," he said. And he went and bought a pack of Belvederes.

And that was the end of that.

He left town at the end of that week. They didn't settle the marriage thing. Morley said no one had ever asked before. She said she wanted to think about it.

"What's to think?" said Dave. "I love you."

She said, "I have to know I'm not just marrying you because you were the first to ask."

Dave was sure there was another guy in the picture. Morley said that wasn't it at all.

And there wasn't.

Dave stopped smoking again six months later. It was in Huntington, Virginia. Still with Doctor Hook. They pulled into town at five in the morning and nothing was open so he had to mooch fags off the soundman, who smoked menthol.

He needed the smokes to calm down. He was gripped by the agitated, excited buzz that always seized his stomach when they pulled into a town he had never visited before. No matter how small the place, Dave always snapped awake the moment the bus geared down.

By the time he had checked into the hotel the sun was already coming up. He sat on the edge of the bed and inhaled the three borrowed cigarettes one after the other, trying to tranquilize himself. Then he drank a root beer and ate a chocolate bar and fell asleep.

He woke at noon, disoriented and confused. The first thing he remembered, before he could even dredge up the name of the town they were in, was the menthol cigarettes. That was because his mouth tasted like chewing gum that had been left in an ashtray too long. Like toothpaste that had been mixed with road tar.

He couldn't decide whether it would feel better to brush his teeth or get his hands on a regular cigarette. He didn't have the appetite for either.

This is ridiculous, he thought. And he stopped smoking again.

He started again that night.

He quit once and for all the day he married Morley. He didn't make a big deal about it. It was a silent promise he made to himself during the ceremony. It happened when Morley said, "I do."

"I do," said Morley, looking directly into his eyes.

Me too, he thought quietly. *I do too.*

And he meant it.

Dave and the Duck

One idle morning, when Dave was sitting behind the counter in his record store, fiddling unconsciously with his wedding ring, he realized—first with mild interest, and then with growing alarm—that he couldn't get the ring off his finger. Not that he wanted to get it off. Until, that is, he noticed he couldn't remove it. Then he wanted to very, very much.

He tugged and twisted the ring until his finger turned red and puffy. Then he put his finger in his mouth and tried to pull the ring off with his teeth, but it wouldn't slide over his knuckle. And that was the moment when Dave—sitting alone in his store with his finger in his mouth—entered the world of irrational fear. One moment he was listening to a Lee Hazelwood album circa 1973, trying to decide if Hazelwood was making a deep cosmic statement or perpetrating some kind of elaborate musical joke. The next he was tugging at his finger like a wolverine caught in a trap, struggling to catch his breath.

In the blink of an eye his store felt airless. As if all the oxygen had been used up. As if there was no air left to breathe. In the blink of an eye, Dave was overcome by a need to move. As if the only way to get air into his lungs was by moving.

And still the ring wouldn't budge.

He locked up and flipped a sign into the window that read "Be Right Back" and hurried down the street, twisting the ring as he went. He didn't have a clue where he was heading. He was too overwhelmed by this sense of the world collapsing upon him, too overwhelmed by the need to get going to pay any attention to where he was going to.

He called Morley from a pay phone. "I can't get my wedding ring off," he said.

Morley was sitting in her office at the theatre she manages, going over a budget for a season thirty-five thousand dollars in deficit and heading south.

"Not that I want to," added Dave into the silence.

"Or need to or anything," said Dave.

The knowledge that he was talking to his wife was calming him down.

"It's uncomfortable," he said later that night as they sat in the kitchen after supper. "Like an itch you can't reach."

Morley took his hand in hers, and Dave felt the panic returning—looming like a swamp monster over some swamp horizon that he had thought was far away but turned out to be right there in his own kitchen.

It was getting hard to breathe again. It was like he was in a hole at the bottom of the swamp . . . and the ring was on his finger and his finger was on his hand and his hand was being held and he was starting to feel as if he should get moving again. And if he was going to move he would need his hand back. Most of all, he needed to get the ring off his finger or he was going to go crazy.

"You are not the shape you used to be," Morley was saying. "There has been . . . growth. This happens."

He removed his hand from hers and held it in front of his face as if examining his fingers. In truth, he was getting his hand out of her grip.

"You could always have it sized," said Morley. "They could make it bigger."

He went to a jeweller before he went to work the next morning.

"It's a nice ring," said the jeweller.

"We had it made," said Dave. "It's one of a kind."

First they tried lubricating Dave's finger with soap. Then with olive oil. When neither of those worked, the jeweller got a roll of electrical tape and taped Dave's finger like a hockey stick. Everything except the ring. "Can't be too careful," he said. Then he took Dave to the back of the store and pointed to a grinding stone.

"You have to be careful," said the jeweller as the stone began to whirl. "One wrong move and I could take your finger right off."

When he was finished, the jeweller said, "You can have it back in a week."

That night, Dave showed Morley the indentation on his finger where the ring had been. It was like a phantom ring.

"It feels good to have it off," he told Morley.

They had been married twenty-three years.

Morley's eyes narrowed but only imperceptibly.

"I've had that ring on my hand almost as long as I haven't." Dave said. "It felt like it was squeezing me."

"Oh," said Morley. "Oh," was all she said.

By lunchtime the next day things had shifted. The missing ring had begun to worry him.

"It's weird," he said. "I keep feeling for it and it isn't there. I do it all the time without thinking. I feel naked. Emotionally naked."

"Interesting," said Morley.

Then it shifted again. It started to bother Dave that it bothered him.

He said, "I'm so set in my ways that all it takes is a stupid ring to throw me off kilter. I am fat and I am almost fifty and every morning I have orange juice and cereal for breakfast at more or less the same time and more or less the same place, and I take the same three sandwiches to lunch every day and . . . and look," he said, pulling his sweater up over his stomach, "every time I wear this sweater I wear this *shirt*."

Morley didn't say anything.

By the end of the week, Dave wasn't talking about the ring any more.

He knew enough to keep quiet about it.

He noticed that every time he brought up the ring Morley would get prickly. Would talk only in monosyllables.

"Would it bother you," she asked on the weekend, "if I took my ring off? Would you be upset if I stopped wearing my ring?"

"I am just getting it sized," said Dave. "I haven't taken it off. I haven't stopped wearing it."

Dave got the ring back a few days before he flew to Nova Scotia. His sister, Annie, had called and said, "Elisabeth had a stroke."

His father's sister, Elisabeth.

Annie said, "I have to go to Boston for a week. I think you should come."

He went the following Monday.

Morley drove him to the airport.

"I don't know when I'll be back," he said. "It depends on what I find."

He had everything packed in a satchel that had once been his grandfather's. Elisabeth, who was always handing him stuff, had given the satchel to him. It was the sort of satchel you don't see any more. Leather. Lumpy. But soft, nice to touch. And stylish for its unstylishness. As Dave reached in the back seat for the bag, Morley noticed the ring back on his finger and smiled.

"I love you," she said. "Look after Elisabeth."

He checked into the Lord Nelson Hotel and went right away to the hospital. Elisabeth was confused. At first she recognized him. Then she had no idea who he was. The doctor said, "It's early. Don't worry. She is going to be okay."

He had dinner by himself in an Italian restaurant on Spring Garden Road. He had two glasses of Merlot and pasta with roasted vegetables and a cup of dark coffee.

It had been two years since he had been in Halifax. It was a bittersweet feeling to be in Halifax alone.

The next morning, coming down in the elevator, Dave realized he had left his key in his room. He would get one at the front desk later. It was early. He went for a walk and bought a book at one of the bookstores near his hotel. Then he wandered into the Public Gardens.

Inside the gates there were tulips of every colour—Chinese red, lemon yellow, coral pink, lilac purple. *I should take some flowers to the hospital,* he thought. He sat on a bench for a while near the bandstand. Then he bought a bag of peanuts in a plastic bag and, in a preoccupied-not-paying-attention sort of way, he began to feed them to a duck that was hanging around his bench. Before long, Dave had a fluster of ducks squabbling for peanuts.

It made him happy just to be sitting there, feeding ducks.

He was trying to be fair about it. He was trying to spread the peanuts around so all the ducks had a chance—not only the aggressive ones. There was a tentative duck on the edge of the circle.

Dave reached deep into his bag of peanuts and threw some to the diffident duck. The others turned and waddled furiously towards it.

In the midst of the commotion Dave caught a flash of metal in the sunlight among the peanuts on the ground, and he thought, *Some poor sod has lost a ring.* And then he felt for his own ring. To his horror, he felt only finger. He realized *he* was the poor sod—it was *his* ring glinting in the sun. He looked again, and then it dawned on him with a sickening clarity that the hungry, left-out duck had just gobbled up his ring.

Dave stared at the duck in disbelief.

The duck stared back at him.

Dave looked at his bare finger and a wave of dread settled on him. It was the same feeling he first had sitting in his store. The ring, which belonged on his finger—his wedding ring, which he had just had sized so it would be easier to get on and off—was in the stomach of a hungry quacker.

His heart began to race, he was short of breath, he was dizzy, he felt faint. The world was collapsing again.

Dave dropped his bag of peanuts and lunged at the duck. The duck squawked in outrage and fluttered up about five feet in the air. It landed in the middle of a group of ducks on the other side of the path.

Dave knew that if he looked away for even an instant he wouldn't be able to tell his duck from the others. With his eyes locked on the culprit, he made another wild and unsuccessful leap. The duck fluttered up again and Dave slid along the grass on his knees. He was like a football player chasing a bouncing football around an end zone.

The duck stood up on its legs and began to flap its wings. It looked as if it was going to take off. In desperation, Dave pulled off his jacket and flung it in the air. For an instant it hung there like a shadow, and then it enveloped the bird. There was a moment of confusion and feathers and squawks, and then Dave was standing in the park with a duck wrapped in his jacket.

A duck, tucked under his arm like a loaf of bread.

He looked around to see if anyone had noticed.

There was a woman, holding the hand of a small boy, staring at him.

"What are you going to do with that duck?" she said.

Dave had no idea what he was going to do with the duck.

"Roast it," he said as he passed her.

The only thing he did know was that he was getting out of the park as quickly as he could. He was heading towards his hotel. Where else could he go?

The duck was surprisingly quiet as they crossed South Park Road. Surprisingly well behaved. The duck seemed relatively happy under the coat.

Dave was almost at the elevators when he remembered he didn't have his room key.

He lined up at the front desk, thinking that this wasn't the first time he had stood in front of a hotel clerk with a bird under his arm.

The clerk looked down to check his name on the hotel computer.

Dave tried to rearrange the duck.

The duck quacked.

The clerk looked up abruptly.

Dave said, "I beg your pardon. Excuse me."

He squeezed the duck against his body as he walked across the lobby. Apparently he squeezed too hard. Halfway to the elevators the duck had a dump.

People sometimes use the expression "as loose as a goose." Not, however, people who know about these things. People who know about these things know that goose pellets come out pretty well packed. A duck dump, on the other hand, comes out, well, as loose as a goose.

Once the elevator doors closed behind them and Dave and his duck had a moment of privacy, Dave opened his jacket to see what was going on. Which is something he wouldn't do if he had it to do over. It was a mistake. An understandable mistake. But a mistake, nevertheless.

As soon as the duck spotted the elevator lights it began to beat its wings furiously. In an instant, the quiet duck had become a wriggling mass of kicking and quacking feathers. It had become a scratching and biting duck. When the elevator doors opened, on the fourth floor, Dave was barely holding on to the duck by its little duck feet while it beat him mercilessly with its wings.

The elderly couple waiting for the elevator didn't say a word. Not to Dave and not to each other. They didn't step forward into the elevator, nor did they step back. They simply stood motionless and speechless and staring as the feathers flew and the doors opened and then closed.

Two floors later, when the elevator doors opened again, the duck gave Dave a mighty whack with a wing. Dave loosened his grip for an instant and the duck was free—flying down the corridor, with Dave in pursuit.

An art dealer from Toronto, a coiffed women of a certain age, opened the door of her room just as the duck winged past at about shoulder height and ninety miles an hour. She was still standing in her door with her mouth hanging open when Dave screeched to a halt and fixed her with an air of steely authority.

"Hotel security," he barked. "Get back in your room and lock the door." For good measure he added, "The duck is rabid."

The woman stepped backwards and slammed her door without a word. Dave peeled off.

He rounded the corner at the end of the hall and had already taken three steps before he stopped. And gasped. And spun in the air and headed back the way he had come. The tables had been turned. The duck was coming towards him now with fire in its eyes.

Dave lurched back down the corridor, bouncing off a fire extinguisher, glancing over his shoulder, looking for an open door, thinking, as he heard the beat of the wings, that this was closer than he ever wanted to get to the running of the bulls in Pamplona, Spain.

It took twelve minutes of utter madness before he got the duck under his arm and into his room. And then the duck bit him, and the chase was on again. Around and around the bedroom, Dave after the duck, the duck after Dave. The two of them with enough adrenaline coursing through their bodies to fuel a British soccer riot.

When Dave finally got the duck into the bathroom, and the bathroom door was shut with Dave safely on the other side, feathers and duck muck were everywhere. It took Dave almost an hour to clean up. He carefully checked each duck defilement for his ring. Then he collapsed into the wing-backed chair in the corner of his bedroom and stared at his empty finger.

He looked at the closed bathroom door. It was eerily quiet in there. He got up and cracked the door to see what was going on. The duck had pushed one of the hotel towels up against the edge of the tub and fashioned a sort of nest. It seemed content as Dave slipped through the door.

"It's nice here, isn't it?" said Dave.

"Quack," said the duck.

He checked each duck dropping in the bathroom, but there was no ring there either. He filled the tub with water and, having once again shut the duck in the bathroom, lay on the bed, wondering what he should do next.

Before he had developed a plan of action there was a knock on his door.

The young man standing in the corridor was wearing a blue blazer and holding a notebook and a walkie-talkie.

"Hotel security," said the young man.

"Yes?" said Dave.

"We have a report," said the young man, "of a loose parrot."

Dave stood back and waved his arms around the room.

"Loose parrot?" he said. "Not in here."

When Dave checked on the duck again, it seemed so comfortably settled in its nest that he felt brave enough to leave the bathroom door open. Half an hour later, the duck waddled out and walked around the room, pecking at the carpet. Dave got some corn chips from the mini-bar and left them in a pile near the television.

He called Morley.

"I have to tell you something," he said urgently. "It's about the wedding ring."

"You've lost it," said Morley.

"I haven't lost it," said Dave.

"I don't think I could go through a missing ring again," said Morley.

And that is when the duck started quacking furiously.

"What is that?" said Morley.

"The television," said Dave.

"It's sounds like you're watching some nature thing," said Morley.

"I am," he said. "I am watching a duck lay an egg."

He *was* watching a duck lay an egg.

"You never watch that stuff," said Morley.

"This is unbelievable," said Dave, genuinely startled.

"You sound like you've been drinking," said Morley. "What is going on?"

"Nothing," said Dave. "I have to go."

After the phone call Dave fell onto his bed and tried to sort out his thoughts. He was exhausted. Why hadn't he been able to tell Morley what had happened? Where were these feelings of fear coming from?

He looked at the duck.

He could feel a wave of panic building again. Morley would be furious if she knew where the ring was.

"This isn't about us," he told the duck. "It's about my wife."

The duck quacked and had a dump.

Dave dropped to his knees and peered at the refuse.

No ring.

"If I feel like this," he said, "imagine what my wife would feel like. I'm doing this for her."

He put the duck back in the bathroom and a "Do Not Disturb" sign on the door. Then he went to the hospital. When he came back at dinnertime there was duck slop everywhere. But still no ring.

Dave opened the bathroom door and phoned room service and ordered himself a beer and a half dozen oysters on the shell. When the duck saw the oysters, she ran across the room and sat at his feet. So he ordered another dozen for her and they watched the early news together.

After the news, he went through the latest mound of duck dirt. Her production was beyond belief. At this rate, he figured, the time from bill to butt couldn't be more than twenty-four hours. He ordered another dozen oysters and they watched *The Simpsons*. Dave had seen the episode before, but the duck seemed to enjoy it.

He was woken at five the next morning by loud squawks. He headed for the bathroom door but stopped when he realized the cries were coming from the other side of the room. From the window. He threw back the curtains and, to his horror, found a male duck pacing back and forth on the window ledge.

He opened the bathroom door. There was a second egg in the makeshift nest but his duck was paddling around the bathtub.

"You have a visitor," said Dave.

She rushed to the window and the ducks pecked at the glass like prisoners. His duck looked accusingly at him, but Dave didn't open the window.

A few hours later Dave stepped outside to get a taxi. The doorman, who was holding the cab door open, suddenly screamed and dropped to the ground. Dave looked up just as the duck husband executed a tight dive-bombing manoeuvre past their heads.

"Holy crow," said the doorman, brushing himself off. "That was just like the movie."

Dave looked up and saw the duck wheeling over the Public Gardens like a fighter plane. He jumped into the taxi and went to visit Elisabeth.

While he was at the hospital, Dave was seized by a spasm of anxiety. It was only a matter of time, he thought, before someone at the hotel found him out.

He looked up motels in the hospital room phone book. He chose the cheapest-looking ad on the page.

At suppertime, instead of heading back to the Lord Nelson, he took a taxi to the cheap motel. It looked even more rundown than the ad in the phone book had suggested.

There was a grille in the front office, like in an old western bank.

"How much are the rooms?" asked Dave.

The manager was wearing an undershirt. "Hourly rate?" he asked.

A young woman with a short skirt walked in the front door and sat down in the broken lobby chair. She was chewing gum. She eyed Dave.

The manager nodded at the girl. "Is Melanie with you?" he asked.

Dave shook his head. "Do you allow animals?" he asked.

The manager's eyes narrowed. "What kind of animals are you talking about?"

"My pet," said Dave.

The manager didn't say a word.

"My pet duck," said Dave.

"A duck," said the manager.

Dave nodded.

The manager spat in the wastebasket. He said, "We're not that kind of place, mister."

On the way back to the motel, Dave went to a drugstore and picked up a pair of rubber gloves and a box of Ex-Lax. But when he got back to his room he found a little pile of corn chip droppings in the bathroom. The duck was already passing the things he had given her the night before.

Dave dropped the Ex-Lax in the garbage.

After supper he went to the library and learned that everything a duck ingests goes to its crop before it goes to its stomach. The crop, a muscular processing plant, is full of little stones that grind food up before it is digested. According to the book he found, Dave's ring would be ground to gold dust before he would ever see it. Or, more likely, it would stay in the crop until the duck died. Dave could, he supposed, cut the duck open, but, he thought, remembering the words of the odious little motel manager, he wasn't that kind of guy.

He went back to his room and wrapped the duck back up in his fouled jacket. Then he took her across the street to the Public Gardens and let her go. When he put her down she flapped her wings a few times and then waddled away without a backward glance.

"Good luck," said Dave.

She didn't seem to want it.

As he watched her slip into the brush Dave wondered where his ring would end up, and who would find it, and how long from now. What they would think, what story they would make up when they found the ring in a circle of duck bones.

He knew his duck wouldn't touch the eggs she had laid, now that they were no longer in her nest, so he threw them into a Dumpster behind the hotel, along with two large bags of paper towels and duck deposits.

He didn't sleep well, wondering what he would tell Morley about the ring. Worrying about what she would say.

Early the next morning Dave took his jacket to the front desk. He asked the concierge if he could have it cleaned. The concierge stared at the fouled jacket and his lip began to curl.

"It's clam chowder," said Dave.

"Of course," said the concierge, flicking a feather off the counter with disdain.

Dave visited Elisabeth again. She was less befuddled each day. The doctor told him she would have to go to rehab for at least a few months.

Dave told Elisabeth he had to go back home.

"I'll be back in a month," he said.

At lunch he went to a jewellery shop not far from the hotel and, with a heavy heart, bought an extravagant silver bracelet for Morley. He had never bought her jewellery in his life. The store, the clerk and the enormous quantity of jewellery overwhelmed him. He almost fled without buying anything. But the clerk was fussing with him so attentively that Dave didn't want to disappoint him. The bracelet cost a small fortune. But if he was going home barehanded, he couldn't go empty-handed. He thought it was a pretty bracelet. But he wasn't sure. Morley would have to tell him.

He went back to the hospital to see Elisabeth one last time, but she was asleep, and he didn't wake her.

He had two hours before his plane.

He went to the hotel to pick up his jacket, but when he got there he couldn't find his ticket stub. He looked at the concierge hopelessly.

"It's all right," said the concierge with a smirk. "I remember you. You're Clam Chowder."

He handed Dave the jacket on a hanger and passed him a small envelope.

"The cleaners found a ring in your pocket," he said. "Imagine you would want to wear it home."

Dave had time to take the hotel bus to the airport. As they pulled by the Public Gardens he put the ring back on his finger and stared at it.

Twenty-three years was a long time.

He didn't have any regrets.

He had a window seat on the plane and was served a surprisingly good meal. He knocked back two glasses of wine with supper and a drink later. He flew the final hour with his face pressed to the glass, watching the sun setting ahead of him and holding the silver bracelet in his hands, thinking that nothing happened without a reason. He was still holding the bracelet as the wheels bit into the runway. It made him anxious to hold it, but it was a new kind of anxiety. It felt fresh and exciting. He had never done anything like this before. It made him happy.

Tree of Heaven

SUMMER ARRIVED during the second week of June. The week *began* hot and sticky, and the temperature kept rising. By midweek the sky had settled into a gloomy opaqueness that wasn't blue but wasn't grey either. It was just heavy and thick. Oppressive and hot.

They began issuing smog warnings on Wednesday. By Friday there had been a run on fans in hardware stores all over town. Drivers were crankier than usual and pedestrians jostled each other with grim determination.

On Saturday night, the movie theatres were overflowing with people looking for a way to beat the heat. When shows began filling up, people began buying tickets to *whatever* was available.

"Just let us in," said one man desperately in a downtown complex, pushing a twenty-dollar bill across the stainless-steel counter. "I don't care which movie . . . just let us in!"

The heat broke on Sunday evening, but the week had left everyone drained. On Monday morning you could tell the people who didn't have summer plans by the edginess that had settled upon them.

One morning, in the middle of the hot spell, Dave met Susan Thompson pushing her daughter, Jennifer, down the street. Susan and her husband, Bob, had moved into the Dillingham house during the winter. Susan looked distracted and harassed.

"Oh," she said, glancing up and down the street. "The babysitter didn't show up."

Susan was on her way to the bank, the grocery store and the dry cleaners. She was going to be gone only half an hour, forty-five minutes at the most.

Dave said, "Give me Jennifer. You can pick her up on your way home."

And that is how Dave came to be standing on his front porch, holding a baby girl in his arms, ringing his own doorbell.

When Morley answered he tried to look concerned.

"She followed me home," he said. "Can we keep her?"

While Dave was looking after Jennifer, his son, Sam, blew in the front door. "Can I have a loonie?" asked Sam. "We're going for ice cream. Whose baby? Can we keep him?"

Dave arrived home with Jennifer again a week later. This time it was a Saturday afternoon and Morley wasn't home. Neither were the kids. This time Dave sat happily on the front stoop while Jennifer slept in her stroller.

When she woke up and started to cry, he felt a flare of panic. He went inside and fetched a Popsicle from the freezer, and the two of them shared it. By the time Susan arrived to pick up her daughter, Dave and Jennifer were fast friends.

Dave waved goodbye.

"Bye-bye," he said. "Bye-bye." Opening and closing his hand, as if he were squeezing a ball.

Jennifer leaned forward in her stroller, waving back. "Bye-bye."

When they were gone, Dave surveyed the mess Jennifer had left behind. There was melted Popsicle everywhere. On his pants and his shirt and his hands, for starters. And on the porch. And in little puddles on the walk where Jennifer's stroller had been parked.

Dave had forgotten what it was like to live with little children.

He went inside to change. As he walked across the living room, he remembered that there had once been a time when he'd had to kick a path through the toys to get from one side of this room to the other. A time when fatigue had been such a constant companion that doing something as simple as putting Lego away had required more energy than he'd thought he would ever see again.

He went upstairs and changed his shirt and pants and washed his hands and came downstairs to make a sandwich.

Even eating had seemed impossible then. He and Morley had had to eat in shifts if they went somewhere with the kids. He remembered the night he had paced the sidewalk in front of a Chinese restaurant, with Stephanie howling in her Snugli, while Morley ate anxiously in the restaurant window.

Now, at three o'clock on this Saturday afternoon, he didn't even know where his teenage daughter *was*.

There was a certain relief in that. That he no longer had to be on constant patrol. That if they were left alone for five minutes, his children wouldn't necessarily stick their fingers in an electric socket, or fall down a flight of stairs, or crawl across the room and help themselves to the cat food.

But there was a certain loneliness too.

Dave poked at his cheese sandwich. The mess of childhood was gone from his life forever. He had had two cracks at it: his childhood and theirs. But it was over now. The end of childhood.

A melancholy thought.

Lost in melancholy, Dave couldn't even say for certain if his children would remember their childhood as the best of times.

He had always thought *he* had had a happy childhood, but on this melancholy afternoon he couldn't even be sure of that.

"Remember," he said to Morley that night, "how Eugene and Maria used to take Sam and Stephanie for walks? Remember they would get ice cream?"

"Of course," said Morley. Then she added, "You took them for ice cream too, you know."

When Dave woke up on Sunday morning, his first conscious thought was that he should clean the car.

He used to do that every Sunday morning. The exterior one week, the interior the next. Rotating. That was years ago, when he'd bought his first new car and there were no children messing up his life. When having a clean car seemed important. Back in the days when Dave thought he would keep the car maybe three years, four tops, then he would trade it in and get a new one. Trade up.

Now, he knew he was never going to trade up. He wasn't even going to trade in. He was going to be the last person on earth to drive this car.

As he lay there in bed, being careful not to move abruptly, being careful not to wake his wife, Dave remembered when he had stopped cleaning his car each week. It was the autumn Stephanie was—what? Six? Maybe seven. They'd driven to Detroit one Saturday to have dinner with Mark Knopfler and then watch his concert at the Olympia. On the way home, somewhere around Leamington, Stephanie had leaned forward from the back seat and said quietly, "I feel sick."

Before Morley had even had time to turn completely around, Stephanie threw up. It was a disgorgement of heroic proportions, erupting out of her with freight-train fury. She opened her mouth and delivered a spout that cleared the front seat and splattered against the dashboard—most of it, with pinpoint accuracy, disappearing into the heating vent.

When they got home, Dave scrubbed the car within an inch of its life. He used detergents and disinfectants—scrub brushes and toothbrushes—but all that winter the sour smell of vomit returned every time he turned on the heater. Even now, even after all these years, even after he had emptied bottles of air freshener and jars of essential oils into the heating system, Dave was convinced he could still smell it whenever he switched on the heat.

It was vague and far away, like the frowst of souring milk—an odour young parents know all too well. How many times had Dave wandered into his home, minding his own business, and become aware that there was, without doubt, a sippy cup of milk ripening somewhere? Maybe it had been there for three days. Maybe it had been there for three weeks—there was no way to know. All he knew was that it was there. And all he could do was get down on his hands and knees like a dog and sniff under chairs and around the couch, praying to God that he would see the cup before he stuck his nose into it.

The Schellenbergers, who live on the same street, have a smell in their car. Every time the Schellenbergers start *their* car it fills with the distinctive odour of lamb curry.

"It just started one day out of the blue," Bernie Schellenberger will explain if you should remark on it.

Bernie took his car to three mechanics before he found one who could explain it. Some belt in the bowels of his engine was rubbing against some block. He could have it repaired for four hundred dollars or he could live with the five minutes of lamb curry.

"It's kind of a pleasant smell," Bernie decided.

The smell of Stephanie's misadventure was otherwise, and its incessant presence had gradually worn away at Dave's pride of ownership. Unlike Bernie, he couldn't come to terms with it.

And so, over the years, Dave's car had fallen into an inexorable decline. He hardly noticed the mess any more. For years there had been a constant dusting of Goldfish crackers on all of the seats. And raisins, little black pellets, as if he were sharing his car with a warren of rabbits. One morning when he looked at the mess of his car he wondered if, while he slept, a family of rabbits didn't munch their nightly way along the shadows of his alley, nudge his car doors open and sit there listening to the radio, leaving their little piles of pellets behind.

Ever since she'd got her licence, Stephanie, his own daughter, the agent of his downfall, had begun to complain about the state of the car. She referred to it as The Slothmobile. "It is embarrassing," she said.

This was the first indication of the reversal of roles that Dave knew awaited him. The first indication of the father becoming the child.

So, on this Sunday morning, when Dave woke early and was seized with this faintly remembered urge to clean his car, he slipped out of bed quietly and went downstairs.

On a shelf in the basement he found a yellow bucket with an old chamois so hard and stiff he couldn't imagine it being of any use to anyone. He brought the chamois upstairs and filled the sink with hot water and let it soak while he made coffee. When he reached into the water and found the deerskin slippery and soft he felt a surge of satisfaction. That he had even found it was good—that he could renew it like that, with hot water, made him feel mildly competent. He was a man. He knew about things like chamois. He was about to do things to his car. Life was pretty all right.

Dave's dad had never cared much about the cars he drove, though in his later years he grew to care more and more about the odometers.

After he retired, Charlie used to carefully note the mileage of every trip he took. He would drive into Sydney and come back with a little piece of paper on which he would have written the day's mileage and the time, down to the minute, that the journey had taken.

"I was to town today," he would tell Dave on the phone. "Three hours and seven minutes." Dave was never sure if his father was delivering good or bad news. He tried to keep his responses to noncommittal murmurs of acknowledgment.

When Charlie died, Dave found a neat stack of these little notes in the back of a drawer in his father's bureau. Dave couldn't bring himself to throw them out. He put them in a small cardboard box and carried the box back home. He put the box in the back of a drawer in his bureau. The box was there, still.

Morley's dad, Roy, developed his own automotive fascination in his later years, though he became more concerned with place than with time and space.

A good half hour could go by on an afternoon drive without Roy saying a word. Then he would suddenly look around and announce, "You'll be interested to know we are in Harrowsmith County now."

These were the melancholy thoughts that Dave carried with his yellow bucket and his damp deerskin into the driveway that Sunday morning.

Only moments before, life had seemed pretty all right, but it was with a lingering sense of sadness that Dave got down on his knees and began emptying his car of the detritus of the years, thinking, as he pulled candy wrappers and old pencil stubs from under the passenger seat, of how the generations that bracketed his had grown too old. Both his mother and father—and his son and his daughter—had deserted him. Abandoned him. No one needed him any more.

He filled a small plastic bag and went inside for another. He found a bleached rayon scarf on the back window ledge that looked as though it had been lying in the sun for years. And a pot of congealed lip gloss. And a pair of sunglasses he had never seen before. And wizened apple cores. And a leathery, hard plug of something that he first thought was a cigar and then realized was a mummified banana.

He ran his fingers over a mottled stain where a package of crayons had melted. The stain reminded him of the afternoon he had parked the car in the sun and come back to find his favourite King Crimson album curled like a dry sandwich.

He found a cucumber under the front seat. When he reached out to pick it up his hand went right through it. It had been over a week since Morley had been shopping.

The cucumber reminded him of the summer afternoon something had distracted Morley while she was unpacking groceries and she had forgotten a bag of meat in the trunk. The babysitter had found the meat days later and had phoned Dave at work to ask if he thought the hot dogs would still be all right.

"I don't think so," he said. "How do they smell?"

"They smell disgusting," said the babysitter. "But I was going to boil them."

He picked at a brown crust on the carpet on the floor of the back seat with pride. No one else would know what it was. Another summer memory. He had bought Sam a plastic cup of green Jell-O with a summit of whipped cream. He had found it a week later, minus the whipped cream, lying on the floor, both the plastic cup and the Jell-O fused into the carpet. He had removed what he could, but the Jell-O had baked into a resin-like blob the size of a hockey puck. Over the years the blob had slowly turned from green to brown and gradually worn away.

With growing despondency, Dave realized he would never be able to return his car to its pre-child state. In a way, it no longer mattered. Once there was a time when he would have cared. He didn't care any more.

Dave was on his knees by the back door on the driver's side, trying to pluck a reluctant coin out of a crevice, when he noticed a slight haze of green between the driver's seat and the front door. When he reached out to wipe the haze it felt soft and fluttery, not sticky like he'd expected. He leaned forward and squinted, and then he leaned forward more and blinked in amazement. Something had taken root in the sand in the bottom of his car.

There was a tiny plantlet growing there.

Dave's first impulse was to pluck the little green thing off the floor. But he hesitated for a moment, and in the moment of hesitation he was overcome with the miracle of it.

Somehow a seed had landed on the floor of his car. Somehow it had found enough dirt and sand and decomposing organic matter to germinate.

It was a flower in the desert. It was life, affirming life. It was reproduction. It was happening in his car.

He took the chamois and dripped some water into the well by the door and frowned. There was dirt and sand there, but that was hardly the medium for healthy growth. He went to the front garden and came back with a handful of soil. He padded it carefully around the seedling.

It took him over an hour to finish cleaning the car. He kept coming back to the driver's-side door to examine the plant.

Before he went in for breakfast, he jockeyed the car in the driveway and left the door open so the rays of the early morning sun caught his seedling.

Morley was up and about.

"I have to go in to work," she said. "I'll be home . . . I don't know, three, four."

And she breezed out the side door and climbed in the car. When she saw how clean it was, she smiled and gave Dave the thumbs-up. Then she drove away.

Dave, standing in the driveway, horrified.

He had once heard a story on the radio about a little girl. Was she two years old? She had climbed onto the back of her father's delivery truck just as he was leaving for work. Dave had imagined that her father worked for FedEx and that the little girl was standing on the back step of a big FedEx delivery van. This was in the country, and the man travelled for several miles up hills and around sharp corners before anyone could stop him.

When someone asked the little girl what she was thinking during the ride, she said, "Hold on, hold on."

As Dave stood in his driveway watching Morley drive away, he was muttering the same words to his little plant: *Hold on*.

He hadn't warned his wife. There wasn't enough time.

Or maybe it was because he was worried what Morley might do if he told her something was growing in the car. He was worried that she might not understand.

Morley didn't come home until supper.

When she pulled into the driveway, Dave ran out to meet her.

"How was your day?" he asked. He was staring at her feet as she opened the door, not at her face.

She almost put her heel down right on top of the seedling.

"Look out," Dave barked.

Morley looked at him as if he were crazy.

"What's the matter?" she said.

"I thought . . . " And that was the moment of truth. That was the moment he could have said: *There is a seedling in the car and I don't want you to kill it, because it is not just a seedling, it's the struggle of life itself.*

But he didn't say that because—well, it is hard to know why, isn't it? Hard to know why we say, or don't say, anything. Maybe he didn't say anything because in his heart he knew that Morley felt no insecurity about her role as a nurturing human being. She had, after all, carried their children in her belly; she had, after all, risen in the night and nursed them. She knew the ache of motherhood.

All Dave knew was that he didn't want anything to harm this plant, this life that had fallen under his care. And he knew that he had no confidence in his ability to explain this.

He found excuses all that week to use the car every day. It was something he hardly ever did. He would invent lunchtime errands that would take him great distances from work. Then, when it was time for lunch, he would drive to a quiet lane that ran along some railroad tracks and park in a sunny spot with the door open. He brought sandwiches in brown paper bags. He bought bottled water, amusing himself by changing brands each day.

"Today," he told his seedling, "you are drinking from a French glacier."

The first day he did this he poured out so much water that he almost washed the seedling away. He had to scratch a handful of earth from the hill by the railroad tracks and add it to his little garden to soak up the flood.

The next day he tried using a plastic coffee cup, with the same disastrous result. On day three he bought a small bag of potting soil at the hardware store and had it open by the car door.

For the rest of the week he filled his mouth with water and carefully measured the water out, squirt by squirt. Life to life.

By Friday his seedling had grown an inch.

That night he dreamed it was summer and he was driving his car along a winding mountain road, down some Mediterranean mountain towards the sea. Maybe it was in Monaco. It was hard to tell exactly because in his dream his plant, which must have been jungle ivy, had filled the car. It had twisted around the handbrake and up the steering column and around the mirror and in front of the windshield. Sitting in the driver's seat was like sitting in a jungle. Dave kept trying to brush leaves away from his face. The car kept going faster and faster, and suddenly Dave realized he wasn't driving any more. The plant was driving. The ivy had the wheel and it was driving too fast. There was a corner coming and they were going too fast for the corner and they were drifting into the oncoming lane and there was a truck coming the other way like in a James Bond movie. It was a FedEx truck and it was laughing at him. As it passed, Dave spotted Morley and the kids. They were standing on the ledge at the back of the truck and they were screaming, *Hold on, hold on*.

He woke up sweating, his heart pounding.

He went downstairs and made a cup of tea and added a shot of brandy. He stood by the window and watched a raccoon the size of an industrial vacuum cleaner waddle along his neighbour's fence.

When he finished the tea he picked up his car keys and stepped outside. It was hard to see in the dark. He got a flashlight. He opened the car door. His seedling was over two inches tall now. Two inches of wobbly green stem that looked entrancing in the yellow spotlight of the night. It had begun to branch out. The fresh green leaves were mysteriously serrated and impossibly well formed for something so small. It looked like a miniature shrub. Dave was enchanted.

He was still terrified that someone was going to see it and pull it up. Or worse, not see it and inadvertently step on it.

When the children were young and she'd had no other time, Morley used to garden by moonlight. *No time like the present,* he thought. Looking up at the moon, Dave reached down and tugged at his plant. To his great surprise it didn't come. He'd thought it would slip out of the ground like a carrot. With willing forgiveness. But it was resisting.

"I have to," he said quietly, and he tugged harder.

And it came.

He carried it to the back of his yard, the way you might carry a baby to its bed, to a corner by the fence. He broke the grass, placed the little seedling in the earth and said, "There."

And he went back to bed.

And he forgot about it.

And he did not remember it for three weeks.

And when he did he went to the corner of his yard by the fence and, to his great surprise, he found that his plant had grown as high as his knees.

He did not show it to Morley for two more weeks, not until the beginning of August, when it was higher than his waist.

He showed it to her and told her how he found the seedling in the car and how, one night, he planted it in this corner, and look what came.

Morley looked at his plant and rubbed the leaves and told him it was a sumac.

But it is not a sumac. It is an ailanthus, known as the *Tree of Heaven*. It is a persistent and resourceful little tree that was brought to New York years ago from Asia and thrives in urban environments. A tree that can sprout in a crack of the pavement and under porches and decks and, apparently, in cars.

Unlike a sumac, Dave's plant will keep growing until it is nearly sixty feet tall. At the end of every summer it will produce small yellow-green flowers, and in the early fall the flowers will be followed by a beautiful reddy fruit, bearing seeds with little wings, like maple keys.

Its leaves will come late in the spring, and every spring Dave will think his tree has died until, astonishingly, it comes alive. Every spring a miracle.

And every spring when the leaves finally come, Dave will stand in his backyard and think of the summer he found the tiny seedling in his car, and he will look at his tree and think that things survive—even without his presence. Even without him, life goes on. Life has a will of its own and he needn't worry. His job isn't to worry or do things. His job is to watch—and to wonder.

Lazy Lips

IT WAS ONE OF THOSE FUNERALS that just didn't make sense.

Dave drove down the night before and checked into the old Fox Hotel on George Street. The Fox had been gentrified since Dave had last seen it. There was a girl in a uniform standing behind the front desk, for heaven's sake, with a bowl of apples beside her. You wouldn't have eaten an apple that you picked off the front desk of the *old* Fox.

Dave wasn't unhappy to see the change. He had made the reservation for old times' sake, not because he actually *wanted* to stay in a dump. As he signed the register he was thinking that, since he had last stayed here, he had probably gone through about the same upgrade as the hotel. He picked up a local paper, selected an apple and took them both to his room.

Scotty Hornickel had played drums with Burton Cummings. Before Burton got famous. Scotty saw the fame coming before anyone else and quit.

"This is not the life I want," he said.

He ducked the fame and instead opened a little music store.

He was the kind of guy you wanted to know. Over the years everyone went to his store: Deep Purple,

Alice Cooper, Ozzie Osbourne, Iggy Pop. Dave had lost track of the nights he had sat around Scotty's store talking, listening to musicians jam.

Scotty watched everything philosophically. He was one of those guys you thought would go forever.

The funeral was just what you would have expected. There was a doo-wop group and a six-foot-eight, hundred-and-twenty-pound Wayne Newton impersonator. He looked ridiculous, but he sure could sing "Danke Schoen."

It was after the service, when a fog of sadness had settled on Dave and he was staring vacantly into his cup of coffee with sadness and regret, that Austin Shoop emerged out of the fog. Shoop, a bald man with bad clothes and earrings in both ears, looked at Dave and said, "Dave. Geez. I didn't know you were still around. Someone told me *you* were dead."

For the melancholy drive home, Dave put on a George Harrison tape and brooded his way through the night. "My Sweet Lord." "All Those Years Ago." The music didn't make him feel any better.

Over the years, Dave had worked with a lot of performers who had been snatched prematurely from life. Plane crashes, drug overdoses. But Scotty Hornickel and George Harrison had both died of natural causes. It was one thing living through unexpected tragedy. It was another thing to deal with natural, everyday, cycle-of-life tragedy. A nasty reminder that one day, and sooner now than it used to be, it was going to be his turn.

It was two weeks later when Austin Shoop called Dave at work.

"I've been thinking about you," he said. "I teach at the university, you know."

Dave didn't know.

"Ethnomusicology," said Austin Shoop. "Pop culture. The sixties. Anyway, Scotty used to come to my class every spring and, you know, talk to the kids. And now, well, being dead and everything, he isn't going to be available this year, and I was thinking, you could take his place."

Dave never went to university. When the kids he grew up with were going to university, Dave headed out on the road instead. He stayed out there for fifteen years, working as a technical director, and a road and tour manager for many of the biggest acts in the music business—certainly some of the craziest.

It was a decision he had never questioned—not seriously—not until his daughter, Stephanie, left for college. When Stephanie headed out to have this experience that he had never had, Dave began, for the first time ever, to wonder about the choice he had made. And that sneaky, most vexing of all questions raised its nagging head: "What if . . . ?"

The call from Austin Shoop made Dave feel good. His experience obviously counted for something in the world of academe. The life he had constructed was obviously not unimportant.

As soon as he hung up the phone, however, he had second thoughts. *Now why did I agree to that?*

Dave hated speaking in public.

He didn't mind speaking one on one, especially if he was speaking to people he knew. But if he was in the spotlight, if he was asked a question in front of others, the moths of anxiety began their dance.

Giving this speech was going to be a big deal.

Dave began to prepare three weeks before he was scheduled to visit Austin Shoop's class. He began writing out ideas on index cards. He decided he would begin by talking about Scotty.

Dorothy, who runs Woodsworth's Books, just down the street from Dave's record store, brought him an out-of-date pamphlet on public speaking. She meant it as a joke.

Dave read it from cover to cover.

The booklet said you should be able to wrap your lips around each word of your speech, as if it were a tasty morsel. It featured a series of lip exercises for "lazy lips."

Dave began the lip exercises. Stretching his lower lip over his upper lip, then stretching the upper lip down over the lower one. Alternating with increasing rapidity. Humming while he did it.

He did the exercises when his store was empty—sitting behind the counter with the booklet in his lap, rounding his lips tightly, as it advised, grooving his tongue and pushing it through the opening as fast as he could.

Twice, he was so caught up in these oral calisthenics that he didn't notice people coming through the front door. Both times, when the customers came in and caught him—sitting there with his tongue flicking in and out, his eyes crossed as he tried to follow it—they left without announcing themselves.

Dave made presentation notes on his index cards. *It is imperative,* he wrote, *to keep your breathing quiet and natural so that it remains unobserved by the audience.* He underlined "breathing quiet and natural."

But it was the pamphlet's section on body language that really caught his attention. He came home one evening and told Morley that over half of all human communication takes place on the non-verbal level.

"This is documented," he told her. "By research."

Smile at the audience, he wrote, underlining it three times. *Select one person in the crowd and talk to him or her personally.* He underlined "one person" three times.

And gestures. He should use gestures. All good speakers use gestures.

He stood in front of the bathroom mirror and tried out various gestures. Holding out his hands, palms up at shoulder height. That implied openness.

He put together a bag of his favourite records. The only album ever released by The International Submarine Band, Gram Parson's first country-rock group. A copy of the ultimate cult album, *Forever Changes,* by the doomed psychedelic group Love. A 45 rpm recording of the Nancy Sinatra–Lee Hazelwood duet "Some Velvet Morning"—a song his friend Richie Unterberger says is a strong candidate for the strangest song ever to enter the top forty.

The night before he was supposed to leave, Dave went upstairs into the attic to get a suitcase. He came downstairs in a Grateful Dead T-shirt, a leather vest and a pair of bellbottom jeans with embroidered cuffs. He was grinning gleefully. The pants were not done up at the waist, because they couldn't be done up at the waist.

"Because my hips have apparently gotten bigger," he said. "I'm hipper than I used to be."

He didn't *look* hipper than he used to be.

Morley stared at the fleshy lumpiness of Dave's belly hanging over his jeans. She was thinking, *I remember those jeans*. But she looked so distressed, so horrified, so defeated, so beyond speech that Dave didn't wait for her to say anything.

"I'm just joking," he said uncertainly. But he wasn't joking. He was holding his all-time favourite poncho behind his back. It was fashioned from a grey blanket.

"Seriously," he said. "How do you think I should dress for this?"

"Like an adult," said Morley.

The night before his speech, Dave stayed up until two-thirty in the morning copying onto paper everything he had written on his index cards. He wrote instructions in the margins. *Breathe. Smile. Gesture.*

When he finished, he carefully numbered each page so they couldn't get mixed up.

Dave arrived on campus four hours before he was scheduled to give his talk. He found the dormitory where he was going to spend the night and a young woman took him to his room—a spacious suite with a granite fireplace and a tiny bed.

"Stephen Hawking stayed here when he received his honorary degree," she told him. "And Pierre Trudeau."

She was standing by the door the way they do in hotels. Dave wasn't sure if he was supposed to tip her. Before he could decide, she had left.

He laid his clothes out on his bed. The Grateful Dead T-shirt and the vest. But not the jeans. Not the poncho.

The auditorium was bigger than he had expected. He had been thinking *classroom*. He had been thinking *grade six*. This was more of a theatre. It was three-quarters full when he arrived.

Backstage, Austin Shoop introduced him to a fussy young man.

"I'm doing audio," he said. "Where's your disk?"

Dave stared at him blankly.

"You're not doing PowerPoint?" he asked, incredulous.

Dave looked at Austin Shoop in confusion.

"Am I?" he asked.

"Just a microphone, Dwayne," Shoop said. He took Dave by the arm and led him to a small group of students standing by the Coke machine.

"My committee," he said.

"It is so good of you to come," said a well-scrubbed girl in a bright yellow sweater. "It is so important for us to hear about the sixties before everyone has passed away and everything is forgotten."

A second girl leaned forward. "We imagine you may not want to stand for the whole thing," she said. "We have a chair for you onstage. In case you want to sit while you talk."

Before Dave could protest, Yellow Sweater looked at him and said, "That's a very cool shirt. Is it from the sixties?"

Dave stared at them. They were smiling solicitously at him. They were all wearing chinos, fancy sneakers and pastel shirts.

He felt old. He felt intellectually bereft.

Austin Shoop, now at the podium, was not making him feel any better. Dave was sitting in his easy chair, in the middle of the stage, and mostly he was not understanding a word of what Austin Shoop was saying. Something about upcoming lectures. Something about the process of canon formation and the contemporary understanding of musical meaning. Shoop was in full academic flight. He was on about semiotics and critical theory and the neo-republicanism of Elton John, and

Madonna, whom he was describing as a postmodern goddess of commodification who had proclaimed the long-awaited emergence of matriarchy in the decay of the fallen western, male-dominated, post-war, post-industrial world.

Dave glanced at his speech nervously. He was doing his best to look as if he understood what Austin Shoop was saying. But he wasn't understanding. He wasn't even trying to understand. A horrible thought had occurred to him. What if, when it was his turn, he went to the lectern and froze? What if his mind went blank? What if he got to the podium and opened his mouth and nothing came out?

It had happened once to his son. His own flesh and blood, Sam, had stood onstage at a spring recital. Stood and stood and stood. And then, into the immense and awful silence that had settled over the auditorium, Sam had said one small word. He had said, "Sorry," and then walked offstage. What if it was genetic? What if Dave froze?

Dave's reverie was interrupted when he heard a ripple of polite applause and, looking up, realized Austin Shoop was staring at him. He glanced around uncertainly. There was some uncomfortable laughter. He looked back at Austin, who was nodding.

Dave stood up and took a tentative step towards the podium. He felt as if he were being led to his execution. He set his notes down awkwardly. Then he began to search for his glasses, patting his pockets. He found them, and leaned forward, and gripped the podium stiffly with both hands. There was dead silence now.

He grimaced, cleared his throat, sighed heavily and began reading his notes.

"It is a great pleasure to be here this evening," he said unconvincingly.

Of course, that's not what the audience heard him say. They heard him say, *I would rather have a needle in my eye than go any further.*

"It is a great pleasure to be here this evening," he said again, gripping the podium with all his might.

Then he remembered what he had practised, and he leaned forward and squinted at them. He was looking for someone with whom he could make eye contact. There was a shuffling as people looked away uncomfortably.

He couldn't catch anyone's eye.

Dave felt a stirring of anxiety in his stomach.

Then he spotted the girl in the yellow sweater.

When their eyes met, she swallowed nervously. But Dave felt a sense of relief.

He looked down at his speech and then back at the girl. And he began again.

"It is a great pleasure to be here tonight," he said, for the third time.

There was some nervous laughter at the back. But Dave didn't hear. Dave was remembering that it's the first couple of minutes that set the tone for the whole speech. Dave was thinking, *If I screw up here, I am going to spend the whole speech thinking about what I should have said at the beginning instead of thinking about what I should be thinking.* Dave knew if that happened, his brain could split, and that could lead to disaster.

And that's when he noticed his hands. They were gripping the podium so tightly his knuckles had turned white.

He looked out to see if the girl in the yellow sweater had noticed.

He looked at her so plaintively that she nodded at him. She was trying to be encouraging.

He misunderstood. He thought she was telling him, *Yes, I see them too.*

And suddenly his hands felt like big clown hands—like swollen, white-gloved cartoon hands two times too big for his body. Spatula hands. He had to get them out of sight before everyone noticed them.

He started to inch his hands slowly off the podium. And as he did this, he realized that his arms didn't feel like his own arms any more. They felt like penguin wings—big, flapping penguin wings with his swollen hands stuck on the end. They were sliding down the podium as if they had a mind of their own. And it was while Dave was watching them move and wondering where they might be heading that it occurred to him that he had already begun his speech.

He looked down and saw that he was, in fact, on page six. Words had been—and in fact were still—coming out of his mouth, though he had no idea whatsoever what he was saying. He had been too busy thinking about his spatula hands to pay attention. And now he heard himself talking and his voice sounded peculiar to him—it didn't sound like his voice. It sounded like someone doing a not very good imitation of his father.

That was when he noticed that he had reached the bottom of the page. He turned the paper over quickly so that no one would notice his big fat cartoon hands and he began reading at the top of the other side.

He was a third of the way down before he realized that he had been there before. He had turned back to page five, instead of ahead to page seven.

He said, "Sorry," flipped the page over and started down page six for a second time.

He did not notice what he had done because he was too busy looking for the girl in the yellow sweater, who had stopped nodding and had begun to frown.

That was when Dave remembered what he was supposed to do with his hands. He was supposed to make gestures.

Where are *my hands, anyway*? he thought. He began to pat himself down, looking for his hands the way you would look for a pair of glasses.

And he thought, *Isn't that silly*.

And precisely at that moment, his mind clicked over.

Dave had been reading the words on the pages in front of him mechanically while he fretted privately about everything else. Now, unbeknownst to Dave, deep in his brain a synapse misfired, or perhaps some wires got crossed, and he began reading his speech silently and speaking out loud everything that was going through his head.

And what was running through his head at that moment were the instructions about breathing.

"Breathe easily and at a natural pace," he said to the startled class. "If you are using a microphone, it is especially important to be careful that your breathing sounds aren't picked up by the mike and magnified to your audience."

Students began to glance at each other uncomfortably. Except, that is, for a boy in the first row, an engineering student who was taking the course as an elective and had been mystified by everything Austin Shoop had said. This boy was nodding earnestly. He opened a notebook and began writing.

Dave was so totally focused on the girl in the yellow sweater that he had no idea what was happening. And the expression of alarm that he read on her face wasn't helping. Her look of horror activated Dave's adrenal glands. His heartbeat quickened. His breathing became shallower and more rapid. His muscles tensed. Dave was scaling a summit of anxiety he had never visited before.

A body will do almost anything to rid itself of tension. Anything at all. Dave began to sway back and forth and to rock from side to side. His head was moving around like an oscillating fan. His right hand was jerking up and down like a parking lot gate. Dave thought he was making emphatic gestures with his hand. He had failed to take into account, however, that the gestures had nothing whatsoever to do with what he was saying.

His arm movements did make him *feel* more comfortable, and Dave thought, *Maybe I should switch positions,* so he leaned into the mike and said, "If you change your speaking position during a speech, you should always lead with the foot nearest your destination."

The boy in the front was writing everything furiously into his notebook.

But Dave wasn't looking at the boy in the front row. He was staring at the girl in the yellow sweater, and the more he focused on her, the more anxious she got. This maniacal speaker—waving his arms and weaving back and forth and saying all these crazy things—was speaking directly to her!

"If you are going to step to your left, lead with your left foot," said Dave. "Never cross one foot over the other when you begin a movement."

When Dave said that, his arm jerked violently up into the air and his watch flew off his wrist. It flew off his wrist and out into the stunned silence of the auditorium.

And everything stopped.

Dave stopped talking.

The boy in the front row stopped taking notes.

Everything stopped as they all watched the watch sail over the crowd. It sailed over ten rows—students swivelling in their chairs to follow it. It sailed over ten rows and landed in the lap of the girl in the yellow sweater.

She screamed in horror.

"Not me," she shrieked. "I'm only eighteen!"

That was more or less the end of the formal presentation. After people settled down, of course—after the girl in the yellow sweater had been led to the counselling offices, after some semblance of order had returned to the hall—Austin Shoop suggested that Dave might agree to answer questions.

Dave nodded, and a hand shot up in the air. It was the engineering student in the front row.

"Excuse me, sir," he said, flipping through his notes frantically. "Which leg did you say you lead with?"

After the rest of the questions—*mostly* about music—a small group of students gathered around Dave.

A young man with a soul patch, wearing army surplus pants and a V-neck blue sweater, looked at Dave and said, "That was incredible, man. Do you want to go for a beer?"

A beer was just what Dave needed.

They went to the student pub, and then about ten of them went back to the boy's room, because he had a turntable and they wanted to hear the records Dave had brought. Dave more or less gave them the talk he had meant to give in the auditorium. Except this time without his notes. This time, without worrying about his hands.

The kids would have stayed all night, but sometime after midnight Dave got overwhelmingly tired and left the albums with them and went to bed.

"Get them to me in the morning," he said.

The next day, Dave woke early and went for a walk—across the campus to the river, where he watched the scullers practising in the smoky morning mist. He sat on the bank and felt glad he had come. Even though the speech had been a disaster, talking with the kids afterwards had been nice. He'd been surprised to learn that none of them were musicians. Most of them were taking Austin Shoop's course as an elective. They were just normal kids getting ready for normal lives.

It made him feel good that they wanted to know what he had to say and what he had done with his life. It made him feel good that they saw value in his experience.

He liked the kids, and liked that they were interested in things. He was glad Stephanie had chosen to go to university. If she was meeting kids like this, she was going to be okay.

And he was happy with his choice, too. He had done what he wanted to do.

He got on the train to go home just before lunch. For the first while he sat quietly and watched the country rock by—the highways and the towns, with their rivers and old stone mills. He waved at some kids on their bikes by a level crossing. He bought a coffee when the porter came by, and then he opened his briefcase and pulled out his Discman. He put on his headset and slipped in a homemade Beatles CD. Both John and George were gone. But Paul was still here, and he was doing the one sure thing he could do. He was still singing. Dave turned up the volume.

Now Scotty Hornickel was gone too. Dave shook his head. They'd sure had some good times together. Laughing. Carrying on. Doing what they did. He turned the music up loud. So what if it would deafen him? It made him happy. Like it had so many times before.

Morley

Morley Writes

Meg Masters
Editor
Penguin Group (Canada)

Dear Ms. Masters,

Just a quick note to confirm what I am sure you already know. Stuart talked to me about the possibility of writing a brief note for his upcoming Vinyl Cafe book. Although the project sounds like fun and I am flattered by the invitation, I'm afraid I don't really have the time to do this. Best of luck with the book.

Cheers,
Morley

Dear Ms. Masters,

Thank you for your thoughtful note.

I understand how you might feel that we are "almost friends" and why it seems that you know me better than you know your own mother. (Although I would have preferred it if you had said "sister"!) And I am glad you enjoy my "frenetic wisdom." However, I haven't changed my mind about the introduction. Given that, I don't want to waste your time meeting for lunch.

I appreciate the invitation.

All the best,
Morley

Dear Ms. Masters,

Thank you for your lengthy letter. I sympathize with your desire to achieve some "symmetry" in the design of your book and understand that the other members of my family are participating in the project.

To be perfectly honest, however, I don't feel I have anything of substance that I could possible say about Stuart or about his radio show.

I don't tend to listen to his program much these days.

Sincerely,
Morley

Dear Ms. Masters,

In reply to your fax, I appreciate your offer to send me the book in galley form, but, as I have tried to explain, I haven't read Stuart's previous books and I don't want to change that now—in galleys, or final pages or whatever you call them.

Nor do I want to say anything about Stuart himself. He is a friend of my husband's and is over here more often than you would imagine. He's a nice enough fellow, if a bit absentminded. In fact I am looking at a pair of his reading glasses right now, which he left on the kitchen counter last night—leaving me once again with the dilemma of deciding: do I walk them over to his house or wait for him to call? If I do wait, you can bet he will call my cellphone in a panic when I am miles from home. Sometimes I think his glasses are more a hobby than a tool.

But why am I telling you this? You work with him—which I imagine is not without its challenges.

At any rate, that's a long way of saying no, I haven't had a change of heart about the essay. But thanks for checking.

Respectfully,
Morley

Dear Ms. Masters,

In reply to your email, I understand that "this little blurb" needn't be "a thesis," but I still haven't changed my mind.

Stuart swung by yesterday to pick up his glasses, but I suspect that was a pretext for bending my ear a bit more about this book. Even if I weren't so busy, I have heard enough about The Vinyl Cafe *and this book to keep me going until next spring.*

I remain,
Morley

P.S. If you are speaking to Stuart today, could you tell him that he has now left his ball cap at our place?

Dear Ms. Masters,

Thank you for the flowers. Most unexpected. So, too, your offer to have someone in your department write my "little essay thing" for me. As the "essay thing" is supposed to reflect what I think about the show, I find it hard to imagine how someone in your department could do a "preliminary draft" for me. Did Stuart put you up to this?

Puzzled,
Morley

Dear Ms. Masters,

I spoke to your publisher today. I told her that you have been making every effort to convince me to participate in the project. I explained my position to her. I don't think she will be bothering you anymore. Dare I expect the same from you?

Hopefully,
Morley

Dear Ms. Masters,

In response to your phone message—in a word, no.

With absolute
certainty,
Morley

Dear Ms. Masters,

Dave told me of your concerns. Not to put too fine a point on it, I don't think you would want to publish what I am thinking right now. You are going to have to come up with some way of filling these blank pages yourself. I am sure you are up to the challenge.

Morley

Labour Pains

THERE WAS A SATURDAY a few summers ago you might remember—so smudged and feverish that you might have thought, like Dave, that the city was about to ignite, that any moment the temperature would soar through a critical flashpoint and all the front lawns in sight would begin to smoulder.

It was the Saturday Dave staggered into his basement in search of his children's inflatable swimming pool. Not for the children. For him. When he found the pool, Dave lugged it onto the front lawn, inflated it, filled it with water, flopped down beside it and sat there in his shorts and his T-shirt, with his bare feet in the pool, holding, for dear life, on to the shards of his sanity.

He was sitting there looking as if he had been hit on the head with a rubber mallet when Amy Lane and her husband, Jim, walked by. Jim was wearing their week-old infant on his chest in a corduroy Snugli. It was the first time Dave had seen Amy and Jim since the birth of their baby.

"Congratulations," he croaked, barely summoning the strength to wave. He fully expected them to continue down the street. He had forgotten that Jim Lane was a first-time father.

Ten minutes later, Jim and Amy were sitting beside him with their feet in the pool. Dave was holding their daughter, and Jim Lane was well into the story of her birth.

"It was an amazing day," Jim was saying.

"Two days," said his wife pointedly.

"Thirty-six hours, *actually,*" said Jim, smiling at Dave, "of *actual* labour. But the pain wasn't that bad."

"Thirty-six and a half hours, *actually,*" said Amy.

"And we didn't take any drugs," Jim said proudly. "We did the breathing thing. I was the coach."

If he hadn't been so hot, Dave might have let that go by. If he hadn't felt so sticky and utterly exhausted, Dave probably wouldn't have said a thing.

But he was hot beyond belief. And feeling cranky. So instead of letting it go, Dave said, "I understand the breathing thing can be very helpful. I hear a lot of women recommend it to their husbands for root canal work."

It has almost been twenty years since Morley was first pregnant, with Stephanie. It wasn't the easiest of pregnancies. On Dave, that is. It was hard on Dave right from the start.

When Morley learned she was pregnant, she phoned Dave at work, at the record store. She called from a phone booth outside her doctor's office.

She said, "It's me. I have something to tell you."

She was feeling so tender and sentimental, so full of

hope and fear and great love, so full of so much emotion that she burst into tears.

She cried for five minutes.

Dave was holding on to the phone imagining horrible things—all the worst things. She was incurably ill. She had fallen in love with someone else. She was leaving him.

When she stopped sobbing, he said, "For God's sake, what's the matter?"

She said, "I have something to tell you," and then she burst into tears again.

When she finally blurted it out, when she finally said it—"I'm going to have a baby"—he was completely overwhelmed. He couldn't believe this was happening to him. It was too momentous, too God-like, to be part of the creation of life. Something bigger than him must have been involved.

She said, "I'm going to have a baby."

And Dave blurted out, "I didn't do it."

He closed the store and went right home.

They both cried.

For a week, Dave was buffeted by waves of anxiety. How could he, of all people, be a father? Then something clicked. He went to bed one night worried and woke up the next morning feeling oddly pleased with himself.

He also woke up with a new and dramatic aversion to chicken. Suddenly, he couldn't stand the smell, the texture or the taste of chicken. He couldn't stand the sight of chicken. He couldn't stand the idea of chicken.

He would break into a cold sweat driving past the Swiss Chalet.

Morley agreed to cut chicken from their diet.

By the end of the first trimester, Dave had put on twelve pounds. He'd gained the weight because the same morning the chicken thing happened, Dave developed a king-size yearning for dill pickle potato chips. By the end of the thirteenth week of Morley's pregnancy, Dave was eating a family-size package of dill pickle potato chips every day. He carried them around with him like a blankie.

Morley, however, was okay.

Morley had gained only eight pounds.

And it didn't really show.

Not like Dave.

At the beginning of the fourth month, Dave forgot to pay the rent at the record store.

"I'm worn out," he said to Morley. "I'm all fuzzy. I'm finding it hard to concentrate."

Everything seemed less important to him than the impending birth.

Morley began to worry. He was so wound up. She wanted to calm him down. She decided to cook a special meal—a romantic meal for just the two of them. She roasted a chicken. She'd completely forgotten.

When Dave came home from work, she sat him down at the kitchen table. There were candles flickering as she poured him a glass of red wine. Everything was beautiful. Until she produced the chicken and Dave started to cry.

This happened on and off for the next two months. Dave would be happy one moment and crying the next. He barked at her for the first time since they had been married.

She said, "You just barked at me."

He said, "You don't understand. What if there's something wrong with the baby? What if I'm a bad father? What if the baby doesn't like me? What if I lose my job?"

Morley said, "You own the business. Who is going to fire you?"

It didn't help.

She put her hand on his head. She said, "Dave, I love you."

He said, "What if you love the baby more?"

When they were six months pregnant Dave and Morley went, with their pregnancy class, on a tour of the hospital birthing rooms.

Like most men, Dave was pretty ignorant about his wife's reproductive system. He thought he understood in the broadest of terms what was going on, but he really didn't have a clue. It had all been explained to him once, but he had never got it clear.

It was as though someone had registered him in a book-of-the-month club without going over the rules. Dave was aware that there was a monthly mailing—but he wasn't at all certain what was sent. Or where it was sent from. Or, for that matter, where it went. Whenever he tried to remember any details, all he could summon up were disconnected words. Mostly nouns. Mostly place names, places that sounded like stops on the Paris Métro: the Oviduct; the Fallopian Tubes.

And the truth was he had belonged to this club for so long it seemed a little late to be asking about the rules. It would be like meeting someone on the street you don't recognize. There is that brief moment when you can say, "I am sorry, I have forgotten your name." But if you let that brief moment pass, there is no turning back. You have to fake it. Dave had been faking it for too long.

Taking everything into consideration, it was probably better he didn't know all the details of this book club.

The only trouble was he liked reading so much.

And so it was that, while Dave was navigating this foggy sea of uncertainty, he sailed into the hospital for his tour of the birthing centre.

It was all blue water until he nosed into the sterile field and fetched up in front of the stainless-steel table, face to face with the forceps and stirrups, face to face with the moment of truth. He made a weak signal and tried to paddle backwards, feeling dehumanized, feeling embarrassed, feeling seasick, but mostly . . . feeling faint.

As the class began to troop out of the room after the instructor, Dave went white and ghosted against the delivery room wall. Morley spotted him just before he pitched over. She leaned into him and pinned him to the pale-green wall until three of the other fathers came to her rescue. They picked Dave up and laid him on the birthing table. Before he came round, Ron, the class clown, tenderly placed Dave's feet in the stirrups. Then they scooted out, leaving him with Morley—shipwrecked.

When he came to, he made her promise she wouldn't tell anyone what had happened, especially the other fathers.

She never told him how he had ended up on the table.

It was a week later, at a regular meeting of their birthing class, that the nurse in charge asked the women to divide themselves into two groups.

"Everyone who is planning on a natural childbirth stay here," she said. "With me.

"Anyone who thinks they are going to have to take a chemical painkiller go to the far end of the room." As if they were being banished.

The husbands scuffed to the side while their wives guessed their way to either end of the room.

Morley was well aware that, if there was any truth in statistics, most women in this class would take something during their birth. She resented the nurse standing there, setting everyone up to feel bad. Morley didn't want to take painkillers during the birth, but she didn't want to disappoint herself either.

She joined the one other woman at the painkiller end of the classroom. When the room was finally sorted, there were just the two of them facing the ten women standing beside the nurse.

The fathers were all looking on anxiously. All except one. Only Dave had misunderstood the instructions. Only Dave among the men had moved numbly into the non-painkiller group. He was standing there amid the other mothers, staring bleakly at Morley, who was at the opposite end of the room glaring back.

The male and the female mourning dove are both involved in nest building. The male collects grass, weeds, twigs and pine needles and brings them to the female at the nest site. They both arrange the materials, and the nest is completed in one to six days.

Dave began to nest during Morley's eighth month. The nesting began unexpectedly at five o'clock one Saturday morning. It began when Dave sat up in the darkness and said, "I can't sleep. I'm going out to the garage to organize stuff."

Morley, who had spent the hours between midnight and four thrashing around, muttered, "Good idea." At three-thirty she had become convinced that this child she was carrying had a firm grip on her left kidney and was trying to stuff it over to the right side of her body so it would be more comfortable. She had been so sure this was happening that she had stumbled out of bed and checked the index of the book that was guiding her along this strange journey—a journey she had begun to call "the Watermelon Highway."

Morley, who had finally fallen into a restless sleep at four, muttered, "Good idea," but she had no memory of that moment when Dave appeared before lunch and told her proudly that he had sorted every last nut, nail and screw into little glass jars.

"I'm glad we got that done before the baby," he said.

"Me too," said Morley as she slumped in a kitchen chair and stared vacantly at a pile of laundry. She had been sitting there for forty-five minutes. She had been struck by the certainty that she was going to have twins and was wondering how the ultrasound could have missed this most obvious fact.

That was the weekend they bought the crib—a task they sailed forth to accomplish in high spirits only to flounder in the showroom, only to come aground on the rocky shore of choice.

"Would that be a traditional crib or something a little more contemporary?" said the saleswoman as they stood at the door of a place called Rock-a-Bye Baby. "Or perhaps a contemporary rendering of a traditional design?" she added before they could get away. "Or," she said as she put her arm around Morley's shoulder and chivvied her into the store, "perhaps something altogether different. Perhaps . . . a rocking crib."

Morley had a weepy moment in front of an Amish Sleigh crib and the women quickly turned to Dave and said, “We have it in pecan or mahogany.”

Dave stared at her dumbly so she continued, “Well? What colours are the nursery?”

Dave gestured helplessly towards Morley.

“We don’t have a nursery,” he said. “Do we?”

Wrestling with the profusion of choice there in the showroom turned out to be nothing compared to the mountain of misery they had to scale when they got home and Dave headed upstairs to assemble the crib.

“It shouldn’t take long,” he said.

He laid the pieces out on the floor and stared at them in mounting horror.

After an hour and a half he had all but given up hope—there was, as far as he could see, no visible way of attaching the bottom to the sides.

But even sure of this fact about this crib, he pushed on.

Three hours later he went downstairs and got Morley.

“I’m finished,” he said.

And then, as they stood in the bedroom doorway, their arms around each other, admiring what they had done, the cat purred past them and glided to the middle of the room. She stopped there and flicked her tail. When the air current she had disturbed hit the far side of the room, the crib shuddered, the sides folded in and it collapsed into a heap.

It was another two hours before Dave called Morley upstairs for the second time. He was standing beside the crib, his arm resting on the headboard.

"See?" he said, shaking it. "Solid."

Solid, certainly, but now the side went up instead of down, so if you wanted to take a baby in and out of the crib you would have to slide it in and out—the way you would slide a turkey in and out of an oven.

They didn't get it right until the next day. Not until Dave had phoned the crib helpline.

"I bet you get a lot of calls like this," he said.

"Not really," said the earnest young woman who had walked him through the instructions.

All he could think was, *If I can't even assemble a crib, how will I cope with being a father?*

Later that week Morley walked by the baby's bedroom and caught Dave bending over the crib. At first she thought he was admiring his handiwork. She stopped and watched him from the hall. As she watched, he bent over and fumbled with the latch and slid the crib side down. It was only then that she saw he was cradling the cat in his other arm. It was only then that she realized what he was doing. He was practising. She sneaked away without saying anything. She sneaked away filled with love.

It wasn't until the next morning that she realized the cat smelled of talcum. It wasn't until the next afternoon that she found the diapers in the garbage covered in cat hair.

She bought a breast pump and left it on the baby's changing table. Dave found it and thought it was a development toy. He suspended it over the crib.

"I put the mobile up," he said at supper.

They talked endlessly about how they were going to handle things. Dave didn't want the baby sharing their bed with them. He was adamant about this.

"What about the middle of the night?" asked Morley. "What if the baby is sick or crying? What if I fall asleep feeding her?"

"Her?" said Dave.

He wouldn't budge. He finally told her what he was afraid of. He was terrified he might roll over and smother his own child.

"But there is an instinct to stop you from doing that," said Morley.

"How can you be sure I have it?" he asked. "They might have missed me."

He filled a white plastic bag with five pounds of margarine, sealed it tightly and drew a stick-picture baby on it with a black marker. He set the bag down between them one night.

"I didn't say anything about a margarine instinct," said Morley. "I said a baby instinct."

"We'll see," he said.

Morley woke up at three in the morning to find Dave beside her, holding his hands out like Lady Macbeth. He was covered in margarine.

"I killed her," he said. "I killed her."

Dave, who had his face almost pressed into hers—Dave, who was staring right into her wide, white eyes—said triumphantly, "It's *our* spot."

And that was when Morley's eyes got even wider. When she moved even closer and said, "*My* spot! Not *our* spot, *my* spot, Dave. I'm the one having this baby! I want you to tell me what *my* spot is!"

Dave nodded at her earnestly, prying her hand off his arm. He pushed a chair to the middle of the room and stood on the chair. While Morley huffed and puffed he peered at the spot on the ceiling and said, "I think it's a squished fly."

Their nurse winced.

There was the briefest moment of silence.

Then Morley began. She said many things, most of them mercifully forgotten and never repeated. The gist of what she said was that she was not about to focus all her life-producing energies—all her God-like, child-producing strength—on a dead fly. You idiot. The gist of what she said was that Dave had to find another spot or he might as well forget about fatherhood. But Dave couldn't see another spot. He had never heard her speak like that. He was terrified.

Then Morley wasn't talking to him any more. She was talking to the doctor, she was telling the doctor (in what might be described as an assertive tone) that it would be a good idea if he gave her something for the pain.

Dave thought to himself, *This is the moment I am supposed to step up to the plate*. They had agreed that

Dave—the birth coach—was, at this moment, to dissuade Morley from taking painkillers, to encourage her to keep at the breathing, to focus and visualize away the "discomfort."

Dave faced the doctor and said, "We aren't going to take anything for the pain."

The doctor looked at Dave and then glanced at Morley, who had just been hit with a contraction so powerful that she was moaning like a wounded beast. Dave turned to the doctor and, in a small, faraway voice, said, "On the other hand, could I maybe have something for the pain too?"

The book had said there might be moments like this. Moments when he would feel uncomfortable and queasy, and he had thought he understood that, but nothing he had read had prepared him for this. There were sounds coming out of his wife that were making him afraid. Sounds so frightening that he didn't want to hear them. She was bathed in sweat and making extraordinary sounds. He was sitting in the corner of the room now, and that's when he realized what the breathing was for. The breathing they had learned in class and had practised together wasn't for Morley. What she was doing now was beyond breath.

The breathing was for him. He was breathing in and out, in and out, and while he breathed, she was bringing life into the world. All he could think was, *In and out, in and out.*

He looked at the pathetic bag of fresh fruit he had brought. Offering his wife a kiwi fruit at this moment would be as ridiculous as trying to tame a mythological beast with a plate of olives. The doo-wop tape he had made seemed so ludicrous. Why hadn't anyone told him what this would be like? Why hadn't they told him he should have been wearing mountain-climbing gear? Next time he would be ready. Next time he would wear a helmet and crampons. This wasn't a breathing thing, this was an Everest thing. This was a survival thing. A life-or-death thing. The next time he would bring rope. Lots of rope so they could tie themselves together. And maybe a large mallet. He would bring a large rubber mallet for the pain. This is what he was thinking as his daughter's head crowned. He was thinking about rope, and then he remembered he had to keep breathing—in and out. Just as long as he didn't have to do anything but breathe in and out the way they had taught him in class, he would be all right. He closed his eyes and concentrated on his breath. He didn't feel uncomfortable and queasy; he felt terrified. He was involved with something much too big for him. And suddenly there was another cry and the doctor was holding a baby in his arms.

Suddenly the two of them were three. Dave felt a rush of wonder. The doctor was holding their baby. Their daughter. Their Stephanie. He took her in his arms and the very first thing that came into his mind was *One day this girl is going to break my heart*. And he began to cry.

This is what Dave was thinking about as Amy and Jim continued to talk about the gory details of their daughter's birth. He realized he had missed some of their story, but now he had no urge to rush them along, to hurry them through their own Everest tale. He peered down into the baby's remarkable, tranquil face and smiled.

"What happened next?" he said. "What happened next?

Birthday Present

THE DAY MORLEY TURNED FORTY—a Tuesday afternoon that seems long ago and far away now—her friend and neighbour Mary Turlington came over after lunch with a little box wrapped in gold foil. It was just a token. The sort of trinket women give to each other to mark special moments. It was a ceramic creamer in the shape of a cat—the creamer's handle fashioned from the cat's tail, the cream designed to purr out of the cat's mouth. It was the sort of thing you would pass with a smile and a shake of your head at a garage sale. But, if you happened to get one from your best friend on your fortieth birthday, it would be the sort of thing you might grow fond of, the way you grow fond of certain Christmas decorations.

Women understand these things. In fact, only women possess the grace to pull something like this off. A man is not likely to drop in on a friend, unannounced, on his friend's birthday, and give him a ceramic creamer in the shape of a cat. Not in a thousand years. And if he did—if, say, Bert Turlington were seized by some inexplicable spasm and bought Dave a ceramic creamer for his birthday, wrapped it and took it to his house after dinner—no matter how cool it was (because a cat creamer could possess a certain retro coolness), the transaction would leave a trail of awkwardness and confusion that could hover between Bert and Dave for . . . well, quite possibly for the rest of their lives. For months they would avoid each other, in case the subject of the creamer arose.

But Mary isn't Bert, and Morley isn't Dave, so on Morley's fortieth birthday, Mary Turlington knocked on Morley's front door after lunch, holding her dog's leash in one hand and the wrapped creamer in the other.

When Morley opened the door her eyes were watery and red. She was holding a wad of Kleenex. She looked as if she had been weeping. She had, in fact, been weeping on and off all morning.

"Morley," said Mary right away, "what's the matter?"

Now that's another thing a man wouldn't do. If Bert knocked on Dave's door to give him a ceramic creamer in the shape of a cat (of course it wouldn't be in the shape of a cat, it would be in the shape of a dog) and Dave answered the door with tears in his eyes, Bert would not ask what was wrong. Not if he was thinking clearly. If he was thinking clearly, Bert would do one of two things. He would remember something he needed to check at home: "I'll be back in a minute," he might say. Or, if he wasn't overwhelmed with the need to escape, if he wanted to stick around, Bert still would not risk an emotional encounter. He would help by handing his friend a plausible excuse.

He wouldn't ask, "What's the matter?" He would say, "You cutting onions?"

But because she is a woman, and therefore possessed of an emotional fearlessness, Mary looked at Morley's red and watery eyes and she drove right to the heart of the matter. Mary said, "Morley, what is the matter?"

Morley's shoulders began to shudder. She opened her mouth, but no words came out. She shook her head, turned and walked into the kitchen.

Mary followed her.

They sat at the kitchen table.

Finally Morley said, "How could he live with me so long and not know I would hate it?"

"You mean tonight?" said Mary.

"I don't want a birthday party," said Morley. "I hate birthday parties."

Morley had, in fact, hated birthday parties since she was a little girl, hated them ever since she could remember.

She hated birthdays so much she had burst into tears at her own fifth birthday party the moment everyone began to sing "Happy Birthday."

Morley didn't like being the centre of attention.

And she hated everything else about birthday parties. She hated greeting people at the door. She hated games like Pin the Tail on the Donkey. She hated bursting balloons. She even hated presents. When she attended her friends' birthday parties, Morley would watch them unwrap their presents with her heart pounding, her anxiety rapidly escalating. She would grow frantic because she wanted the birthday girl to like her present the best.

The year she turned seven, Morley sat in front of her pile of unwrapped presents and started to weep. "I don't want to open them," she said to her mother between sobs. She was certain there would be a present she wouldn't like. And she was sure everyone would know. She was afraid she would hurt someone's feelings, afraid she wouldn't be a good enough actor.

And now, thirty-three years later, Morley felt much the same about the neighbourhood party Dave had planned for her fortieth birthday. She didn't want to be the centre of attention on her fortieth birthday. She was afraid she wouldn't be a good enough actor.

She had hoped the day would just slip by.

Dave had known that she would *say* that she didn't need a party. So he hadn't told her about it until two days beforehand.

She begged him to call it off.

"But I've already invited everyone," he said.

Morley didn't want the entire neighbourhood knowing she was forty. "You announced it?" she said.

"Not exactly announced," said Dave. "I asked people to come. To a party."

"You announced it to the neighbourhood," said Morley.

"Just people we know," said Dave.

"You told them I was forty?"

"Well, *turning* forty," said Dave. "Not *actually*. Forty. Not yet. Technically."

This was information that Morley had not planned on releasing. She didn't want children on the block running around chanting, "Lordy, Lordy, your mom's forty!" It was a fact she had thought they could keep within the privacy of their own home.

"It is just so insensitive," said Morley to Mary Turlington. She was fiddling with the little cat creamer as she talked.

"What do you guys normally do?" asked Mary. "What do you do on his birthday?"

"I never throw a party," said Morley defensively. "Never. Ever.

"Last year," said Morley, "I gave him ballet tickets."

"Oh," said Mary, nodding.

"The year before," said Morley, shutting her eyes, "I gave him a Shaker blanket box."

"And the year before that?" asked Mary.

"Cooking class," said Morley.

"Cooking class," said Mary.

"I enrolled him in a vegetarian Indian cooking class," said Morley.

"He must have liked that," said Mary.

"Actually," said Morley, "I'm not sure."

If truth be told, it wasn't just the notion of being the centre of attention that was upsetting Morley. Honestly, a part of her was charmed that her husband had planned to make a fuss over her fortieth birthday.

But she was anxious about the *kind* of fuss her husband might organize.

As Morley understood it, Dave's notion of a party involved a keg of beer, a few bags of chips and a crowd of people drinking the beer on empty stomachs.

"I hired caterers," said Dave.

"You what?" said Morley.

"I have hired caterers," said Dave. "You don't have to do a thing. The caterers will come in the afternoon and bring the food and set everything up. They'll clean up before they start, and they'll clean up when they're finished."

What could she say? He wasn't begging her, but almost.

So the party was on. And that's why Mary found Morley crying on the day she turned forty.

The caterers were supposed to arrive at three.

Morley had agreed to go out for the afternoon. She would get her hair done. She would have a facial. She would go shopping. They would leave a key under the mat. The caterers would let themselves in and get ready.

"No cleaning, no cooking, no nothing," Dave had said. "You go out. You come home. Everything will be ready."

"I have to get ready to go," said Morley to Mary Turlington. She stood up and began to clear off the table.

"Let the caterers do that," said Mary.

Morley looked around her kitchen. There was a laundry basket on the counter. There were dirty breakfast dishes in the sink. There were footprints on the floor.

"I was going to wash the floor," said Morley.

"No cleaning," said Mary.

"I can't leave the house like this," said Morley.

"Yes, you can," said Mary. "That's the deal. Right?"

So off she went.

And at ten past five, there she was, walking up the street towards her house. Except she wasn't walking up the street—she was swinging.

Forty years old and Morley had just had her first facial. Her first manicure. She felt elegant. She felt sophisticated. Her hair was light and bouncy. It felt as if it was swaying back and forth like TV commercial hair. She glanced down at her hands. Her nails were sparkling. Her face was glowing. She was moving with grace. She sensed that her posture had improved. She was standing tall. She was utterly . . . presentable.

She held her nails up to her face, and she looked around the street and she thought, *Please Lord, let this be the moment I run into someone I haven't seen for years.*

And then she was thinking about what was waiting for her. She was thinking that, in a moment, she would walk into her house, and there would be a caterer to greet her. She thought how good it was to be rich. *My servant is waiting,* she thought, *my servant who has been with me all these years. I should give him the weekend off.* And that made her smile, and she thought, *How would I cope without him? I don't even know where he keeps the coffee.* She laughed out loud and thought how wonderful it was to be so calm and elegant. How wonderful it was to have a faithful servant laying out plates of hot food on your dining room table while you sashayed along the street looking so good that birds were falling out of the very trees you were walking under.

Morley could hardly wait to get home. She would breeze into the kitchen, check one of the dishes casually, as if this were something she was used to doing. And then she would go upstairs and stand in front of the mirror and check herself. She would look so good.

It was five-twenty when she walked in the side door.

She expected to be wrapped in the steamy aroma of a kitchen going full blast. She expected her dining table to be groaning with hot plates and platters. She expected hors d'oeuvres and entrees, salads and desserts. She expected an abundance—no, she expected an overabundance, she expected excess.

She walked in the side door and up into the kitchen and stopped dead in her tracks.

She looked around in disbelief.

There was a laundry basket on the counter. There were dirty breakfast dishes in the sink. There were footprints on the kitchen floor. Not only was there no food, there was no sign of a caterer anywhere. There was a deficit of caterers.

She phoned Dave at work.

Dave wasn't at work.

"He left an hour ago," said Brian, who comes in part-time. "He said to tell you he went to get a keg of beer."

"A keg of beer?" choked Morley.

"And chips," said Brian.

Morley's mouth fell open.

She hung up.

"That was a joke," said Brian. But she didn't hear him.

Brian phoned back.

"That was a joke," he said. "Dave went to buy flowers. Is everything okay?"

"The caterer isn't here," said Morley.

"Don't worry," said Brian. "He'll show up."

"But people will be here in less than an hour."

"Those guys work fast," said Brian. "Don't worry."

Okay, thought Morley.

She went upstairs and stood in front of her full-length bedroom mirror. Her elegance had evaporated. She looked distressingly familiar. Her hair, which had been so flouncy on the street, had flounced into a tangled mess.

She looked at the clock radio. Five-thirty.

The invitation had said six.

She went downstairs to the kitchen. The laundry basket was still on the counter, the dishes still in the sink, the footprints still on the floor.

The telephone rang. She looked at it with apprehension.

"Hello?" she said.

It was a man. An unfamiliar voice.

"Is that you, Mrs. Dave?"

"Yes," said Morley. "Who is this?"

"I am Frank. Your server," said the voice on the phone.

"Frank," said Morley. "Where are you?"

The voice said, "I am right here. Where are you?"

Morley said, "I'm in the kitchen."

There was an uncomfortable pause.

The voice on the phone said, "I don't see you."

Morley said, "Well, where are you?"

The voice on the phone, Frank, said, "I am in the kitchen too."

There was another pause. A longer pause.

Then Frank said, "I don't think you are in the kitchen. When are you coming home?"

Morley said, "Frank. Where are you exactly?"

Frank said, "By the stove."

Morley couldn't help herself. She glanced across her kitchen towards the stove. She almost said, "No, you're not." But she suppressed the impulse and said, instead, "Frank, what house are you at?"

"I am at your house," said Frank. "Fifteen Chestnut."

"Frank," said Morley, "we don't live at Fifteen Chestnut."

Morley could hear the gears grinding in Frank's brain.

"But," said Frank triumphantly, "if you do not live here, why am I all set up for your party at Fifteen Chestnut?"

"Frank," said Morley, "we live at Fifty Chestnut."

There was another pause. Longer still.

"Frank," said Morley, "why did the people at Fifteen Chestnut let you in to set up for a party they're not having?"

"You are not home yet," said Frank.

"Frank," said Morley, "how did you get in?"

"There were men working on the deck," said Frank. "*They* let me in."

"Frank," said Morley, "I don't want to upset you . . . but I think you're in the wrong house."

Morley had the portable phone in the crook of her shoulder. She had already picked the laundry basket off the kitchen counter. She was running upstairs. She stopped on the landing.

"Frank," she said. "Don't cry."

"I just lit the Sterno," he said. "All the food is in the warming dishes." Frank's voice had risen an octave. He said, "The house wasn't ready for a party. It took me an hour to tidy everything."

Then he said, "What happens if you come home?"

"Frank," said Morley. "Frank, stay calm. I have a plan."

"This is not a good situation," said Frank. "I have no training for this."

"Frank," said Morley. "Listen to me. I want you to turn the warming plates off. I want you to walk up the street. No, Frank, listen to me. I want you to run up the street. I want you to run up the street to my house. I want you to run to Fifty Chestnut Street. There is a station wagon in the driveway. I am going to put the key in the ignition. Bring everything down here."

There was a sob on the other end of the line. Frank said, "What about the Millers, Mrs. Dave?"

"Who are the Millers, Frank?" said Morley.

"There is an envelope here on the counter by the fridge. It is addressed to Mr. Don Miller. If you don't live here, is it possible that Mr. Don Miller does?"

Morley took a deep breath. She said, "The Millers aren't expecting you, Frank. I am."

She felt as if she were in the thick of a hostage-taking. She felt as if she were trying to talk a hostage-taker out of his hideout.

"Mrs. Dave," said Frank, "what happens if the Millers come home and find their house tidy and clean and smelling of chicken pot pie and vegetable cannelloni?"

"Frank," said Morley, watching herself in the mirror, "that is a risk we are going to have to take."

It took Frank five minutes to get down the street. When he knocked on the front door his face was white.

"Frank," said Morley, "the key is in the car."

"Mrs. Dave," said Frank. He was wringing his hands. "You don't understand. You don't understand how much I cleaned up there. The house . . . it doesn't look like the same house any more."

"Just go, Frank," said Morley. "We won't say anything to anyone. Just go and get the food."

Frank was nodding his head. But he was staring into the middle distance and he wasn't moving.

"Frank!" shouted Morley.

The tires squealed as he backed onto the street.

Halfway up the block he honked his horn, jammed on his brakes and swerved around a man on a bicycle.

It was Dave.

Dave watched in disbelief as his car screeched to a halt. He watched as a man he had never seen before, a man in black pants and a white shirt, leapt out of his car and ran into Dr. Caudwell's old house.

Dr. Caudwell had sold his house just before Christmas.

Before Dave could work out what to do, the man ran out of Dr. Caudwell's old house carrying a large chafing dish. He threw it in the back of Dave's station wagon. And then he ran back into the house again.

Dave couldn't believe his eyes.

He was witnessing a robbery.

As he watched, the man came out carrying another piece of silver.

Without stopping to think, Dave dropped his bike and began to lumber along the street. He launched himself across the sidewalk at Frank, feeling like Sergeant Preston of the Yukon—about to get his man—but looking, sadly, more like the last kid chosen on the schoolyard football team. Frank looked up at the last moment and stopped dead in his tracks, watched Dave fly by him like an off-target human cannonball. Dave hit the car instead of Frank and slid to the ground. Frank stared in amazement as Dave struggled to his feet. Frank couldn't believe his eyes when this strange, deranged man shook himself off and came at him again. This time they went down in a tangled heap.

Frank had been carrying a dish of tomato bisque. When the steaming soup hit Dave's chest, he looked down and saw what he determined was his own blood and gore streaming down his flannel shirt.

"I have been stabbed," Dave screamed. "Help me!"

And that's when the second car pulled into the driveway.

And Don Miller stepped out.

He surveyed the scene and pulled out his cellphone and called the police.

It took a while for everyone to calm down.

For Dave to understand he hadn't halted a crime in progress.

For Frank to stop fretting about Dave's chest wound.

When they did straighten things out and they all went inside, Don Miller couldn't believe what Frank had done to his house. The house had been full of contractors when Don had last seen it. Frank had rolled up the painters' drop cloths and swept up the sawdust and lugged a table up from the basement.

They were standing in the empty living room.

"It looks incredible," said Don Miller.

"I know," said Frank.

And that is when Don Miller said, "My wife and kids come in tonight. But we're staying in a hotel until

Monday, when the movers come. Why don't you leave everything here? Why don't you have your party here?"

And that's when Dave said, "Only if you bring your family."

There is something liberating about a house without furniture. There is something musical about voices when they bounce off empty walls. There is something about the way bare wood floors invite people to move—to slip, to slide, to become dancers.

Dave loaded up a box of his favourite party albums—*Gimme Shelter* by the Rolling Stones, *OK Computer* by Radiohead, *Hip Hugger* by Booker T and the M.G.'s, *Aretha's Greatest Hits*.

By the time Don Miller arrived with his wife and two kids, the music in the living room was cranked. People were dancing.

It was a grand party.

Frank recovered his equilibrium and glided around the house with his bow tie askew and his sleeves rolled up. People perched on countertops with plates in their laps. People sat all the way up the stairs sipping wine from glasses and beer out of the bottle. Someone ordered pizza for the kids.

At eleven-thirty, while they were dancing in the living room with their shoes off, Morley leaned against Dave and said, "I feel like a teenager."

Which is exactly what Sam, eleven years old, said not five minutes later to Molly Miller, age twelve, as he smoked his first cigarette with her in the Millers' garage.

The Millers come from Indian Bluff, Saskatchewan, a town of two thousand people, where Don taught high school and Susan worked in the bank.

"This is great," said Don Miller to Dave as they leaned against the kitchen counter just before midnight. "We were scared of coming. I don't mean tonight. Not to this. To the city. Susan was offered an opportunity and we had to try it. But we were scared we wouldn't meet anyone. We were scared Molly would meet the wrong kind of kids."

By the time they brought out the cake, Morley had forgotten it was her birthday. Mary Turlington had got at the icing anyway and it now read *Happy Birthday Morley* across the top and *Welcome Home Millers* on the bottom.

Don Miller gave a speech, and he was funny and everyone applauded and no one even noticed Morley when she sat down quietly in a corner and opened her presents.

It was a perfect night. A night of spilled drinks and laughter and general youthfulness. A perfect night to turn forty.

Sometime after midnight Sam came to Morley and said he didn't feel good.

"I think I'll go home," he said.

"Too many Cokes," said Morley.

"I smoked," said Sam.

"Oh," said Morley. "That always makes me feel sick."

"Me too," said Sam. "Do you think I'll get cancer?"

"Probably not," said Morley. "Do you think you can quit?"

"I think so," said Sam. "I'm going to quit tomorrow."

It was well past midnight when Dave and Morley slipped quietly in the back door of their house. Dave poured himself a glass of water and leaned against the kitchen counter.

"Was that okay?" he asked.

Morley walked across the kitchen and put her arms around Dave's neck. She leaned into him and whispered in his ear.

"One more dance," she said. "One more dance."

And they danced slowly around the kitchen. Dancing to the sounds of night cars and crickets.

There was a laundry basket on the counter. There were dirty breakfast dishes in the sink. There were footprints on the floor.

It was perfect.

Rashida, Amir and the Great Gift-Giving

IN THE MIDDLE OF NOVEMBER, when Jim Scoffield was cleaning out his attic, he came across a box of children's books he neither recognized nor remembered. He brought them downstairs, intending to do what he always does with books he doesn't want. He was going to take them to the library and push them through the return slot.

By Friday afternoon, the books had made it as far as his front hall, which is where Jim happened to be standing when he spotted Rashida Chudary pushing her daughter, Fatima, up the street in her stroller. Rashida and her husband, Amir, had moved into the neighbourhood in January, and everyone had taken great delight in helping the Chudarys through their first winter. When it snowed, people woke up all over the neighbourhood wishing they could be at the Chudarys' to see their reaction.

Jim grabbed some wrapping paper from where he keeps it, under the sofa, and quickly gift-wrapped the books.

Then he ran outside.

"An early Christmas present," he said, handing the children's books to Rashida and pointing at her daughter.

Jim said the thing about the books being a Christmas present so she wouldn't think he was odd, running out like that. He gave her the books and then he went inside to fix dinner and forgot about them completely.

Rashida didn't, however. Rashida went home and went into a tailspin.

Rashida and Amir are from Pakistan. This was going to be their first Christmas in Canada.

"Jim clearly said it was an early Christmas present," she told Amir that night when her husband arrived home. "Do you know what that means?"

Amir shook his head disconsolately.

Rashida was pacing.

"It surely means this whole neighbourhood gives each other presents," she said.

It was not two days since the start of Ramadan. Amir hadn't eaten since sun-up. His head was throbbing. He couldn't think about neighbourhood gift-giving. All Amir could think about was the carrot muffin he had seen in the doughnut store at lunchtime. He had only gone to the doughnut store to look at the muffins.

"I don't understand why we don't have muffins in Pakistan," he had said when he'd first tried one. "They are truly wonderful things."

Rashida could see that Amir was thinking about food—he had a certain muffin-hungry look about him. She wasn't about to be distracted.

"He was waiting for us . . . on his porch," she said. She was holding out the books Jim had given Fatima.

"They were beautifully gift-wrapped. If Jim did this," she said, "imagine what Gerta Lowbeer will do. And what about Betty the Baker?"

When they'd first arrived in the neighbourhood, Betty Schellenberger had brought them home baking countless times.

"Maybe if you walked by her house tomorrow," said Amir, "Betty the Baker would give you delicious carrot muffins for Christmas."

Rashida snorted. "Amir," she said, "this is not a joking thing. Remember what happened in October."

What happened in October was Hallowe'en, and Hallowe'en was a disaster at the Chudarys'. No one had warned them about trick-or-treating. When the doorbell had rung unexpectedly during supper, Rashida had opened it to find a mob of chanting children. She had thought they were teasing her. Rashida shooed the children away and shut the door as quickly as she could, hoping Amir wouldn't notice.

Children kept coming to the door all night, of course.

When they finally figured out what was going on, they were horribly embarrassed. Rashida didn't want to repeat the disaster.

"Amir," she said, "we have to get to work."

Amir and Rashida spent November in a frenzy of preparation. They assembled elaborate gift baskets for everyone in the neighbourhood. Each basket had little packages of aromatic rice and tamarind and home-made chutneys. They stayed up late sewing little cloth bags for the spices.

Things at Dave and Morley's house were more comfortable in the run-up to Christmas. Morley has been paring back her Christmas responsibilities over the years. She has pruned her shopping list. She doesn't do as much baking as she used to. And Dave always does the turkey now. So as Christmas approached, Morley felt uncommonly sanguine about the season. She felt as if she were floating above it, as if she were a seabird floating effortlessly over the waves. She felt such a sense of control that she even sat Dave down one night and they sent Christmas cards to his Cape Breton relatives.

On an impulse, Morley sent a card to Amir and Rashida. By coincidence, it arrived the morning Rashida and Amir finished making their neighbourhood Christmas packages.

"Oh my golly," said Amir. "Not cards too."

Unlike Morley, Dave had been preoccupied with Christmas since the end of October. The neighbourhood arena holds an annual skating party every December—a fundraiser to raise money for a new Zamboni.

Dave went to an organizing meeting. When he set off, he knew he wouldn't be leaving without something to do.

Before the meeting began, Dave overheard Mary Turlington talking to Polly Anderson.

"He flips a few steaks on the barbecue and he thinks he has cooked a meal," she said disparagingly.

She was talking about her husband, Bert.

"Baking," said Polly Anderson. "That's the final frontier. Show me a man who can bake a cupcake and I'm all his."

They both cracked up.

At the end of the meeting the chairman passed a typed list of jobs around the table. Dave looked down the list and without a second thought said, "I'll bake the Christmas cake."

He said it for Bert Turlington. He said it for Ted Anderson.

He said it for all the men in the neighbourhood.

He said it for men everywhere.

He saw Mary Turlington shoot Polly Anderson a raised eyebrow.

And that's how, on a Saturday in the middle of November, Dave came to be in his kitchen, surrounded by brown paper bags of sultanas and currants and lemons and figs and dates and prunes and nuts and glazed cherries and various sugars. And a giant jug of bourbon. He was wearing a Santa Claus hat.

Morley had taken one look at him and said, "I think I'll take Sam to a movie."

Dave had imagined his family at home while he baked—Sam licking the beaters, Morley with her arms around him.

But Dave and Morley have been married over twenty years now. Morley knows how these things go.

"So we won't be in your way," she'd said, struggling into her coat. She couldn't get out of there fast enough.

Autumn dimmed and the rains of November arrived and the street lights went on earlier each night. The wind came up and the leaves blew off the pear tree in the backyard, and it was good to be inside. And inside at Dave's house, life was sublime.

Dave had his cakes wrapped in cheesecloth and aging on a shelf in the basement.

Two or three evenings a week he would head downstairs and sprinkle them with a soaking mixture he made with the bourbon.

"It is very European," he said one night. "It's like having a goat down there."

Sometimes on the weekends Kenny Wong came over, and they would go into the basement and sprinkle the cakes together.

On Grey Cup weekend, Dave and Kenny watched the entire game without touching one beer. They sucked on half a fruitcake each.

By the middle of December, Dave was ready for the arena. Big time. His cakes were moist and mature and, truth be told, delicious. Dave had eaten two of them. He had nibbled them both to death. He had the remaining dozen lined up like gold bars in a vault.

Amir and Rashida had their gift baskets ready to go too—wrapped in Cellophane, tagged and waiting in the front hall.

But a sense of anxiety had descended upon the Chudarys. Amir and Rashida didn't know when the neighbourhood gift-giving would begin. Knowing nothing about Christmas traditions, they didn't want to jump the gun.

"It wouldn't be right, Amir," said Rashida. "We must wait."

And then there was a party at Fatima's daycare, and all the children were given presents.

That night Rashida said, "I am thinking, Amir, that the gifting has obviously begun. We have not been included because they do not want to make us uncomfortable. If we are going to be part of this neighbourhood, Amir, it is up to us to make the first move."

Amir thought otherwise, and they had a steamy argument about what to do. In the end, Rashida said, "I am going tonight and that is all. If you are coming with me, Amir, you must come tonight."

And so they set off after supper, pulling their wagon full of twenty-eight gift baskets.

When Rashida handed Morley her Christmas basket, Morley experienced a stab of guilt. She was ashamed of herself. She had been working so hard to minimize the hassle of Christmas, and these new neighbours, these new Canadians, had so clearly embraced the spirit of the season.

She invited them in and she put their basket under the tree. Then she said, "I have your present upstairs."

She flew upstairs and, in a panic, grabbed a glass bowl she had picked up at a craft show. It was already wrapped. She had been planning to give it to her mother.

"See," said Rashida to Amir fifteen minutes later as they pulled their wagon along the sidewalk. "They were waiting on us, Amir."

It took Amir and Rashida three hours, but when they'd finished, they had left baskets all over the neighbourhood.

The next morning, Morley noticed a tiny rash in the crook of her elbow—a spot that often flared when she was feeling pressured. While she was drying her hair she told Dave what was bugging her.

"I gave the Chudarys that pretty glass bowl. We have lived right next to Maria and Eugene for eighteen years and we have never given them anything. And Gerta, too. If I give something to the Chudarys, surely I should give something to Gerta."

She could feel the muscles in the back of her neck tightening. As she headed downstairs for breakfast she was trying to figure out when she would have time to shop.

Morley went to a flower store at lunch and bought two bunches of holly. She was planning on taking one to Eugene and Maria next door and one to Gerta. She was planning to do it after supper. But before she could do that, the doorbell rang and there was Gerta—standing on the stoop beside a wagon full of presents.

Christmas cookies.

"I baked for everybody in the neighbourhood," she said defensively.

There was a small muscle ticking under her left eye.

On the weekend Morley dug through her emergency stash of presents looking for something to give Mary Turlington.

"I wouldn't want Mary to find out I gave something to Gerta and not to her," she told Dave.

She found a pair of hand-dipped candles. They were warped. Perhaps, she thought, if she warmed them up, she could straighten them. She took them downstairs and put them in the microwave.

After she had scraped out the microwave, Morley dashed to a neighbourhood store. She arrived just before closing and bought a gift basket of herbal teas for Mary.

On her way home she bumped into Dianne Goldberg. Dianne was pulling a wagon up the street towards her house. The wagon was full of presents.

Morley couldn't believe it. Everyone knew the Goldbergs didn't celebrate Christmas.

Morley said, "What a coincidence. I just put something under the tree for you."

When they got home Morley ducked into the living room ahead of Dianne and slipped the tea under the tree.

"Hey," said Sam, when Dianne had left. "Eugene was here while you were out. He brought a present. It's in the kitchen. Can we open it?"

Morley rubbed her arm. The eczema on her elbow was the size of a tennis ball.

By the Friday before Christmas, Morley had received ten gifts from neighbourhood families, including two baskets of herbal tea identical to the one she had given Dianne Goldberg. One of them looked as though it might have been the same basket.

Her rash had extended down to her wrist.

And then, with only three shopping days left, Morley came home from work and found a small bottle of strawberry-flavoured virgin olive oil from a family down the street she had never met before.

She stood in the kitchen staring at the oil and scratching her arm.

"Damn it," she said.

Unfortunately, that was also the afternoon Dave closed the Vinyl Cafe and came home early to ice his Christmas cakes. His plan was to fit them together like a jigsaw puzzle and seal them with a sugar-paste. The man in the bakery said the paste would harden up like marzipan.

"Tougher than marzipan," said the man.

When the paste had boiled into a sticky syrup, Dave took it off the stove and began to pour it on his cake. But instead of hardening up, the icing flowed around like lava, pooling in the low spots. The cake soon looked like something Sam might have made for a geography project—like a papier-mâché model of the Rocky Mountains.

It hadn't occurred to Dave that the cake surface had to be flat.

He went downstairs and got his belt sander.

It took him longer than he'd thought, but Dave finished icing the cakes before anyone got home. When he finished, he realized his cake was now far too big to fit into the fridge, which is where the baker told him it belonged. The only place Dave could think of that was both large enough and cold enough for his icing to set was the garage.

Ever so carefully he picked the cake up and struggled out, backwards, using his elbow to push open the door. On the way into the garage he stumbled against the door frame and knocked one end of the cake. A piece fell off. Dave headed back into the kitchen. He set the cake on the table. He went outside to fetch the broken bit, but the piece was not where it had fallen. Dave looked around the yard.

And there, heading towards the pear tree, backwards, was a squirrel—dragging the broken bit of cake in its mouth.

Dave squeaked and leapt in the air. The squirrel dropped the cake and disappeared up the tree.

Dave retrieved the piece of cake. He brought it inside and cut off the bit that he thought had been in the squirrel's mouth. He tried to set what was left of it back in place. The more he fiddled with it, the more the piece refused to fit. It was rapidly losing its shape.

Eventually, using a mixture of honey and icing sugar, he made a sort of cement and glued the hunk of cake back on. He used the last of the sugar-paste to cover the join. It was like masonry.

Dave carried the cake carefully out to the garage, the squirrel nattering at him as he walked under the tree. He set the cake on the roof of the car. And he made sure the garage door was tightly closed on his way back inside.

It was an hour later that Morley came home and found the strawberry-flavoured olive oil.

"Every night," she said with exasperation. "Every night I come home and someone else has left a present. What is *wrong* with these people?"

She was scratching her arm vigorously as she left the room.

Dave, who was sitting at the kitchen table making little marzipan snowmen for his Christmas cake, didn't risk an answer.

Morley came back into the kitchen with her coat on. She looked at Dave and said, "I'm going to Lawlor's. Anyone else who shows up here is getting chocolate."

As she stormed out the door she said, "Those look more like mice than snowmen. You can't put marzipan mice on a Christmas cake."

Dave waited until she left, then he flattened the ball of marzipan in his hand and threw it across the room for Arthur, the dog.

"Arthur," he said, "I am having a hard time with these mice. I keep squishing their little paws."

Then he said, “Uh-oh.”

And he jumped up and ran out the door.

He got to the driveway just in time to hear a squeal of tires, just in time to see the red lights of his car disappearing down the street. With his Christmas cake on the roof.

He began to run down the street waving his hands wildly, calling to Morley.

He was running and waving when she hit the speed bump and the cake flew off.

He was still running and waving when Morley glanced in the rear-view mirror and spotted him.

“Now what?” she muttered.

She jammed on the brakes. The car skidded to a halt. She threw it into reverse.

Dave stopped moving. He watched in horror as the car engine roared and the wheels changed direction and the station wagon reversed over his cake.

He started running again.

But he wasn’t alone any more.

Pounding along the pavement beside him like a racehorse stretching for the finish line, matching him step for step in a rush for the cake, was the squirrel.

“Get out of here,” bellowed Dave.

Morley thought he was talking to her.

She threw up her hands and then gunned the car—and drove over the cake for a second time.

Dave carried the cake home the way he would have carried a dog who had been hit by a milk truck.

He set it down on the kitchen table.

He picked a piece of gravel out of the squished part. He got a screwdriver from the basement and a flashlight. He held the flashlight in his mouth and leaned over the cake like a surgeon. It took him twenty minutes to flick out all the gravel he could see.

Then he tried to pat the cake back into shape with his hands. But the icing was too hard and the squished part was too squished.

He felt totally defeated.

What would Polly Anderson say? What would he tell the arena committee? Who would believe that his Christmas cake had been flattened in a hit and run?

He went to the basement and poured himself a glass of the soaking mixture.

He came back half an hour later with a solution.

He would cut the cake into individual servings and wrap each serving in Cellophane—like at a wedding. No one would have to know a thing.

He got out the cake knife.

It bounced off the sugar-paste icing.

He tried again. The knife began to bend but it didn't break the surface.

He got out his carving knife.

He leaned over it and, using his body weight, managed to get the knife into the cake. But try as he might, he couldn't get it out.

He headed into the basement to find his old electric carving knife. He hadn't used it for years.

When he came upstairs, there was Arthur the dog with his back legs on one of the kitchen chairs and his front legs on the kitchen table. There was Arthur slowly and methodically licking the entire surface of the sugar-paste icing.

When he spotted Dave, Arthur leaned forward and put his paws protectively around the cake.

As Dave stepped towards him, Arthur started to growl.

Dave used a damp dishcloth to smooth out the traces of the dog's tongue on his icing.

He plugged in the carving knife. The first cut was picture perfect. On the second, however, a piece of walnut came flying out of the cake and ricocheted off Dave's forehead.

On the third cut, the carving knife started to shudder. Then it began to smoke, and then it seized up completely.

When Morley came home Dave had just finished the job. He had used Bert Turlington's jig saw.

He pushed his safety glasses onto his forehead.

"Hi," he said.

Morley was carrying a large cardboard carton. At first, Dave thought she had gone grocery shopping. She hadn't. She had bought every box of chocolate miniatures left in the drugstore. And a bottle of cortisone cream.

The skating party was the next night. Dave took his cake up to the arena an hour early and set it out on the refreshment table by the skate-sharpening machine.

He wanted to hang around and serve it to people.

Fortunately, he had to go back to work and close his store.

When he returned an hour later there was a man standing by the arena door. He didn't look happy. He was holding his jaw.

"Are you okay?" asked Dave.

The man shook his head. "Some idiot baked a fruitcake and left the pits in the dates. I broke a filling," he said.

"You're kidding," said Dave.

When he got to the table beside the skate-sharpening machine his cake had hardly been touched.

Someone had altered the sign that he had carefully lettered before leaving home.

"May contain nuts," it read.

Except someone had scratched out the word "nuts" and written a new word in its place. His sign now read, "May contain gravel."

He was going to go home.

But he spotted Sam waving at him from the ice and he thought, *Who cares?* He waved back and held his skates up and headed towards the changing room.

Christmas Day is going to be a little strained in Dave's neighbourhood this year. On Christmas morning,

Dave will get seventeen boxes of chocolates.

"Oh look," he will say, when he opens the twelfth box. "Miniature chocolates. My favourites."

There will be little surprises like that all over the neighbourhood. Gerta Lowbeer raided her freezer of all her Christmas baking to make the cookie plates she gave to everyone. Gerta's relatives will be stunned when they arrive for their traditional Christmas Day visit to see plates of crumbly Peek Freans in place of Gerta's delectable shortbread.

On Boxing Day, old Eugene from next door will realize he has given away the last of the year's home-made wine. To his horror he will find himself between vintages and will head off to the liquor store for the first time in fifteen years. Dave will bump into him staring morosely at the labels in the Yugoslavia section.

Mary Turlington, who prides herself on her detailed Christmas record-keeping, will get so flustered with the neighbourhood gift-giving that she will completely forget to buy a present for her husband, Bert.

"I can't believe it," Mary will say, scrolling through her Palm Pilot on Christmas morning. "I must have deleted you."

The only house where Christmas will go without a hitch will be Jim Scoffield's. When Jim's mother arrives as usual a few days before Christmas, she will be amazed at all the festive flourishes. The hand-dipped candles, the home baking, the Christmas CD.

"It's all from people in the neighbourhood," Jim will tell her. "I've never seen a Christmas like it.

People kept coming to the door with wagonloads of presents."

On Christmas Day, Jim and his mother will go out for a walk and run into the Chudarys in the park. They will stop and talk for ten minutes, and Jim's mother will make a fuss over Fatima. As they say goodbye, Jim will look at Rashida.

"What are you planning for New Year's?" he'll ask.

"New Year's?" Amir will say as soon as they are alone. "New Year's! Rashida, don't these people ever stop?"

"It will be all right, Amir," Rashida will say.

"*Inshallah*," her husband will reply. "*Inshallah*."

If it is God's wish.

Book Club

CHANGE, IMPORTANT LIFE-ALTERING CHANGE, seldom comes in by the front door. Change—be it a change of circumstance or even monumental, ground-shaking change in the landscape—tends to creep up on you. Change doesn't often stand on the stoop and ring the front bell, looking around and tapping its foot impatiently while it waits for you. Change, more likely than not, slips in when you are not at home, or when you are there but too preoccupied to notice, when you are busy trying to remember some difficult thing like whether this week is garbage and recycling or just garbage.

Change is a sneak.

And after twenty years of motherhood, change had sneaked up on Morley.

Everything had seemed frozen and immutable until one day, standing in the supermarket, her hand hovering over a package of frozen vegetables (corn), it occurred to Morley that her daughter, Stephanie, who was away at university for the second year, might never move back home. Her son, Sam, was now old enough to look after himself at lunch, if you didn't mind scraping dry peanut butter off the kitchen counter. And Morley, for the first time in years, had time on her hands.

A few minutes later—exactly how many minutes Morley couldn't say with certainty—she found herself in a fog, staring at a display of dried mushrooms. She was holding a one-ounce package of organic Maitakes: $24.95.

Morley had no idea what one did with dried mushrooms—most particularly, she had no knowledge of the evidently remarkable qualities of dried Maitakes—but she felt a need to take them with her, nevertheless. Maybe, she thought to herself, turning the package over in her hands, this was what it was like for birds. Migration. Maybe one moment they were sitting there, somewhere, staring into the middle distance, and the next they were seized by a need to get going. For birds it was South America, the mystery of migration; for Morley it was dried Maitakes.

But before that, before she'd started to think about migration—and why, until that day, she'd never even considered buying dried mushrooms and whether you were supposed to soak them and for how long—she'd been thinking about . . . nothing.

She had just been standing there in the supermarket, staring at the mushrooms thinking . . . nothing.

Now she was thinking about how she could have lived so long knowing nothing about mushrooms. Or dried mushrooms, anyway.

This wasn't necessarily an important thing, except in a collateral sort of way. Except you should know about these sorts of things. If you are a curious kind of person, that is.

Morley nodded slowly. She said, *"I am,"* under her breath.

When she went to put the package of mushrooms in her basket, she couldn't see her basket anywhere. Her smile turned to a puzzled frown as she realized she had no idea where she had left it. No idea where she should look.

Ever since she'd had kids, Morley had wondered what it would be like to have time as a friend again. To have time on her hands. She had passed years imagining the things she might do.

Now that she suddenly had time, Morley wasn't sure what she should do with it. She was like the first skater at the rink, hesitating before she stepped onto the clean white ice. Not wanting to spoil the perfect surface of potential. Not wanting to make a mistake.

If it had been spring, instead of the depths of another endless winter, Morley might have sunk herself into her garden. But it wasn't spring. There was a blanket of snow over everything. She was lost in the snow.

One Sunday afternoon, with Dave at his record store doing God knows what and Sam still upstairs, still asleep, Morley lay down on the living room couch. With a pillow behind her head and a chenille throw over her legs, she began to read a novel she had been given for Christmas. There had once been a time when this was a normal thing in her life. A time when, on a

Sunday afternoon, she would brew a pot of coffee and lose herself in a book, or magazine, or maybe the *Sunday Times*. But that was Morley B.C.—Before Children. And that, unbelievably, was decades ago.

This is great, she thought as she stretched out on the couch and cracked her book. But it wasn't great. She felt fidgety. She felt a pang of guilt. She was so used to being interrupted, so used to having to squeeze out little moments of time for herself, that she couldn't relax. She had lost the knack. Reading had become a thing she did at night, just before she fell asleep.

She got up and wandered over to her desk. She paid some bills.

But being the woman she is, Morley wasn't about to stand on the edge of the rink forever. Perhaps she just needed something more active than reading. A few Christmases ago she had enrolled in a chair-making course. At first it had been fun, but her chair had, in the end, been a disaster. It had looked more like a go-kart than a chair. She had put wheels on it. She had given it to Sam. She needed something less practical.

A week after her unsuccessful attempt to relax with her Christmas novel, Morley enrolled in a yoga class. She went for three weeks. It didn't work out. She kept falling asleep during the deep-breathing part. *Something more dynamic,* she thought. She let Polly Anderson talk her into joining a local tennis club.

There was a tennis ladder, and new members had to be on the ladder. A way to meet everyone. Morley's and Polly's names were written on little round discs and hung on the middle rung. Morley watched in despair as Polly scooted upwards—like she was making some sort of determined mountain assault. Polly headed north, while Morley's little disc sank inexorably, game by game, step by step. She didn't last two months. The club was pretty decent about it. They refunded half her initiation fee.

Dave brought home a catalogue of continuing education courses for Morley.

"How to Make Your Own Soap," she said, flipping the catalogue over. "Why would you do that? Isn't there enough soap out there already?"

"I was thinking something more practical," said Dave, picking up the calendar. "I was hoping you might consider Dolphin Healing."

He was flipping through the pages.

"Here," he said. "Dolphin Healing. Page thirty-two. 'A course of conscious breathing techniques to help you access the realm where dolphins exist. Once you get there, you tap into dolphin consciousness and transform the dolphin energy to awaken the healer within.'"

"Would it," asked Morley, "unleash the power of joy in my life?"

"Guaranteed," said Dave.

"I would rather eat the dolphin," she added. "Okay, okay," said Morley. "I would rather make soap."

To make Dave happy she signed up for a course called Anyone Can Draw.

At the end of the second class, the instructor asked her to stay behind.

"There is something I have to tell you," he said glumly.

They refunded her course fee.

It was two weeks later that Mary Turlington invited Morley to join her book club. Morley was delighted. She realized the idea of finding *new* interests was forced. This was perfect. She would go back to old interests. She had been a voracious reader, B.C. She just needed a push to get going again. A book club would help her wade through the overwhelming choice that she faced every time she walked into a bookstore.

Morley took the calendar that hangs on the side of the refrigerator, sat down at the kitchen table and wrote "Book Club" on the first Tuesday of the next month.

The calendar was normally filled with the kids' activities. The only event on it that involved Morley, aside from family vacations, was, *oh joy,* her annual physical.

She hung the calendar back up. She walked into the living room. She walked back into the kitchen and glanced at the calendar, pretending she didn't know what she was going to see. Pretending she needed to check what she was doing Tuesday night. *Oh . . . of course . . . Book Club.*

It made her proud to have this social event involving her on the family calendar. She took the calendar down and wrote "Book Club" on the first Tuesday of every month. Then she hung it on the front of the fridge instead of the side. She wanted someone to notice.

Morley arrived at her first book club meeting five minutes early. She found herself in a house full of women in business suits. Many had scarves draped casually around their necks. It looked more like a board meeting than a book club. Morley was wearing a cable-knit sweater with khakis. She looked as though she were there to serve coffee. Worst of all, Mary Turlington wasn't anywhere to be seen. No, worst of all, the woman on the other side of the dining room was holding the book they were going to discuss and it was covered with a flurry of yellow Post-it Notes. Morley hadn't even brought her copy of the book. All she had been planning on saying was that she had had a hard time keeping the characters straight. That was when she noticed the woman in the corner flipping through a binder of typed notes. The woman looked as if she were preparing to defend a thesis.

A few of the women had begun to drift into the living room. Morley followed them. She chose a red chair in the corner by the fireplace—a chair out of the spotlight. Conversation in the room stopped abruptly when she sat down. She sensed something was wrong. Maybe it was the way she was dressed.

How was Morley to know that the women always sat in the same seats at each meeting? Dana Regan, a real estate agent, had sat in the red chair by the fireplace for as long as anyone could remember. It ensured that Dana was always the last person called upon to talk. Dana always said the same thing at every meeting: "There is nothing I could possibly add. Everyone has already said everything I was planning to say." It was the prevailing opinion in the club that Dana Regan hadn't read a book in years. At one time or another, everyone in the room had thought about sitting in Dana's chair to force the issue, but Dana was such a bombastic woman no one had the guts.

Every eye was on Dana when she walked into the living room. She made it halfway across the floor before she spotted Morley sitting in her chair. It was a sight so beyond anything Dana had considered possible that it stopped her dead in her tracks. She stared at Morley. The room fell dramatically still. Dana was standing immobile, except for her shoulders, which had begun to shiver like a hound on point. If it had been anyone else sitting in her chair, Dana would have bellowed something rude and authoritative. But this was someone she didn't know, and some unexpected remnant of manners asserted itself. She stood there for a beat more, her mouth opening and then closing. Then she snorted and flounced into Taylor Wever's seat.

Not a moment later, Taylor Wever came in. When she saw Dana in her seat and Morley in Dana's, Taylor sat in Alison Morin's place. Once she was settled, every head in the room swivelled, as one, to face the door, waiting for Alison. It was as if they were watching a tennis match.

Alison, the curtest woman there, pulled up short, surveyed the room, frowned and said, "What the hell is going on?"

Exactly what I was thinking, thought Morley.

"We'll start," said Fay Struthers, who runs the meetings, "on the left and we'll go clockwise."

And so it happened that Dana Regan was called upon to start the discussion—for the first time in five years. Dana Regan, who had never, ever commented on a book, was on the spot.

The room fell deathly quiet. Dana cleared her throat and leaned forward. She stared directly into the faces of every woman there and then, with her eyes drilling into Morley, she said, slowly and dramatically, "There is nothing I could possibly add."

It was Kerry Lukaweski's turn next. Kerry was the woman holding the book so festooned with Post-it Notes that it looked as if it were about to take wing and fly away. Morley straightened herself, preparing to pay particular attention to Kerry. *This will be good,* she thought. Kerry, with all her notes, would explain the book to everyone.

"Well," said Kerry, "I have to admit that I had a hard time getting into this book. But after fifty pages I thoroughly enjoyed myself." Kerry's voice was beginning to get shaky. "Sebastian's epiphany at the garbage dump was a tour de force . . ." Her eyes were filling with tears. "His pain . . . her pain. It was just, so . . . so . . ." To Morley's astonishment, Kerry's voice broke completely, her sentence ending in a sob. She dabbed at her eyes with a Kleenex. She hung her head and waved her hands as if to say, *I can't go on. Move to the next person . . . Please!*

Morley was trying to figure out which character Sebastian was and when he had been at the garbage dump.

Next was Fay Struthers. *Fay will have something helpful to say,* thought Morley. With her short, clipped hair, her no-nonsense shoes and her wire-framed glasses, Fay struck Morley as a woman of efficiency and practicality. A woman who would cut straight to the point.

"It is a deeply flawed novel," said Fay authoritatively. "But at the same time utterly, utterly luminous."

There was a moment of silence. Everyone nodded. Everyone but Morley, that is. Morley wasn't sure you could jump in and ask questions when it wasn't your turn, but it didn't look as if Fay was going to say anything else. Morley wanted to know about this flaw. She opened her mouth and was about to speak when Fay snapped her head around and glared at Morley accusingly. "*What?* You don't think it was luminous?"

Morley phoned Mary Turlington first thing the next morning.

"Why weren't you at the meeting?" she asked.

"I've dropped out," said Mary. "That's why there was a space for you."

It was too late to do anything about that. Morley wasn't going to quit after one meeting. Besides, the dates were already marked on her calendar.

When she arrived for the next meeting, Fay Struthers's husband, Shane, answered the door. There was no sign of any women in the kitchen or dining room.

"They're in the living room," said Shane as he took her coat.

All of them were sitting in their proper places. Mary Turlington's empty chair was waiting for Morley.

That month's book was a story set in Napoleonic France and told backwards from the point of view of a soft, ripened cheese. It wasn't made clear that the narrator was a cheese until page 268. Even then it was only a passing reference.

"I found it totally unbelievable," said Alison Morin. She crossed her legs and picked up her coffee cup. "A cheese would never behave like that in post-revolutionary France."

"Of course it was flawed," interjected Fay Struthers. "But it was utterly, utterly transcendent." She gazed at Morley defiantly.

When the conversation marched around to Kerry Lukaweski, Morley noticed that Kerry was already clutching a wad of Kleenex. "But imagine . . . imagine," Kerry cried, "being a cheese . . . the pain of it all . . . I never knew . . ." That was as far as Kerry managed to get before she was totally overcome with tears.

Morley, sitting there in Mary Turlington's chair, felt as if she had been punched in the stomach. Morley had missed the cheese reference completely. She had assumed the narrator was an old person with a skin disorder.

The next book was over eight hundred pages long. A novel about five minutes in the life of a Polish railroad baggage handler. Morley was determined to read every page, come hell or high water. As she read, she was hyper-aware of all dairy references.

The Monday morning before the meeting, however, Morley still had four hundred pages to go.

By the time she fell asleep on the couch that night, she had read only one hundred more. She woke with a start at one in the morning. She brewed coffee and tried to read more, but it was useless. She couldn't keep her eyes open. When she went back to bed, she couldn't fall asleep.

In the morning, Morley divided the book into sections with Post-it Notes. She marked page six hundred with a note that said 10:00 a.m, page seven hundred with a note that said 11:00, page eight hundred with noon. She took the morning off work to read. She figured she would have half an hour after work to finish the last thirty-two pages. She felt as if she were in a marathon.

When the meeting began it was clear to Morley that no one in the club had read the book except for her. She felt a warm smugness envelop her as the discussion began. But before it was her turn, the conversation had taken flight from the book she had struggled through and had landed on another novel by the same author. A much shorter book that the club had, apparently, read the previous year.

When it was Morley's turn she cleared her throat and said, "I would like to bring the conversation back to this month's book." The book she had spent the last twenty-four hours struggling through.

Everyone stared at her blankly. It was Dana Regan who said, "Why would you do that, dear? We're not talking about *that* book."

At the next meeting, it was Morley's turn to go first. For once she had understood the book. She hadn't liked it. She felt sure of her opinion.

"The early parts were okay," she began, "but I have to say, the second half of the book . . ." Morley was rather pleased with herself now. She was about to try out a new expression, something she had never said before. "I have to say," said Morley, "that I think this book is . . . deeply flawed."

There was a snort from the other side of the room.

"Why on *earth* would you say that?" said Fay Struthers.

Alison Morin jumped in. "I thought it was the most important book of the decade."

Everyone, apparently, agreed.

Maybe, thought Morley, *maybe I have read the wrong book.*

She hadn't read the wrong book. That was the following month. The month they were supposed to read *The Still and Quiet Heart* and Morley plowed through a dreadful antebellum romance called *Stay Still My Heart*.

Fay Struthers called her in the middle of the following week. They were assembling the next year's book list. Would Morley please bring a book recommendation to the upcoming meeting?

The message sent Morley into a tailspin. The women in her group had hated every book she had liked. Every book that had confused her they thought was a work of genius. And any time she'd asked one of the members if they had read a book that she had liked, they'd dismissed it out of hand.

Morley was not about to bring something she loved to this group and watch them eviscerate it. She felt too protective of the books she loved to offer them up to some sort of ritual sacrifice.

She spent three days of utter agony. She pored over the books in their house. She had a crying fit at Woodsworth's, the little bookstore down the street from Dave's store. She spent an afternoon in the library wandering up and down the rows, her fingers walking along the spines of the books. She read the jacket copy searching for words like "luminous" and "transcendent." She looked lost. She was.

She found *To Kill a Mockingbird* on Stephanie's bookshelf and sat on Steph's bed rereading the first seventy-five pages.

That night she went into the basement and opened

cartons of books that had been sealed up since they had moved. She found a box of books marked "Morley—College." She sat on the basement floor and opened it, piling the books around her.

She came across a paperback copy of *Black like Me*. How could she have forgotten this book? It had changed the way she saw the world. She couldn't believe she had abandoned it to a cardboard box in her basement. She opened another box and then another. An hour went by and then another. Sitting on the floor with these old friends around, she felt a wave of guilt. She had to get them on the shelves again. She couldn't leave them locked in the basement like political prisoners. She might not have the time to read any of them, but at least they would be in sight—at least she could touch them, take one down from time to time and flip through it. Just knowing she could do that felt good.

That night she brought *Black like Me* to supper. As they ate, she told Sam the story of John Howard Griffin, the Texan who, in 1959, dyed his skin black, cut his hair short and assumed the identity of an itinerant black man.

"It's all about walking in someone else's shoes," she said as she passed the book to Sam.

"It's more than just a story," she said. "It's a metaphor. Do you know what a metaphor is?"

Sam had no idea what a metaphor was. "Of course," he said. "We took it in math."

Morley flipped the book open at random and began

reading the part where a white bus driver won't let Griffin leave the bus to use a restroom.

"This happens over and over again," she said. "He is treated with disrespect in nearly every encounter he has. Just because of the colour of his skin."

Suddenly she put the book down and stared at Sam intently. "Have you read *To Kill a Mockingbird* ?" she asked.

Sam shook his head tentatively. This was beginning to worry him. Was she going to make him read *To Kill a Mockingbird* ?

"What about *Little House on the Prairie* ?" said Morley.

Sam shook his head. Now he *was* afraid. He had never seen his mother like this before. Maybe, he thought, it would be better if he lied about these books. It was making him uncomfortable the way she was staring.

"What about *Never Cry Wolf* ? Have you read *Never Cry Wolf* ? Or anything by Farley Mowat?"

Morley wasn't looking at him any more. She already knew the answer.

"*Dandelion Wine,*" she said. "*Dandelion Wine*. Damn it. You should have read *Dandelion Wine*. I should have read it to you. What have I been doing?"

"You were making supper," said Sam, trying to be helpful.

After supper Morley sat on the couch and called Sam.

"I want to read you some more of this," she said. She was holding *Black like Me*.

Then she said, "The guy who wrote this book was in the war. He got too near a shell that exploded and he was blinded. He lost his sight. Then one day, twelve years later, he was walking on the farm where he lived—I think it was a farm—and his sight came back. Just like that. After twelve years. And that's when he did this thing where he turned himself black."

She got teary halfway through the first page and put the book down.

Sam reached out and touched his mother's face, wiping at the tear running down her cheek. He said, "Are you all right?"

Morley smiled.

"I am very all right," she said.

Morley phoned Fay Struthers the next morning. She told her she wouldn't be coming to book club any more.

"I don't need them," she told Dave.

On her way home from work she bought two bookshelves—the kind that need to be assembled. That night she put them together herself. She set them in the hall and filled them with the books from the basement.

"Old friends," she said to Dave.

She is right about the books, but she is wrong about the book club. Once she starts reading again, Morley will want to share her books with more people. The books she will read will take her to worlds beyond her own, and it is always more fun to travel with friends.

In the spring, Morley and Mary Turlington will start their own book club. There will be seven women at the founders' meeting.

They will agree to five categories for the books they will read during their first year.

1) A book about a man I could marry.
2) A book I read in grade school.
3) A book that mentions chocolate favourably.
4) A book I want to read because I saw the movie.
5) A book my husband would quit after the first chapter.

The book club will last for years. Each meeting will be called to order when Morley stands up and says, "Is there anything anyone could possibly say about this luminous book?" And everyone will collapse into hysterics.

At some meetings that will be the closest they get to discussing the book in question. Some weeks, the wine and the good feelings that come with being among good friends will be all they need.

Stephanie

According to Stephanie

As far as I am concerned this book is total fiction. If it is supposed to be the truth, it isn't. It is so full of inaccuracies. At first I got upset about it, and some of my friends were saying I could sue, because it's, like, defamation or something. And I started to go through it and count the mistakes, and then I started a list, and then I thought this is ridiculous. It is just laughable. And these are just the ones that I know about.

Tommy—and I am still going out with him by the way, *and it is over two years now, not like he says. We had an anniversary in the fall and the way it is in here it looks like . . . no way we would still be going out, because it looks like I just picked him up. And that is just so wrong, it was not like that at all. He was standing there in front of Millhouse in the rain and looking totally pathetic and lost and I asked him if he was looking for someone, which is what anyone would have done if they had an ounce of manners, which I am sure you would have done if you had been me. Anyway, I did not exactly* give him sanctuary*!!! I let him sleep in Jane's room, which is a whole different thing as far as I am concerned. And all that stuff about me having my eyes on another boy at the party we went to that night is so bogus, because I didn't have my eyes on any boy—least of all Tommy. Yes, he did walk back to the dorm with me and yes, we did have the conversation about cartoon characters, and yes, I did say I liked Eric from* The Little Mermaid, *but not in the way he implies, like it was a big deal or something—it is pretty obvious the operative word was* like, *not* love*! The way it is here makes me look like some kind of freak!*

And speaking of parties, I was never at a toga party . . . not ever. I was at one party where people were wearing togas . . . but I wasn't! And it wasn't advertised as a toga party. And I went to all my classes, it was Becky who was skipping, and I took Sociology 110 in first year not Sociology 101 like he says. And in the first class Professor Michaels did hit vegetables with a hammer more or less like he says, but it was a watermelon and a pumpkin and an eggplant, *not a* squash. *So you see what I mean.*

And speaking of that, I didn't keep any of my papers from first year. And I admit in the beginning

I wasn't getting A's and B's—which I am now, by the way*! Not that there is any mention of* that *anywhere—just of how badly I was doing when I started. And there is a huge difference between high school and university so, yes, my marks were lower to start with. Duh! But not as low as he says, which is a total lie because if they were that bad I would have been on probation, which I never was except at the very beginning of the first year. But only for a few weeks. Or a month at the most.*

I could go on and on if I wanted. Like, I don't even know what a Fu Manchu moustache is. And in one story he has me coming home after midnight and my dad is still awake and I come in the house and unlock the door with my key, except I don't have a key and my parents don't lock their house (which is ridiculous if you ask me—but that's not the point). And I am pretty sure I came home on a Friday night, not a Thursday like he says, and I certainly wasn't in tears. And it was my idea, not Becky's, that we live in Millhouse, except it is not called Millhouse, though I am not going to say the name here because I agree with the idea that people shouldn't know who we are, especially if there are going to be so many inaccuracies flying around.

And just for the record when I was in the library that day I was working on a paper about Jane Austen, not Ernest Hemingway!!

And just because Tommy and I have been going out for two years doesn't mean that I am not going to date someone else. I know lots of people who go out for that long and then they break up, and I don't know why he has to make such a big deal of it all the time saying that we are still going out like it is some kind of world record. And if he is going to mention it he should get it right because, like I say, it has been over *two years now, not a year and a half like he says.*

The whole thing about leaving home is just so wrong. I wanted *to leave. My parents were really bugging me in my last year of high school—and he makes them sound so reasonable, and what does that make me????*

And I didn't find the lost TV remote in my room when I was cleaning it up after my dad had bought a new one, and I wasn't crying hysterically on the side of the road over a dead raccoon or whatever. I distinctly remember it was Sam who insisted we bury it, it wasn't me. I didn't even want to stop.

And the part about being a "whining, snit-fitting, foul-mouthed brat," Tommy says I shouldn't even dignify that part with a response. But how would you feel if someone described you like that? And Tommy, by the way, *said that's not how he remembers it either. And I was not fighting with Sam over the last bag of potato chips or whatever he says. It was because Sam kept pushing me and crowding my space, and it was my bag of chips and he took them while I was trying to ignore him, and it wasn't a squabble. It was out and out theft, and if my father had bought plane tickets so we could have flown to Cape Breton like normal people (who drives from Toronto to Cape Breton in December???!!!) none of this would have happened. Anyone could tell you that it is going to snow, and sure it worked out okay with Eustache's motel, but it could have been a complete disaster. We could have left the road like that truck we saw, and all I can say is if Tommy wasn't there maybe that's what would have happened, because it was Tommy who spotted the motel and if he hadn't, who knows?*

And I just want to say that I think the best writing in the book is the poem that Tommy wrote, and if it wasn't for that poem maybe I would sue, but it's the first time Tommy has been published (except for university papers) and we thought it was a good opportunity and didn't want to mess it up.

A Night to Remember

When Stephanie was still in high school and still living at home, Saturdays developed a predictable and not unpleasant rhythm at Dave's house. Having had kids, and thus having forfeited for life their ability to sleep in, Morley and Dave rose (disappointingly) early most Saturday mornings. They brewed tea (Dave) and coffee (Morley), then read the Saturday paper together in the kitchen while the kids, the agents of their sleeplessness, slept on.

Not always, but more often than not these days, when they had finished the paper, Morley headed to work on Saturday mornings. And so it fell to Dave, by circumstance more than design, to do the Saturday morning chores. The weekly run around town.

This was never, for Dave, an unpleasant activity, as it often involved reunions with lost friends whom he might stumble on exiting the dry cleaners as he was entering. And if no friends rose to the surface, he could always count on a moment or two of at least civility and at best shared pleasure from the merchants whose company he enjoyed. Mr. Harmon at the food store. Debby at the dry cleaners.

So Dave always set off on Saturday mornings, his list in hand, with a degree of optimism—but never with quite the sense of well-being that enveloped him on a particular Saturday in October when Stephanie was still in grade twelve.

That Saturday he tripped around town in an unusually chipper frame of mind—feeling so darn good about things that he caught himself whistling on his way out of the hardware store.

Happiness, as anyone who has known unhappiness can tell you, is *not* a condition of hardware, or clean clothes, or of any circumstance for that matter. Happiness is a condition of the mind, or more specifically, the imagination. And that Saturday morning as he moved around the city, Dave's imagination was blasting along full steam ahead.

American newspaperman H. L. Mencken once said that the only truly happy people in this sad world are married women and single men.

As if to prove Mencken's point, Dave was, in fact, going to be single that Saturday night. Morley was going out with friends, Sam had been asked to a sleepover at his pal Ben's house and Stephanie was babysitting for the Maddens.

But it wasn't the mere fact of this evening of solitude that had Dave whistling as he glided around town. When he whistled his way out of the dry cleaner's, Dave wasn't thinking about solitude at all. He was imagining, in exquisite detail, the things he was going to *do* while he was home alone.

He had a plan for something so wonderfully self-indulgent that he couldn't stop himself from whistling.

When everyone had gone their separate ways, when he was all by himself, Dave was going to carry the small portable television set down from his bedroom and balance it on top of the television set in the living room. Then, when he had the two televisions carefully stacked, his *tower o' television,* Dave was planning to watch *Hockey Night in Canada* on the small set and a couple of his all-time favourite movies on the other one.

Simultaneously.

The movies were already sitting on the back seat of his car, along with the family-size bag of Doritos, the six-pack of cream soda and the jar of jalapeño peppers. *The Dirty Dozen,* starring Lee Marvin. Beside that, *True Grit,* featuring John Wayne's Academy Award–winning performance as Rooster Cogburn, the crotchety, straight-shootin', one-eyed U.S. marshal.

All Dave needed was a jar of salsa and some of that runny blue cheese from France to make this a night he would never forget—a night to remember.

By the time Dave got home that Saturday afternoon, Sam had already left for his sleepover.

Morley and Stephanie were in the kitchen talking. Dave was so wrapped up with his plans that it took him a few minutes to realize something was wrong.

Stephanie was sitting at the table holding her head in her hands. When she looked up at her father, her eyes were watery and red. Her face was pale.

"What's the matter?" said Dave, looking first at his daughter and then at his wife.

"We have an unhappy little girl," said Morley.

"This," said Dave, setting the cream soda down on the counter, "I can see."

"I just threw up," said Stephanie. "I have a fever."

"Oh no," said Dave.

He meant it with his heart and soul.

"I'm supposed to babysit at the Maddens'," said Stephanie.

"Yes," said Dave, "I know. I guess you're not going?"

It was part question, part statement.

Stephanie shook her head.

And then Dave uttered eight fateful words: "Who did you find to take your place?"

It was six-fifteen on the nose when Dave pushed the Maddens' doorbell.

"This is very kind," said Jim Madden, opening the door almost before the bell had stopped chiming, as if he had been waiting with his hand on the doorknob for Dave to arrive.

"We tried everyone," said Jim.

And then he frowned and pointed at the portable television that was resting on the stoop beside Dave.

"We have a TV," said Jim, as Dave picked up the portable and walked in. Then he glanced at his watch.

"I'm sorry," he said. "We're running a bit late."

He looked upstairs.

"It's Rhonda's sister. She's getting married tomorrow. Tonight's the rehearsal."

Jim and Rhonda Madden have three children: Jade, age seven; Kenneth, who is three; and the baby, Warren, nine months.

Dave supposed it was Warren, the baby, who was crying.

He was wrong.

But before he'd worked that out, Rhonda Madden appeared in a flurry of high heels and a waft of perfume—Kenneth, the three-year-old, trailing her in his pyjamas, like a pull-toy.

"Warren is in his crib, but he needs to be fed," she said, as Jim helped her struggle into her coat. "Jade knows the routine. She'll fill you in." Rhonda Madden was peering in the hall mirror, playing with her hair as she talked. "You'll have to go easy with Jade. She is a little upset because *you* are here instead of Stephanie. Stephanie is her favourite. She likes Stephanie better than anyone. She'll settle down. She knows where everything is. This is very good of you. It's my sister's wedding."

And away they went.

Jade. It was Jade who was crying.

Jade, who liked Stephanie better than anyone.

Dave stood at the front door and watched Jim and Rhonda bustle into their black Saab.

"Have a good time," he said. "We'll be fine."

But they didn't hear. They didn't see his raised arm. They didn't wave back.

Dave turned and shut the door. Jade had stopped crying. The silence of the house overwhelmed him.

Dave looked at his knapsack leaning against the small television. It held his babysitting supplies: the two movies, his cream soda, the French cheese, the jalapeño peppers and the Doritos. He looked at his watch. It was quarter to seven. If he could get everyone in bed by nine, the night wouldn't be a complete loss.

He took a tentative step towards the living room, then his shoulders sagged and he turned for one last look out the window. He saw the Maddens' red tail lights disappearing down the street, carrying his grand plans with them. The car slowed at a stop sign, then accelerated through it without stopping.

Dave was about to turn away when something caught his attention. He leaned against the glass and squinted.

Something was following the car.

He shook his head and blinked.

It was a small thing, running. A small thing in pyjamas, running with its arms outstretched in front of itself.

"Kenneth?" said Dave.

And he bolted out the front door.

"Kenneth," he screamed.

Dave was halfway down the walk before he turned and raced back to the house.

"I'll be right back," he yelled into the silence.

Then he slammed the front door and bounded down the street.

He caught up to Kenneth at the end of the block. Kenneth was standing beside the stop sign, pointing at the red tail lights of his parents' car as it vanished around a corner.

"Mummy," he said as Dave picked him up. "Mummy."

It was only when Dave got back to the Maddens' and walked up to the front door with Kenneth slung over his shoulder, kicking and still screaming for his mother, that he realized, in his rush to retrieve the boy, he had locked himself out.

"Mummy," howled Kenneth.

Dave rang the doorbell and waited.

"I want my mummy," screamed Kenneth.

Dave jabbed at the doorbell again, impatiently. Once, twice. And again and again.

Then he leaned on it. But still no one came.

He put Kenneth down on the stoop and walked across the front lawn anxiously. He peered through the living room window. He couldn't see a soul.

When he turned around, there was Kenneth rocketing down the street again, his determined little feet pounding along the sidewalk. Dave didn't catch him until they were halfway to the stop sign.

When they got back to the stoop, Dave got down on his hands and knees and peered through the mail slot, holding Kenneth to his body like a marsupial.

He could see right across the front hall, all the way to the staircase. And sitting there on the third stair he could see seven-year-old Jade Madden glaring back at him.

Jade, who liked Stephanie better than anyone.

She had Dave's knapsack open beside her. She was eating his Doritos.

"Jade," said Dave through the mail slot. "Open the door, please."

"No," said Jade flatly and not without determination.

"Mummy," screamed Kenneth.

"Be quiet," barked Dave.

There was a moment of profound silence.

And then Dave began to scream. Dave screamed and scrambled to his feet, trying to wrench Kenneth *away* from his body now.

But Kenneth, who had sunk his teeth into Dave's earlobe, wasn't letting go—not without a fight.

It was the neighbours who first heard and then spotted the stranger holding the screaming baby while he tried to jimmy open the Maddens' patio door with a tire iron. It was the neighbours who called the police. And it was the police who eventually convinced Jade to open the front door.

"Are you going to be okay?" asked the sergeant with a smirk on his face as he stood on the stoop. "There *are* three of them, after all. Maybe you need backup?"

Dave shook his head.

The cop said, "I have a twelve-year-old daughter who babysits. I could send her in."

"Har, har, har," said Dave. Then he added grimly, "Don't worry about us. We'll be fine." He stood on the stoop and watched the cops drive away.

He waved.

The cops didn't wave back either.

"Well," said Dave, when he was finally inside with the door closed. "Well," said Dave to Jade, "I was hoping we could be friends."

Jade sniffed and walked into the family room and snapped on the television without a word. Kenneth struggled onto the couch and sat beside her.

And that is when Warren started to whimper. Nine-month-old Warren.

Dave had forgotten about Warren.

"Warren," he said.

He bounded upstairs and found Warren's bedroom.

When he opened the door, Warren was standing in his crib holding on to the rails.

Dave walked in and smiled.

"Hi," he said. "My name is Dave. I'm your babysitter."

Warren let go of the rails, dropped onto his mattress like a stone and started to scream.

"I'm sorry," said Dave, "but Stephanie couldn't make it. She's your favourite, right?"

Dave plucked Warren out of the crib and dropped him onto the changing table.

Getting an angry baby out of a dirty diaper may be one of the cruellest jobs in the world. By the time he had Warren cleaned up, Dave looked like a mud wrestler. Standing with one hand on the squirming baby's chest, Dave looked desperately around the room for clean diapers. He couldn't see them anywhere.

He put Warren back in the crib and ran downstairs.

"Jade," he said, "where does your mummy keep the clean diapers?"

Jade didn't flinch. Her determined little eyes did not stray from the television. She sat motionless, as if Dave didn't exist.

Dave ran back upstairs and lifted Warren out of the crib. They were halfway across the room when Warren began to pee.

It was not a polite little tinkle. Warren had been holding back for some time—his tank was clearly full. Without warning, Warren was squirting around the bedroom like a loose firehose.

Dave did the only thing he could think of doing under the circumstances. He grabbed the firehose and clamped the nozzle shut.

Warren looked at him in stunned wonder as they ran for the bathroom.

Half an hour later, wearing one of Jim Madden's shirts and a pair of Jim Madden's pants, Dave was rummaging through the kitchen looking for baby formula. He was getting desperate.

Warren was still crying.

You didn't need Dr. Spock to know Warren was starving.

When Jade wandered into the kitchen and he asked for her help, she left without a word. She returned to the couch and sat with her arms and legs crossed.

Three-year-old Kenneth, who was wound up tighter than a seven-day clock, was clearly up way past his bedtime. He had spent the last fifteen minutes lugging buckets of wooden bricks, Duplo and a toy train set from his bedroom and dumping them on the living room floor.

"It's your bedtime," said Dave.

"No it's not," said Kenneth, who had begun turning in circles to make himself dizzy.

Kenneth didn't know much, but he knew enough to know that Dave didn't know much either. And he had figured out that his sister wasn't going to come to Dave's rescue. He stopped spinning and lurched across the living room on an angle, crashing into a side table and knocking a lamp, a pile of magazines and two china dogs onto the floor.

For Dave, it was a matter—as they say at the management seminars—of setting priorities. A matter of *first things first.*

Kenneth wasn't the first thing. Warren was the first thing. Dave had to get some food into Warren and get Warren to bed before he could work on Kenneth. Or, more to the point, he had to stop Warren crying before Warren drove him crazy.

But he couldn't find the baby formula anywhere.

It had been so long since his kids had drunk formula that Dave wasn't certain what he was actually looking for. He couldn't remember if formula came as a powder or a liquid.

He was looking for either and was coming up dry.

He did, however, find a plastic bottle of corn syrup.

Dave remembered his grandmother feeding his younger sister, Annie, corn syrup off a spoon. He shrugged, opened the bottle of corn syrup and squeezed some onto a spoon.

Warren wasn't interested in the spoon of corn syrup.

In desperation, Dave dipped his finger into the sticky sap and stuck his finger into Warren's mouth.

Warren's eyes widened dramatically. He stopped crying and began to suck on Dave's finger with frightening strength. When he had finished, he plucked Dave's finger out of his mouth with his little hands, stared at it and said, "More."

Well, he didn't really say the word, but it was clear, by the look of wonder on his face, that that was what he was *trying* to say. Dave squeezed more syrup onto his finger and stuck his finger back in Warren's mouth.

He found a baby bottle and some nipples on the counter. Dave considered putting the nipple right on the bottle of syrup and plugging Warren in.

When Kenneth saw what was going on, he said, "Can I have some of that?" and Dave said, "Sure." He got out a bowl and he poured about a half a cup of corn syrup into the bowl. Then he gave Kenneth a spoon and said, "Be my guest."

Kenneth carried the bowl earnestly over to the kitchen table and began to spoon the syrup into his mouth like soup.

"This is good," he said. "Can I have some more?"

It was during this unexpected moment of harmony

that Dave decided it wouldn't hurt, if he couldn't find formula, to give Warren a bit of warm milk.

Oh, he knew the baby might not take to the milk right away. But he had seen some chocolate syrup in the cupboard, and Dave figured that if he flavoured the milk with a bit of the chocolate and a bit of corn syrup, Warren might take it. Actually, he was thinking, maybe *he* could be Warren's favourite.

At first all he could see in the fridge were cartons of soy milk. Unfortunately, he finally uncovered a jug of milk behind the ketchup. How was Dave supposed to know that the Madden kids were all lactose intolerant?

On its own, the milk probably would not have made Warren sick. On its own, the milk might have given Warren gas. Maybe diarrhea. And probably not until well after Dave had left the scene of the crime.

But when Warren finished his bottle of milk—and no baby in history has ever inhaled a bottle of milk with the gusto Warren displayed as he sucked down the chocolate-flavoured, syrup-laced milk that Dave had prepared—Warren sighed, and farted, and a look of great joy settled on his little face. Dave held him up over his head and shook him back and forth and said, "Well done, Warren." Then he threw Warren in the air and caught him, and Warren giggled. Dave threw him higher and Warren giggled again. And because this was the first joy Dave had elicited out of any of these miserable children, he began to dance around the kitchen holding Warren over his head, shaking him like a pair of maracas. Around and around they went,

Warren being tossed back and forth, up and down, Dave dancing a little jig to the tune of a baby's squeals of delight. That is, until Warren stopped laughing.

Dave lowered Warren and looked at his suddenly furrowed little brow and said, "Don't worry. I won't drop you."

And just to prove it, he threw him even higher.

A peculiar expression crossed Warren's face, as if he was experiencing something new, something he had never experienced before.

When he noticed how pale Warren had turned, Dave frowned and said, "Warren?" holding him in front of his face, peering into his eyes.

Warren burped. His breath had the sour smell of milk that had been left in the sun.

Dave held him at arm's length, but still up in front of his face. And a sound began to roll out of Warren's little body, a sound Dave associated with things like werewolves, and mummies, and beasts that might stalk the countryside before the Second Coming. And then Warren opened his mouth and a ball of vomit flew out of him, right towards Dave's face.

Dave had heard about projectile vomiting, but he had never witnessed it before. Somehow, though, he knew just what to do. Dave ducked.

The ball of vomit flew over his shoulder.

This part seemed to be happening in slow motion: the vomit travelling across the room like a rolling cannonball, Jade coming through the kitchen door with her self-satisfied smile and her arms crossed.

As she walked into the kitchen she was saying, “What is going on?” and without thinking Dave was yelling, “Duck!” And just before the ball of vomit hit her in the chest, the word “Why?” was spilling out of her mouth.

The vomit hit her like a bowl of pea soup. It was the most gruesome thing Dave had seen in years.

As the vomit began its descent down the front of Jade’s sweater, Dave replied, “Because.”

The rest of the night was more or less a blur. The phone rang just after they got Jade cleaned up and into her pyjamas. It was Stephanie.

“Just don’t let Kenneth eat anything sweet,” she said, “or he’ll be up all night.”

“Don’t worry,” said Dave. “I’m not stupid.”

The Maddens didn’t come home until after midnight. They let themselves in the front door quietly and stood in the hall for a moment, listening. The house was dark. They could see the glow from the television flickering against the kitchen wall.

They heard a gunshot, and then another, and then John Wayne’s distinctive drawl echoed through the house.

Rhonda Madden looked at her husband and arched her eyebrows.

Jim shook his head and shrugged.

“Maybe he’s hard of hearing,” he said.

Jim and Rhonda Madden reached the living room together.

Nothing in God's creation could have prepared them for what they found.

Dave was asleep on the floor, his head tilted back so far and at such an odd angle that at first glance Rhonda Madden thought he was dead.

"Is he okay?" she said.

But before the words were out of her mouth, Dave snorted. It was a strangled, snoring sort of snort, and Rhonda realized her babysitter was asleep, not dead—though he was clearly *dead* asleep.

But by the time she realized Dave was only sleeping, Rhonda wasn't concerned about Dave any more. By then she had taken in the whole sorry tableau: the two televisions stacked one on top of the other, John Wayne holstering his gun on one, a heavy metal band leering grotesquely into her living room on the other.

And her children. Her three precious children—her children who had never watched anything except *Barney, Sesame Street* and *Mr. Dressup* reruns—staring slack-jawed at the televisions as if they had been hypnotized.

Warren, the baby, was sitting on Dave's chest. His three-year-old brother, Kenneth, was sprawled on the floor beside them. Jade was across the room in a leather chair, leaning forward.

The three of them were watching the television so intently that none of them noticed their mother and father standing in the doorway.

Kenneth was eating something out of a bowl. It looked like cereal. Jim and Rhonda watched in wonder as Kenneth filled up his spoon and, without taking his eyes off the television, held it up over his head for Warren. Warren, who had never had solid food in his life, leaned precariously forward and smacked at the spoon greedily.

As she watched, dumbstruck, Rhonda noticed that Jade was holding Warren's bottle loosely in her hands. As Rhonda watched, Jade brought the bottle absent-mindedly to her mouth and sucked on it for a full minute. It was full of a thick, golden liquid.

And that's when Dave farted.

He farted and stirred restlessly in his sleep, and Warren tottered precariously on his belly. Rhonda moved to steady him, but before she could do anything Kenneth put down his bowl and held his hand up, reaching over his head and holding on to his brother until Dave settled. He did this without taking his eyes off the television. He did this without apparent thought, as if he had gone through it many times before.

Rhonda stepped forward and picked up the bowl of brown mush that Kenneth had been feeding Warren.

She sniffed it suspiciously.

It looked like cereal, but it smelled like Doritos.

That was when Jim recognized his pants and shirt.

"He's wearing my clothes," he said out loud. "Those are my pants. That's my shirt."

Rhonda Madden looked at her husband in alarm and began to weep.

It was two and a half months before the Maddens called Stephanie to babysit again.

Dave had told her everything, all the humiliating details, including the most humiliating moment of all, when Jim Madden had insisted on paying him. Under the circumstances, Stephanie was surprised to hear from them at all.

When she got to the Maddens', Warren was already asleep. Kenneth was standing by the door beside his mother, as usual. Stephanie found Jade in the living room watching television. When she saw Stephanie, Jade frowned, crossed her legs and sighed.

"You'll have to be patient with her," said Rhonda Madden. "She's been asking for your father. He's her favourite, you know."

Dorm Days

DAVE AND MORLEY drove Stephanie to university on the Thursday before Labour Day.

All summer Stephanie had made it clear that she couldn't wait to move away from home. "I can't wait to get out of here," she said, over and over again. Ask her to do the simplest thing, ask her to clear the table, ask her to help with the dishes, ask her the time, and all summer long all you'd get was a sigh, a disconsolate roll of her head and the mantra. It was as though the Maharishi himself had instructed her. "Here is your handkerchief, here is your flower, here is the road to eternal truth: *I can't wait to get out of here. Ommmmm.*"

Newton's Third Law of Motion states that to every action there is an equal and opposite reaction.

Stephanie may be moving through the universe to rhythms never heard before. The trajectory of Stephanie's life may be unique—is certainly unique—but the trajectory of her life does not contradict the laws of physical mechanics.

By mid-August, Newton's Law of Interaction had raised its confusing head.

She couldn't wait to get out of there.

She didn't want to go.

She worried that all her friends were going to other schools. She worried that she wouldn't make new friends. She worried that she wouldn't enjoy her classes. And, to her great surprise, she worried about missing her parents. Once she moved out, there would be no coming back. Nothing would ever be the same.

"For the rest of my life, I'll be a visitor in my own house," she told her friend Becky one night as they sipped mochaccino chillers at a local coffee shop. "A guest of honour, but a guest. You know?"

By the end of August, Stephanie was worried about the family cat. Who would take care of Galway? Galway, the family outlaw, whom even Sam had given up on, lived in the basement in the winter and on the street in the summer. Galway has lived with Dave and Morley for years now, but she has never become part of the family.

"No one knows how to take care of her," said Stephanie, reaching for the sugar. "They just shove her outside so she doesn't bug the dog. I'm the only one who pays her any attention. I'm the only one who has tried to integrate her into the house."

The week before she left, Stephanie began to clean her room. Morley watched with a complicated sadness.

"It's like a Greek myth," she said to Dave. "Although," she said, pausing, "I can't decide if she is Sisyphus or Hercules."

"Hercules," said Dave. "My vote is for the stable."

Stephanie would start cleaning as soon as she had

finished breakfast—around noon. She would shut her bedroom door, put on a CD and settle down among her piles of stuff, filling garbage bags and cardboard boxes.

Every once in a while the bedroom door would open and Stephanie would appear holding a household object that hadn't been seen in years: a bread knife, an old remote for the television, someone's favourite scarf, all long ago written off as Missing in Action. All long ago replaced.

"Maybe," said Dave quietly one night after Stephanie handed him an umbrella he had thought he'd left in a taxi, "maybe we should alert the press. Any day now she is going to stumble across Jimmy Hoffa's body."

Stephanie, however, seemed to be making precious little progress. As the piles on one side of her room shrank, the stacks on the other side were growing taller.

Sam was watching all this activity quietly—not comprehending, at eleven years old, why anyone would want to leave home.

"That won't happen to me," he told Morley one night as they snuggled on his bed. "I'm always going to live here."

"Well, sweetheart," said Morley, watching the headlights of a passing car sweep across his ceiling, "maybe one day you'll have children of your own."

Sam was quiet for a moment. Morley could sense his forehead wrinkle in the darkness.

Sam said, "Couldn't my children live here with us?"

"As long as they could all fit in your bedroom with you," said Morley.

"That would be okay," said Sam. "They wouldn't mind."

What was making the parting easier for Stephanie, what, in fact, was making it possible, was that Stephanie was going to university with her best friend, Becky.

Becky and Stephanie had requested—and to their great joy been assigned—a room together in residence. It was like a dream come true. The dream of all best friends.

Stephanie and Becky had imagined living together ever since grade three. That year they had tried to convince their parents to buy adjacent houses. Their plan was to get adjoining bedrooms. Their plan was to cut a hole in the bedroom wall so they could crawl back and forth from one house to the other.

They began to share clothes in grade seven. They still do—even though they no longer wear the same size. Becky is short and plump. Stephanie is long and lean. Even though their bodies are spectacularly different, there are still things they can share: sweaters, shoes, make-up.

They might as well be sisters.

They met in the park, in the sandbox. Their friendship, which began in sand, sunk its unshakable roots through the limbs of a Norway maple—a tree they have thought of as *their* tree ever since they could climb it. Ever since they were seven. They each have a branch they think of as their own—a branch that is perfect for sitting. They have sat in the tree for hours. For years. They sat in it the night before they left for university.

At first they called it "the sitting tree." They would say to each other, *Do you want to go to the park?* Which really meant, *Do you want to go and sit in the tree?*

When they were teenagers they would go at night, which was fun because they were invisible at night, and whenever people walked beneath them they would shake the branches as hard as they could. Just for a second. Just a fast shake. And the people walking below would inevitably be startled, would often jump and stare up into the darkness, but no one ever saw them sitting on their branches, hiding among the leaves.

It was fun to scare people, but what cracked them up was listening to their explanations. Because everyone always stood underneath them trying to explain away what had just happened. A raccoon, the wind, squirrels playing.

They called shaking the branches *squirrelling.*

Do you want to go and squirrel? they would ask each other.

One August evening they were hiding in the branches and two teenagers sat beneath them. They were holding hands.

It was obvious the girl wanted the boy to kiss her.

It was obvious he was scared.

He held her hand for the longest time. He even put his arm around her shoulders. He told her she was his love.

"I love you," he said.

It was so beautiful. It was true love.

"Here it comes," whispered Becky.

But she was wrong.

The boy was too scared.

"He should have kissed her," said Becky.

"She should have kissed him," said Stephanie.

Another time when they were up there Ronnie Tomlinson's mother and father had a big argument right below them.

"That was horrible," said Becky. "When I get married, we are never going to fight."

For better or for worse, Stephanie finished packing for university the night before they were supposed to leave. Dave brought the rented minivan home. He went upstairs, picked up a cardboard box and said, "I'll help you with the boxes."

"The boxes stay," said Stephanie.

She had been using the garbage bags to pack.

They went out to dinner, to their favourite Chinese restaurant. Stephanie had to wear reject clothes because everything she liked was already in garbage bags.

As they left the restaurant, Morley saw Stephanie studying her reflection in the glass of the door.

"I packed all wrong," she said.

The plan was to leave early the next morning. The plan was to find Stephanie's room, unpack and then have lunch with Becky and her parents.

By the time they got to the dorm, Stephanie had worked herself into a complete lather. All the other girls on her floor looked weird. There were no other parents around. The room was unbelievably small.

It was a single room with bunk beds. A room so narrow that when Stephanie sat at her desk and Becky sat at hers their backs touched.

In fact, when Stephanie and Becky were both in the room at the same time they were always within arm's reach. There was nowhere to go where you couldn't be touched.

Stephanie didn't feel like going to lunch with her parents, but she was going to grin and bear it—until Dave spotted her old boyfriend, Doug. He opened her bedroom window and called out across the quadrangle, "Doug. Hey, Doug. Up here."

Stephanie looked at her father with mortification and said, "You have to go. I want you to go now."

They walked downstairs in silence.

When they got to the parking lot there was a bare-chested man wearing cut-offs sitting cross-legged on the hood of their car. He was playing bongos. His grey, thinning hair was pulled back into a ponytail. He was the oldest hippie Dave had ever seen.

Dave walked up to the car. He smiled wanly at the man, shuffled from foot to foot and pointed at his car keys.

The man with the bongos said, "I'll be finished in a minute, man."

Morley and Stephanie were crying. Dave didn't want to make a fuss.

"We have to go," he said under his breath to the bongo player.

The man playing the bongos sighed, stood up and jumped to the ground. The hood of Dave's car popped with a loud twang.

"Far out," said the bongo player.

He flashed Dave a peace sign as Dave turned the car around.

Then they were gone.

Stephanie and Becky spent their first weekend decorating their room. They put a *Barbarella* poster on their door. And a bulletin board for messages. And around the bulletin board they stuck pictures of themselves when they were children. Baby pictures. Pictures from elementary school. They spent hours on the door. It was just like they had planned. In fact, it was better.

There were no classes the first week. Instead there was a never-ending program of parties, picnics and parades. There was even a panty raid.

By midweek Becky had decided orientation was boring and too rah-rah and she stopped going. Steph hung in. "It's stupid," she said, "but I'm meeting people." She had made a new friend. A girl named Anna, from Nova Scotia.

Anna and Stephanie danced until two o'clock in the morning at a toga party—from midnight until two without stopping.

Becky stayed home.

They had a phone on the wall of their bedroom above a little fridge. From the middle of the week it rang constantly. Mostly Becky answered. Mostly the calls were for Stephanie.

"The guy from Montreal called," she said. "So did Anna. She wants to know if you are going to join the film society. They saw *Metropolis* and the original *Frankenstein* and something called *Waking Dreams*."

It was a week and a half before Stephanie had her first scheduled class—a Tuesday morning at ten o'clock.

Room H110 was as big as a theatre. There was raked seating—chairs for maybe five hundred. When Stephanie walked through the double doors, she thought that she had made a mistake. But there was a chalkboard at the front of the hall that said "SOCIOLOGY 101." And under that: "How Society Works."

She chose a seat on the aisle.

There was a table in front of the blackboard. On the table there was a watermelon, a squash and a pumpkin.

There was a man sitting beside the table.

He was wearing a mauve shirt with a wide collar and massive bell-bottom jeans with an embroidered ribbon stitched around the cuff. He had beads and Birkenstocks and a Fu Manchu moustache. And a floppy hat.

He looked vaguely familiar to Stephanie. There was a black button on his brown leather vest. Stephanie was too far away to read what it said.

The man seemed completely oblivious to the class. He was sitting at the front of the hall as if he were in a trance. At ten minutes past ten, he abruptly stood up, walked shakily to the lectern and peered out at them.

The room slowly fell quiet.

As soon as the man stood up, Stephanie recognized him. It was the bongo player from the parking lot.

She could make out the button on the vest now. It was a peace sign.

Professor Bongo leaned into the microphone. He said, "My name is Brian Michaels."

Then he looked down and consulted his notes and said, "This course is called How Society Works."

And then, without another word, he reached under the table and brought out a mallet. He lifted it over his head and swung it with startling force into the centre of the pumpkin. He destroyed it in three quick blows and quickly turned his attention to the watermelon. It lasted a little longer.

The keeners in the first row were soon covered in seeds and juicy pulp. A girl in a blue cashmere sweater stood up and started to cry, brushing her sweater as if she were covered in bugs.

The boy beside her lifted a large piece of melon off his notebook and started writing notes furiously.

Brian Michaels didn't flinch. He stood at the podium covered in vegetable matter, with seeds and all sorts of gunk dripping from his hat. When the class quietened down, he said:

"I just did violence to those vegetables."

Then he left the classroom without another word.

The girl beside Stephanie was frowning.

"Are you okay?" asked Stephanie.

"I don't understand," said the girl, looking down at her notebook. "Isn't watermelon a fruit?"

The next Tuesday the hall was packed for Soc. 101. Earnest girls were sitting in the aisles near the front. Engineers and hockey players were standing at the back.

As well as her sociology class, Stephanie was taking an English, a psychology, a biology and the bane of her life, statistics.

Statistics was taught by a Hungarian mathematician named Lehrfield Utz. Professor Utz was the only member of faculty who still lived on campus. He did so more or less by squatter's rights. He had been in his house since 1967. The administration had torn down all the other faculty houses.

They wanted him out of his so they could build a new residence but he wasn't leaving, and they weren't about to chuck him out. He was, by all accounts, brilliant. Prior to computerization, Professor Utz had scheduled the entire university in his head. It was his hobby. He would dictate the schedule over two days at the beginning of every June to two secretaries from the admissions department, who would typeset it and have the calendar printed. People who were there at the time said Professor Utz was more reliable than the computers.

He was as eccentric as he was smart. He hated natural sunshine. The windows of his house were boarded up with plywood, making it appear deserted, which made everyone in the president's office—who of course *wanted* it deserted—crazy. There were rumours that he ate nothing but chocolate bars and pop, but no one had ever been in the house to verify it. And you never saw Professor Utz except in class.

Professor Michaels, on the other hand, popped up everywhere.

He was at the toga party.

And the film society.

He brought a hookah and his bongos to Pub Night and he cornered Becky when he saw her standing alone and told her about his novel, chapter by chapter.

He lived in a rambling house in town and invited Becky to a poetry reading on Sunday night. Becky was scared to go. Stephanie went in her place. When she arrived, there were forty other students crammed in the living room. Professor Michaels was sitting in a beanbag chair explaining his novel to a doe-eyed grad student from Maryland.

When Stephanie came home she was bursting.

"He has a goat in the backyard, called Hendrix. And a pet goose named, like, after a writer. Kerouac or something.

"He makes his own yogourt from the goat's milk. And

I'm sure he was stoned. And there was a beaded curtain in the kitchen door. And candles. And he lives with a Ph.D. student from the States, who is, like, sixteen.

"I'm think I'm going to tie-dye some T-shirts," said Stephanie, flouncing onto her bed.

In the 1990s, petitions had circulated around the campus to have Professor Michaels fired.

"I am just coming back into my own," he'd said that night at the poetry reading, as he passed around a plate of brownies.

Stephanie and Becky loved living together. They would sit at their desks, at their computers, their backs touching, and send emails back and forth as they did assignments. Or talk on Instant Messaging.

Do you want to have a break? Becky would type.

I'll meet you at the Hub, Steph would type back.

Living away from home was fun. Some kids had parents who visited the very first weekend. Stephanie told Dave and Morley she didn't want them to come. She had promised herself she wouldn't go home until Thanksgiving. She wanted to establish her independence.

But she was finding the chaos of the dorm more difficult than she had imagined.

Once a week someone brought bulk popcorn from the campus store and tried to microwave it in a paper bag. The bag inevitably caught fire and set off the fire alarm, and they would have to evacuate. The dorm would smell like burnt corn for days.

Maureen, a girl from New Brunswick, broke the floor vacuum cleaner trying to vacuum up water after a forty-five-minute shower.

And then there was Ruth.

Ruth, a private-school girl, began freaking out over her grades at the end of the second week. Ruth showed up in Stephanie's room on the second Friday and asked to borrow a suitcase.

"I'm leaving," she said. "I can't stand it any more. I'm not coming back."

Stephanie spent an hour trying to talk Ruth out of leaving but eventually gave up and lent her a suitcase.

Ruth was back on Monday.

"My mother wouldn't let me quit," she said.

They went through this every Friday for a month and a half.

After the third Friday, Stephanie didn't try to talk Ruth out of leaving any more. When Ruth showed up in her room on Friday afternoon, Stephanie pointed to her suitcase without being asked.

"It's there," she said, not bothering to look up from her computer. "See you Monday."

Stephanie had begun to adjust to the chaos, but Becky was having more trouble.

Becky's boyfriend went to university out west. She had a phone plan that encouraged midnight calls. Calls after midnight were so cheap that they talked most nights. By October, Stephanie had learned to sleep through anything. Happy phone calls. Sad phone calls. She sensed that there were more sad calls as the weeks wore on.

Stephanie noticed that Becky had begun to stay up later and later. She had stopped going to early classes. There was no one looking over her shoulder and she didn't *have* to do anything. And so she didn't.

She did, however, start to put on weight.

The dreaded "freshman fifteen."

They had their first fight in the middle of October.

Becky picked one of Stephanie's sweatshirts off the floor and dropped it on her desk.

She said, "Your clothes are always on my side."

Stephanie hadn't considered sides before. She had been thinking of *her* bed and *her* desk, but she thought of the rest of the room as shared space.

Becky had been thinking otherwise.

"Why is the garbage can always on my side?" said Becky, waving her arms and smacking her wrist on the top bunk.

They agreed to divide the room in two.

It took them an hour to decide where the line should go. The room was so small it was like dividing a raisin.

They got two garbage cans.

Then Becky said they should get an answering machine.

"I can't keep taking all your messages," she said. "I'm not a social secretary."

They owned a set of encyclopedias together. They had bought them at a yard sale when they were in grade ten. They had been saving them for university.

The encyclopedias were stacked by the door. On Becky's side of the room.

One day Stephanie came back to the room in a foul mood, bearing a disastrous English essay: a C–. She found the pile of encyclopedias pushed over to her side. She threw the English paper on her bed and stared at the pile of encyclopedias. She shoved the books back where they had been and stormed out.

She didn't come back until after dinner. Becky was nowhere to be seen. But the pile of encyclopedias was back on Stephanie's side.

Stephanie pushed them back again.

The next morning, when she got up, the encyclopedias had been moved once more. But not as far. Just onto the border—straddling the line. Neither of them said anything.

That afternoon Becky said, "Why is your garbage pail always full of garbage?"

Stephanie didn't answer. She wasn't talking to Becky. She wasn't going to talk to her ever again for as long as they lived. She had taken a pledge that afternoon.

For the first time Stephanie felt homesick and alone.

The next evening, while Becky was at dinner, Stephanie adjusted the pile of encyclopedias, inching them over so they were more on Becky's side than hers.

When Stephanie was in the washroom the next morning, Becky shifted them back onto the border. Exactly on the border. Or the bottom volume, at least. She staggered each successive volume, however, ever so slightly. As the pile grew, each book was slightly more on Stephanie's side than on Becky's. So that the last volume, the volume on the top of the pile, was completely invading Stephanie's airspace.

"This is ridiculous," said Stephanie.

She was right.

A day and a night passed, and then another day. Forty-eight long hours during which not a word passed between them.

The second night, they were both in their room for the whole evening, working on assignments. They were sitting back to back at their desks, clicking furiously away at their computers. Save for the chattering of the keyboards—a chattering that grew louder by the minute—the silence in the room was frightening.

Finally, at 10:30, in the middle of the silence, Stephanie typed something quickly and pressed enter. Then she put her arms on her keyboard and laid her head down.

Becky's computer beeped. It meant someone was sending her a message. Becky clicked on it.

It was from Stephanie.

It was brief and to the point.

Four simple words.

I miss our tree.

Becky leaned over the keyboard and typed her reply.

She pushed enter.

Almost immediately Stephanie's computer beeped.

Me too, she read.

They wrote back and forth like that for half an hour, the two of them, backs touching, typing like maniacs. The words erupting out of them as if they hadn't talked for years. Like twin sisters separated by a war.

They typed and typed, their computers chiming like bicycle bells.

Stephanie came home for Thanksgiving. It wasn't the way she'd thought it would be. It didn't feel as though she were a guest. She felt like she had always felt.

But everything else seemed to be changing. The food tasted different. It tasted better. And her bed felt luxurious.

Her parents were different too.

They seemed more . . . mature.

Mellower.

Even Sam was . . . charming?

Everything was the same. But it was different.

Like Becky. Becky was changing too.

Their friendship was changing.

They had talked about it the night before they'd come home. Lying in their bunks in the darkness.

Next year, they agreed, they would live off-campus. In a house, with other people, so they could have their own rooms.

More privacy.

Just as they were drifting off to sleep Stephanie said, "I love you" into the darkness. "We are going to be friends for life."

"I know," said Becky. Then she said, "I love you too."

Best Things

IT WAS A THURSDAY NIGHT, past midnight. The street lights were on, but not much else. The occasional television was flickering off the occasional bedroom ceiling. Most of the people who had turned the televisions on had long ago fallen asleep. It was the time of night when everything up and about was used to being up and about. A late-night jogger. A cop car. A taxicab. A garbage truck. Night-shift.

In the parkette behind the KFC, a homeless couple were playing Scrabble under a street light.

In front of the all-night doughnut store, the man who sells tomorrow's newspapers to the sleepless looked at the clock on the bank across the street and decided to pack it in.

Two blocks away, Dave, sitting in his living room with a glass of bourbon beside him and a Rheostatics album on the turntable, raised his eyes when a car glided to a stop in front of his house.

He had a Sotheby's catalogue in his lap—the summer auction of pop collectibles.

On the cover was the solitary item Dave had submitted to the sale. The catalogue described it as a previously unseen photo of John Lennon as a boy. It noted that the photo was inscribed in the youngster's own handwriting on the reverse.

The photo had spent the last nineteen years in the attic storeroom above Dave's record store. Five in a file drawer, fourteen in a frame hanging on a north-facing pillar, out of the sun—just above a frame holding Bob Dylan's handwritten set list from the 1965 Newport Folk Festival.

In the photo on the catalogue cover in Dave's lap, the young John Lennon is staring directly at the camera. He is wearing the short pants, blazer and high socks of an English schoolboy. On the back of the photo, Lennon has written, "Me at Fleetwood the year I lost my trunks. In Mr. Shipway's garden."

The picture of Lennon fetched £2,200 at the Sotheby's sale. A little more than the catalogue had estimated—a little less than Dave had hoped.

Dave set the catalogue on the coffee table beside his chair and peered out the window. A young woman was getting out of the car. Dave leaned forward when he realized that the young woman was his daughter. He glanced at his watch. Then he watched his daughter lean back into the car and kiss the driver. It was a casual, familiar kind of kiss. A comfortable kiss.

The car didn't move as she walked towards the house.

Dave heard her key in the lock. He heard the front door swing open. The car's headlights blinked.

Dave had not been expecting his daughter. She hadn't called to say she was coming home.

She dropped her bag by the door and jumped when Dave stirred. She hadn't expected anyone would be up.

"What took you so long?" said Dave. "I was about to give up on you."

Stephanie laughed. "Liar," she said. "How are you, Daddy?"

It wasn't like this last year. Last year when Stephanie came home from college unexpectedly, she came home with tears in her eyes.

Her first couple of weeks at school had been fine. Her first couple of weeks had been a blast—settling into residence, setting up a life.

And then came October, and with October her fateful rendezvous with Professor David Braithwaite.

"*Awkward,*" scrawled Professor Braithwaite on her first paper. "*Your naive syntax tends to undermine the credibility of your argument, which is, in any event, too obvious. C.*"

"*Clumsy,*" scribbled Professor Braithwaite on her second effort. "*If you wish to succeed in this discipline you will have to develop a more sophisticated heuristic approach to the subject. C–.*"

"*Juvenile,*" sneered Professor Braithwaite on her third assignment. "*I am not interested in the world of Hemingway. There is no world of Hemingway. There is only the text. There is only the world constructed by language. There is only the post-colonial textuality of all experience, including, as I thought I explained in class, the textuality of sexuality. D.*"

Stephanie was used to being at the top of her class. When she had imagined life at university, she had not imagined anything different. She had pictured herself sitting in the library at night, drinking coffee, a pile of books spread on the table around her. Her vision had never included someone like Professor Braithwaite lurking among the stacks in his tweed jacket and leather elbow patches. She hated Professor Braithwaite from the start. Now she was starting to hate herself.

In early November, Steph came home in tears. Over the weekend she pulled herself together and went back again.

She and her best friend, Becky, were living in residence in Millhouse, on an all-girls floor. It had been Becky's decision. The building was older and charming in a sort of rundown, retro way. "Besides," said Becky, "who wants to shave beside a football player?"

It made sense. And Stephanie hadn't stopped to think if it made better sense to share a bathroom with a bunch of women who, in this day and age, had opted for the all-girls dorm.

The residents of Millhouse were more or less split into two groups. There were, first of all, the party girls. The girls who had been *sent* to the all-girls floor by their parents and counsellors. The girls who *needed* to be kept away from boys. These were the girls who conspired to ensure that there were more boys in Millhouse than in any other dorm on campus.

There were the party girls and then there were the over-achievers—a group of high-strung, high-maintenance neurotics who kept the intensity of the floor festering at the level of bad therapy.

There was Lorraine. Thin and pale Lorraine, who constantly worried about the food in the cafeteria. Lorraine was convinced the food was unhealthy. Lorraine would head off at mealtime with a sense of doom, peering woefully at the steam table as if she might be able to spot the viruses and bacteria waving their little shrimpy tails as they lurked in the shepherd's pie.

There was Marissa, who was paranoid about her stuff and called a floor meeting in the very first week because, she explained tearfully, someone had used some of her expensive, spa-purchased shampoo. This, of course, ensured that everyone began using Marissa's shampoo. Before long the girls of Millhouse weren't only using Marissa's shampoo, they were deviously, day by day, refilling her bottle with no-name brands.

There was Sandy, an only child, who became flustered by the unrestrained exchange of clothing going on around her. Sandy, who couldn't abide the idea of trading clothes, took disinfectant to the laundromat and ran the washing machines through a complete cycle before adding her stuff. Sandy carried a tube of antibacterial hand gel in her purse. And a spray for toilet seats. Sandy even ironed her bras.

These were the girls Stephanie turned to in early November when Professor Braithwaite started pricking holes in her self-esteem.

"This stuff is really hard," she said.

To a woman they said, "I'm not finding it hard. We did much harder stuff in high school."

How was Stephanie to know they were lying through their teeth?

These were the neurotic overachieving liars who wanted to stay away from boys of their own free will.

Jane Turnbull, a strapping blonde who played on the women's lacrosse team, was a party girl. Jane had the room next to Stephanie and Becky's.

It was Jane Turnbull's fateful weekend trip to Montreal that changed Stephanie's life and was, in fact, the turning point in her relationship with the nefarious Professor Braithwaite.

It was the beginning of October when Jane started talking about Montreal. She knew about a sorority at McGill where you could stay. Cheap. All she needed was someone to go with her. She kept telling everyone about the bistros and the dance clubs, the old port and the old town. But it wasn't the food or wine or the architecture that was calling to Jane. Jane wanted to go to Montreal for the culture. Jane wanted to French kiss someone who could speak French.

Jane found a couple of guys from the men's lacrosse team to drive her. They left on a Friday after lunch. As they pulled off campus, Jane was sitting in front, making cute with the lacrosse guys, a French-English dictionary in her lap. She leaned out the window, high-fiving Becky in front of Kerr Hall. "*Auf Wiedersehen,*" she called as the car disappeared through the stone gates.

"She meant *au revoir,* right?" said Becky to whomever it was she was walking with.

Jane's boyfriend showed up at Millhouse about three hours later.

No one knew it was Jane's boyfriend, of course. No one in fact had ever heard Jane *had* a boyfriend.

He was just this guy standing in front of Millhouse looking lost and confused, which in itself wasn't unusual. There were always boys standing in front of Millhouse looking lost and confused. The difference between this guy and the other dazed guys who stood in front of Millhouse was that this guy was standing in the rain.

His name was Tommy Nowlan—a second-year English major from Trent. Tommy was wearing a T-shirt with a big picture of April O'Neil on the front—the TV news reporter from the *Teenage Mutant Ninja Turtles*. He was also wearing a pair of blue corduroy pants a size too large, and a pair of gold and blue bowling shoes with the number seven on the heel.

He said he and Jane had been going out three years. Ever since grade ten. He had a picture in his wallet, and a letter.

"I got it yesterday," he said.

The letter was less than a page.

"Maybe now that we are at different schools maybe we should see other people. I don't know. What do you think?"

Tommy knew what he thought. He didn't want to see other people. That's why he was there, standing in the rain. He was there to tell Jane that he thought this was a bad idea.

Except he was telling this to Stephanie instead of Jane. Because Jane was long gone, and it was Stephanie who had stopped and said, "Are you looking for someone?" It was Stephanie who had stopped and said, "Can I help you?"

So Tommy told her all about him and Jane.

Stephanie said, "Jane isn't here. Jane went to Montreal."

She didn't say, *Jane was in a car with two guys from the lacrosse team.* She didn't say, *You have just been dumped by a girl who has gone to Montreal to get French-kissed.*

Tommy said, "When is she coming back?"

Stephanie knew she should say, *Never. Jane is never coming back.* Instead, she said, "I don't know."

"I got a ride here from a guy who isn't leaving until Sunday," said Tommy vaguely.

And that's when Becky came along. That's when Stephanie said, "Becky, this is Tommy Nowlan." And then, with exaggerated clarity, added, "You know. Jane's *boyfriend.* From Trent."

And Becky, who didn't get it, Becky, who had no idea what was going on, said, "Jane doesn't have a boyfriend at Trent."

In her eagerness to clear things up, Stephanie blurted out the truth. "Things are not as bad as you think," she said to Tommy. "They are worse." Or words to that effect.

And before long, Tommy Nowlan was no longer standing in the rain in front of Millhouse looking lost and confused—he was standing there looking lost, confused and devastated.

"I don't even have my wallet," he said. Tommy's wallet was in his suitcase. "I left the suitcase in the trunk of the car," he said.

And the car wasn't coming back for him until Sunday at noon.

And it was still raining.

Tommy ran his hand through his hair and started shaking his head. "This reminds me of my worst field trip ever," he said. "I was in grade two. It was just like this," he said, waving at the sky. "One of those gloomy days with the clouds clinging to the ground. We went to a sheep farm. I was wearing my Big Bird raincoat. I got separated from the class and ended up surrounded by sheep. I couldn't see anyone. They always told you if you got lost you were supposed to sit down and stay where you were. So I sat down in the middle of the sheep. Because it was raining, the sheep weren't moving. They didn't find me for two hours."

Stephanie said, "That's awful."

Tommy nodded. "Have you any idea," he said, "what wet sheep smell like?"

Then he looked at Stephanie for what might have been the first time. Noticed her for the first time, anyway, and said, "Do you have any bad field trip memories?"

And before she knew it Stephanie was telling Tommy about the planetarium.

Tommy said, "A lot of people have bad memories about the planetarium."

And that was when Stephanie decided to give him sanctuary. He could sleep in Jane's bed until Sunday morning. Jane's roommate, Sandy, of the ironed bras, could move into Stephanie's room for two nights.

"That would be great," he said. "Thanks."

At supper she told the lady in the cafeteria that her roommate was sick in bed. The lady gave her a tray of food to take back to the dorm. Shepherd's pie. Tommy tucked into it with gusto.

"I love this stuff," he said. Stephanie had never seen anyone so happy with a school meal.

"I worked in the kitchen at Trent, first year," he said. "Do you know how they make this stuff?" He was waving at his plate with his fork. "They pump the meat into the kitchen right out of a truck, through a pipe, like oil. Actually," he said, grinning for the first time since he arrived, "it's not technically meat. It's a ground meat product. You got to love science."

Unfortunately, Lorraine had just wandered by.

"The potato," Tommy said, licking his lips, "comes in preformed sheets."

This was worse than anything Lorraine had ever imagined.

"I knew it," she said. "I'm going to purge."

Stephanie had to spend half an hour talking Lorraine down.

That night, Stephanie had to sleep on the floor of her room.

"This was your idea," said Sandy, who had settled

into Stephanie's bed. "I'm not sleeping on the floor."

Sandy, it turned out, talked in her sleep. Not polite murmurs but loud, dramatic outbursts, like public service announcements. Each announcement was prefaced by a loud, percussive snort. She would be sleeping quietly, and then she'd blow, like a whale coming up for air.

Stephanie would be asleep—or worse, floating in that confusing place that precedes sleep—and Sandy would detonate and then sit up abruptly and bark out something loud and usually aggressive.

"It's too late for that now," she growled at midnight. "I'm not going to allow it."

Each announcement left Stephanie lying on the floor with her heart pounding. And each eruption took her a little further from sleep.

She finally fell into a half-sleep at four-thirty, ruing the impulse that had made her stop and talk to Jane's boyfriend.

Ex-boyfriend.

She woke at eight to yelling and slamming doors.

Marissa, of the stolen shampoo, had walked, bleary-eyed and half asleep, into the bathroom she thought of as hers to confront Tommy Nowlan, nude, holding her bottle of shampoo in one hand and her pink Lady Bic razor in the other.

It took Stephanie a half an hour to convince Marissa not to wake up the don.

"It's only for one more night," she said. "He doesn't have anywhere else to go. We can't turn him out onto the street."

As she said it, she was wondering why not.

Stephanie had a paper to write for Professor Braithwaite. She hadn't even finished the reading, and now she was spending more time conducting therapy than doing the work she needed to do.

On the way to the library she stopped at the Hub for a coffee.

Tommy Nowlan was sitting in the corner, writing something in a black, hard-covered notebook. He had a glass of water in front of him.

He smiled when he saw her and motioned towards the empty chair across from him.

She sat down, to be polite.

"You look tired," he said.

Stephanie shrugged and looked at his notebook.

"Oh," he said. "Lists."

Stephanie didn't say anything.

Tommy said, "All-time favourite UFO movies. All-time favourite songs sung by movie stars."

Stephanie nodded.

Tommy said, "I was just adding to my list of toys that disturbed me when I was a kid."

He has just had his heart broken, thought Stephanie. *Be patient. Try to look sympathetic.*

Tommy shrugged. He opened his book.

"I had forgotten about Mousetrap," he said. "You could spend an entire afternoon setting the trap up and then, just before you started playing, someone would knock something or a gear would stick. I don't think it ever worked for me. Not once. What a stupid game."

He sighed.

"I guess *I'm* feeling stupid," he said.

Stephanie said, "What else is on your list?"

Tommy said, "We had a little dog. You flipped a switch and it would walk around in a circle and bark and then do a somersault. It drove me nuts.

"And my brother had a teddy bear that talked. It was supposed to be cute but it had these eyes and it sounded like Satan and I hated it.

"And the Spirograph," he added. "The Spirograph was torture."

"We had the Spirograph," said Stephanie. "And the Easy-Bake Oven, which worked once or twice and then it didn't work again. We used to make the dough and eat it raw."

Then she said, "Can I get you a coffee?"

When she came back to the table she said, "What about Speak & Spell? Is Speak & Spell on your list?"

"It was pretty critical," said Tommy.

"Critical?" said Stephanie. "It was always so pleased with itself whenever it won. Sometimes I still hear that voice in my head: '*You're wrong! Try again.*'"

Stephanie took Tommy with her to a party that night. It was a disaster. She spent the whole night alone. Someone told the boy who she had her eye on that she had brought the guy in the April O'Neil T-shirt and the boy stayed away from her all night.

Tommy had a wonderful time. Tommy danced with everyone. Tommy seemed to be getting over Jane. And then, when Stephanie finally decided she had had enough, Tommy appeared at her side.

"I should go too," he said.

Great, thought Stephanie. *So now everyone thinks I am* leaving *with him too.*

Halfway back to Millhouse, Tommy said, "Have you ever had a crush on a cartoon character?"

"What do you mean?" she asked. But she knew exactly what he meant. She could feel her heart beating faster.

"When I was really young," he said, "I had a crush on Babs from *Tiny Toons*. Later I crushed on Gadget from *Chip 'n Dale Rescue Rangers*. Then Penny from *Inspector Gadget*. And," he said, pointing at his chest, "there's April O'Neil. From the *Turtles*. Lately, I have been sort of wondering about the Baroness from *G.I. Joe*. What do you think she'd look like in leather?"

Stephanie had stopped moving. She couldn't believe it. She'd thought she was the only one. All these years, she had just assumed she was messed up.

"I liked Eric from *The Little Mermaid,*" she said slowly, watching him carefully, still not completely sure that he wasn't just making fun of her. But he didn't look like he was making fun of her. He was nodding. She kept going. "I had a minor crush on Robin Hood, from the Disney show," she said. "And Peter Pan, of course."

Of course? she thought to herself. *Of course? What did she mean by "of course"? Like this was normal? Like everyone had crushed on Peter Pan?*

"And sometimes," she said, throwing caution to the wind, "sometimes, if I am in the right sort of mood, Bart Simpson can seem sort of cute."

"Who else?" said Tommy.

Stephanie laughed out loud before she answered. Then she looked at Tommy carefully, her eyes widening, seeing *him* for the first time. Not the soaked boy who had stood dejectedly outside of Millhouse the night before, but someone entirely different, someone who made her feel completely normal, completely and absolutely herself.

She said, "I always thought Commander Cobra was kind of cute."

Tommy said, "That's because he always had the best lines in the show."

On Sunday she got up early and went to the library to work on her paper. But it was hard to concentrate on Hemingway. She kept wondering what Tommy was doing.

What he was doing was sitting on the far side of the library writing in his notebook. He wasn't working on his lists any more. He was writing a poem—a poem for Stephanie.

I am writing this
on Sunday morning.
I am sitting at a desk
in the library
with the newspaper open in front of me

and the peace that comes to those with time on their hands.

Behind me there is a large window
bathed in the surprising warmth of this October sun.
And across the room
beside the fat girl in the annoying pink sweater
I can see you
working on your paper about Ernest Hemingway.

My horoscope says
that the moon is in Saturn.
A time for change.
But as I sit here
and watch you work
I wonder
what Saturn could have to do with anything,
when no one even knows whether the rings are shattered moons or snowballs
or why it confused Galileo so when it filled his cardboard and leather telescope
all hazy and yellow.

But most importantly
I am wondering
how you do that thing with your nose,
the way it crinkles like that
every time you stop to think.
And why it makes me feel like this.

Tommy liked his poem. He read it over several times before he put his book in his pocket, stood up and left the library. It was several weeks before he had the courage to send it to Stephanie.

He did send her something in the mail that next week, however.

Tommy's mother, it turned out, had gone to school with the nefarious Professor Braithwaite. Tommy got her to dig out her high school yearbook.

They read the grad profile together before he put it in the mail.

David "Motorhead" Braithwaite, it began.
The wheel is turning but the hamster seems to be dead.
Pet Peeves: Monday mornings
Favourite sayings: "Hey Bruno, can I borrow your math?"
Cherished Ambition: To get into the back seat of Peggy Low's Camaro

Stephanie was a day late finishing her Hemingway paper. She took it to Professor Braithwaite's office on Tuesday afternoon. She was hoping to slip it under his door, unnoticed, but the office was open and Professor Braithwaite was sitting at his desk, fiddling with his pipe.

It was hard to take him seriously anymore. It was so easy to see the pre–tweed jacket guy.

"Professor Motorhead . . . uh, Braithwaite," she said.

She hadn't meant to say it. It was an honest slip. But he didn't know that. His eyes clouded.

She got a B on the paper. *"Much better,"* he wrote.

Tommy came back the next weekend. He got a ride down on Saturday morning and went back that night. They went for a long walk along the river, and out for pizza. He was wearing his Bart Simpson T-shirt. He kissed her when he left.

It was Tommy in the car with Stephanie on Thursday night. It has been almost a year and they are still together. He picks her up at the station if he is in town when she comes home. They spend weekends together whenever they can. Morley sometimes worries that it is hard on Stephanie to be dividing her time between two places. Dave worries that his daughter might not be getting everything she could out of campus life. But Morley and Dave both remember the beginnings of their own romance—when Dave was still on the road and seemed so far away. The letters, the late-night phone calls and the deep, sure knowledge that the best things in life, the great, wonderful things, always take time and never come without sacrifice.

Christmas on the Road

Late on the night of December 23, not far from the town of Rivière-du-Loup, on the south shore of the St. Lawrence River, on a black and largely lonely stretch of Highway 132 between the villages of St-Germain and Notre-Dame-du-Portage—at the point where you must make your choice to continue along the St. Lawrence or drop southeast out of Quebec on Highway 2 into the dark pine forests of New Brunswick—sometime *before* midnight, but *after* eleven, Eustache Boisclair stood in the empty parking lot of the motel he had owned for twenty-seven years, La Vache Qui Rit, took the last drag of his home-rolled cigarette, looked up at the sky and found the Big Dipper, *La grande casserole,* the only constellation he knew by name, flicked his cigarette into the air and reached up to the big lever on the outside wall of the motel office.

He muttered, *"Sapristi."* Then he pulled the lever, and the lights on the motel's road sign flickered, dimmed and snapped off. Except for the ringing in Eustache's ears, the night was suddenly and profoundly quiet.

There were no guests left in the motel except for a trucker from Pisiquit in room nine, who had the flu and whom Eustache hadn't seen for thirteen hours.

Anyway, the trucker was paid up and would probably leave sometime in the night, unnoticed. Good riddance. Eustache didn't want any guests. He had turned off the heat in all the empty rooms.

Eustache was bracing himself for a long and lonely Christmas. Ever since his wife, Marie-Claire, had passed on, God rest her soul, Christmas had been a long and lonely time. As usual, Eustache was going to do his best to avoid it. He had a case of beer and a case of Cheezies on the floor by the kitchen door. He was going to go on the internet and play poker until it was safe to come out.

He wasn't going to Mass, and he wasn't going to watch television. He wasn't going to watch Roch Voisine sing "Silent Night" one more time. *Tabarnouche*.

If he got bored with poker he would start a Paint by Numbers. He had done 437 since Marie died. He had the best 200-odd hanging in every possible nook of his nine-room motel. Last year at Christmas he had completed twelve. Sometimes he did his best work at Christmas. It was Christmas two years ago that he did his first picture using only black and white paint. An effect that pleased him.

Eustache pushed his wool hat back and scratched his head vigorously. He looked up and down the highway—so shiny it looked more like ice than asphalt.

He breathed in deeply through his nose and turned to go inside.

Little did he know what was heading his way.

Coming from the east, from *le Labrador,* blowing already over *le golfe du Saint-Laurent,* a winter storm of a magnitude that hadn't been seen around St-Germain for over a decade.

And from the west, heading *towards* the motel and *into* the storm, a dark-blue station wagon a day and a half out of Toronto.

A dark-blue station wagon pulling out of a dough-nut store near Trois-Rivières, a station wagon over-loaded beyond belief, with a dog shimmied into the luggage compartment, three teenagers in the back seat all wearing headsets, all leaking sound, so whenever anyone wanted to talk they had to shriek at each other, and a roof carrier, which someone had dug into not five minutes earlier and hadn't closed properly. Coming from the east, a storm, and from the west, a station wagon that was about to deposit much of the contents of its roof carrier along thirty miles of Highway 132.

Hurtling in from the east, the mother of all winter storms.

Hurtling in from the west . . . Dave and his family.

They had left Toronto in a last-minute panic. They had left as a result of an alarming series of telephone calls from Dave's mother in the Cape Breton town of Big Narrows. The first call was about Christmas gifts.

"I was thinking, David," she said, "of getting some of those Beanie Babies that Stephanie likes so much and a pair of jumpers for Sam."

Stephanie, who is in second year at university, hasn't shown an interest in Beanie Babies for over a decade.

Dave phoned Morley as soon as his mother hung up.

"It was horrifying," he said. "It was like she had lost track of time. Like she thought the kids were still babies."

There was a second conversation a few days later.

"It's getting weird," said Dave. "She was talking about my father as if he were still alive. She said she was cooking cod cheeks for supper and he was going to have a fit. My father hated cod cheeks."

When he got home that night, Dave said, "I want to go there. For Christmas."

Morley said, "Yes."

It was too late to think about plane reservations.

"We'll drive," said Dave.

Stephanie said, "But Tommy and I were going to spend Christmas together."

So Dave rented the roof carrier.

Packing was a nightmare.

Dave was standing in the driveway with a pile of boxes and suitcases stacked around him. None of the boxes would fit into the roof carrier. He made everyone *un*pack. He made everyone put their things into plastic bags. He stuffed the plastic bags into the roof carrier, as if he were stuffing a turkey.

The turkey, however, went in the back. With the dog. On ice, in an oversized cooler.

It took two of them to close the roof carrier.

"You don't think that it's going to, like, pop?" asked Tommy. But Dave was already slipping into the driver's seat. They were three hours late.

When they pulled out of their driveway, the car scraped the curb. They looked like refugees fleeing a war zone. But they were on their way.

"At least we got the turkey in," said Dave to no one in particular.

It was a twenty-seven-pound, organically raised, free-range turkey. It had cost him over $135. He wasn't about to leave it behind.

What he didn't mention was what he *had* left behind.

When the roof carrier was full, and it looked as though there mightn't be room for the turkey in the car, Dave had removed what he believed to be a non-essential item from the back. Steph had brought it out to the car at the last minute.

"Is there room for this?" she had asked, nonchalantly holding up a blue athletic bag.

Dave had assumed the blue bag was extra Stephanie stuff. When no one was looking he'd carried it surreptitiously back into the house.

They wouldn't notice the bag was missing for hours.

For now, they were on their way. The kids in the back. Stephanie in the middle between her brother, Sam, and her boyfriend, Tommy Nowlan. Stephanie had been dating Tommy Nowlan for over a year.

Tommy is an only child. He had never been on a family road trip. He climbed into the back seat with great expectation.

"I love this," he said.

As soon as they were out of the city, as soon as they were on the highway, Dave barked "Highway," like this was important news.

"Highway," barked Dave again, and Sam slapped the back of the seat and said, "Highway!"

Morley said, "Okay, okay," and reached under her legs and started passing out bags of junk food. Chips, Cheezies, pop.

Tommy chose Cracker Jack.

"I hate Cheezies," he said quietly.

Before he opened his Cracker Jack, Tommy took out a little black notebook from his jacket pocket and, at the top of a fresh page, he wrote "Things I love about this trip." He wrote "Cracker Jack" and labelled it "Number 1." He wrote "Number 2: You, sitting beside me." Then he nudged Stephanie so she could see what he had written.

Five and a half hours passed before he started his second list.

"Things I hate about this trip."

Number one was "Dog farts"—Tommy had underlined "Dog" and written "I hope" in the margin.

It had begun just outside Cornwall. The air in the back seat had suddenly become frowsty and unpleasant, so thick Tommy almost gagged.

He had reached for the window instinctively, but

then his social side had asserted itself and his hand froze in mid-air.

If he was the first to acknowledge this . . . event, it might be misinterpreted as an admission of guilt.

He couldn't believe he was the only one who had noticed this. But no one else had reacted. Maybe it happened all the time in this family. It certainly didn't happen in *his* family. His family didn't even have a word for it.

In search of fresh air, Tommy began to inch towards the door. Soon his face was pressed flat against the cool glass. He began to tug at his turtle-neck, pulling it up over his chin until it was covering his nose.

Everyone else seemed so oblivious that he began to doubt himself.

Maybe, he thought, it was him.

He almost said, *Excuse me.*

He almost said, *Excuse me, I'm sorry, I didn't mean it. I'll open the window.*

That was when it occurred to him that maybe it wasn't the dog.

He studied the car carefully: Dave in the front seat, scratching. Morley dozing restlessly beside him. *More likely Sam,* he thought. Grubby little Sam, stuffing himself with those greasy Cheezies. And then, with horror, he looked at Stephanie. *Impossible,* he thought. *Sam maybe, but not Stephanie. Please God. Not Stephanie.*

The car, which had less than an hour ago seemed

like such a boisterous, happy, family kind of place, was beginning to disturb him.

There were chip wrappers all over the back seat. And Cheezie crumbs. And empty pop cans on the floor. There were CD cases everywhere. The whole thing seemed unpleasant and crude. His head sank lower into his turtleneck. He looked like a ninja.

"Garbage," he added to the list of things he hated about this trip.

The next thing Tommy knew, they were standing on the edge of the highway—the entire family forming a circle around some sort of rodent, though it was hard to tell exactly what kind of rodent because it was a flattish sort of rodent—flatter than it ought to have been, anyway. It might have been something from the hedgehog family. Whatever it was, it was flat and furry and . . . dead.

Stephanie was in hysterics because she had been driving when the thing had bolted out in front of their car. That's what she'd said, anyway. "Bolted, like it was trying to commit suicide or something." At least that was what she'd said when she could still talk. Now she was just sobbing uncontrollably. All Tommy understood was that she wanted to give it a decent burial. But her father was pointing at the frozen ground.

She made him take it with them.

"We can bury it later," she said.

Dave double-wrapped the flat, furry little corpse in a plastic bag. Then he placed it in the only sensible place he could think of. In the cooler with the turkey.

When they were back in the car, Tommy added "Road kill" to his list.

When Stephanie leaned over to try to read what he had written, he closed the book and slipped it in his pocket.

It was after nine when they pulled into a motel on the far side of Montreal.

"Boys in one room," said Dave, "girls in the other."

As soon as they had settled in, Dave called his mother.

"She sounded so excited," he said when he hung up. "She said she put a tree up. For the first time in five years. She was baking shortbread. I'm so glad we are doing this."

Five minutes later, Morley knocked on the boys' door.

"Have you seen my stuff?" she said. "I packed it in a blue athletic bag."

When Tommy caught the look on Morley's face, he reached for his notebook.

The snow began the next morning at midday.

It was the second day of Arthur the dog's upset tummy. Everyone had their window cracked, and it was cold as well as rank in the car.

At first it was just a scattering of snow—nothing at all, or nothing worth mentioning. Thin trails and strands of snow wisping and dancing on the blacktop like powder. But an hour later Dave was hunched over and gripping the wheel, peering at a road that was all white except for the two black tire tracks that he was following—the snow driving at him, almost on the horizontal.

It was as if he were driving his way across a snow planet, through a snow galaxy. He had the feeling that it was going to go on for a while.

He turned to Morley. "It's snowing," he said.

Morley grunted.

Morley was in an unspeakable mood. Finding herself without clothes of her own, Morley had had to borrow clothes from Stephanie. She was wearing one of Stephanie's tummy T-shirts and a pair of underwear that was too small in every way you could imagine. She had been scratching and tugging all morning.

Tommy had spent the morning trying to keep his eyes off Morley, but it was like driving by the scene of an accident.

He began a new list: "Ten reasons why you should never see your girlfriend's mother in your girlfriend's clothes."

Number one on the list was "Genetics."

Stephanie was no longer sitting beside him. After lunch, Stephanie had announced that she was feeling too squished in the middle. She had grabbed the other window seat. Tommy didn't mind. In fact, Tommy was happy for the privacy. This way he didn't have to shield his notebook from her view. It would not have been a good thing for anyone if Stephanie had read Tommy's latest list.

He had started it that morning after Stephanie and Sam had begun to squabble.

The squabble, which had begun over the last bag of barbecue potato chips, had escalated into all-out war.

Tommy had been sitting by his window like a United Nations peacekeeper, watching in horror as his beautiful girlfriend morphed into a whiny, snit-fitting, foul-mouthed, finking twelve-year-old.

Tommy had pulled out his notebook and divided a page into two columns. He wrote "Pros" at the top of one column and "Cons" at the top of the other. At the very top of the page he wrote "My Relationship with Stephanie."

It was December 23. They were supposed to arrive in Big Narrows that night.

By four in the afternoon they were still in Quebec, and it was apparent to everyone that getting to Cape Breton in a hurry was out of the question. It was getting dark. You could barely see the forest on the side of the road. Just the blackness of the night. The white snow. And Dave driving and driving. They had just passed a huge transport lying on its side in the ditch, flares burning pink around it. They were down to thirty kilometres an hour.

A heavy silence had fallen on the car.

Tommy was working on several lists at once, flipping among them as new thoughts occurred to him.

"Ten reasons why you should always spend Christmas with your *own* family."

"Ten things to do if I don't die on this trip."

"Last Will and Testament of me, Tommy Nowlan, killed tragically in a car wreck on this the 23rd day of December . . . dead emotionally two hours before."

And then Dave said, "I haven't seen a car coming towards us for over an hour."

Dave knew they were going to have to stop.

They all knew they should have stopped already.

"Do you know where we are?" said Dave.

It didn't matter where they were. They were going to stop the next place they saw.

And if that wasn't soon, they were going to end up in the ditch—like the transport they had passed, however long ago that was.

And that's when they came upon Eustache Boisclair's motel. It was Tommy who spotted it. Only the office light on.

"That was a motel," said Tommy desperately.

Eustache Boisclair was sitting at his kitchen table rolling cigarettes when he heard voices in the motel parking lot. He rolls a week's supply at a time—thirty-five cigarettes, five a day.

Eustache uses a turquoise plastic rolling machine he has owned since 1978. He sent away for it after he saw an advertisement during a wrestling match he was watching on television. It arrived in a cardboard box from Winnipeg—a town Eustache has thought fondly of ever since.

As he stood up and walked across the kitchen, Eustache put the empty paper sleeve he was holding into his mouth and sucked a lungful of air through the filter. When he got to the kitchen door he leaned one hand heavily on the doorknob and used the other to ever so slightly part the venetian blinds.

There was a car pulled up in front of the motel office. As he watched the family tumble out of it he began to count.

Un, deux, trois, quatre—câlique—cinq. And then, to add insult to injury, Arthur jumping out the back. *"Un chien,"* muttered Eustache. *"Merde."*

As if he'd heard him, as if he understood, Arthur circled three times, squatted and seemed to sigh.

Dave, meanwhile, began banging on the office door.

Eustache ignored Dave as he watched the deposit this dog was leaving in his yard.

Then he was watching two of the kids—the girl and the younger boy—start to hit each other. The other boy, the third boy, was taking notes, as if he were some kind of a reporter.

Eustache put them in rooms six, seven and eight. Tommy insisted on having a room for himself.

"Non," said Eustache, as they left the office, *"on n'a pas d'restaurant. Le restaurant est fermé."*

And no ice machine either.

So before they went to sleep, Dave put on his parka and boots and headed back into the storm. He opened the back of the car, worked the turkey out of the cooler and set it down in the snow outside their bedroom door. He found a shovel leaning by the office door and covered the turkey with snow.

"It will be fine," he said to Morley as he brushed the snow off his head. "No one will see it."

When they woke up the next morning—the morning of Christmas Eve—Morley and Dave went to the window together. They pulled open the curtains slowly and then looked at each other in horror. They could barely see the top of their car. As for the highway—the highway had disappeared. They weren't going anywhere.

"We aren't going anywhere," said Dave, who had opened their bedroom door, then slammed it shut again—a drift as high as his knees was in danger of collapsing into their room.

Dave fought his way to the office and came back with some instant coffee powder in a paper cup.

"Coffee," said Morley.

"And Cheezies," said Dave proudly, holding up a large bag.

Dave went to the pay phone near the highway and managed to get through to his mother. He told her they weren't going to make it for Christmas.

"She started to cry," he said to Morley when he'd stomped back into the room. "She tried to put a brave face on it, but she was crying. I said she should go over to the Carvers' or the MacDonnells'. She said she had told everyone we were coming. She said, 'How can I possibly face them if you don't bother to show up?'"

They spent the morning digging out the car, creating a mound of snow a good ten feet high in the process. Then they cleared a rough path to the highway. But the highway looked like a ski run.

Eustache joined them beside their snow pile and spat on the ground.

He peered down the road and muttered "*Tabarnouche,*" before he scuffed back to his office.

Back in the motel room, Dave rummaged through their luggage looking for something to eat. He was hungry. But there was nothing left save for a few salty crumbs in the bottom of the last chip bag. He imagined the motel office to be a place of plenty. A place with plenty of food and drink, with a fireplace and plenty of wood. *At least we have the turkey,* he thought sourly. And then he was seized by panic.

They had buried the turkey when they'd resurrected their car. The turkey was under the mountain of snow.

"*Tabarnouche,*" said Dave.

Dave retrieved the shovel and began to attack their snow pile—digging like a mountain guide after an avalanche.

It was Arthur who finally pawed his way through the far end of the mound and dragged the bird out. Arthur had bounced the bird fifty yards down the parking lot before Dave spotted him.

Eustache was watching the chase from the office window, a smile playing on his face for the first Christmas in years.

He appeared at their door twenty minutes later with a loaf of bread, a jar of peanut butter and another bag of Cheezies.

"Thanks," Dave said.

Tommy added Cheezies to his list of things he hated about this trip.

It was Sam, grade seven, the only person in the room still studying French, who looked up as Eustache was leaving. It was Sam who said, in a small but audible voice, *"Merci."*

The old man looked at Sam sitting on the far side of the far bed and smiled for the second time in an hour.

An hour later, when he came back, it was Sam whom Eustache talked to.

"Si vous allez rester ici pour Noël, y'a des choses qu'il va vous falloir," he said.

Sam nodded. *Yes, if they were going to stay for Christmas, there* were *things they would need.*

There was an awkward silence, then Sam screwed up his forehead.

"Peut-être un arbre?" he said.

"Alors," said Eustache Boisclair, pointing at the door.

Sam stood up and put on his coat. He turned and looked at his parents.

"I'll be back in a minute," he said. "Monsieur Boisclair and I are going out to cut a Christmas tree."

He was out the door before anyone could say anything.

They were gone an hour.

When Sam came back to the room he was beaming. His cheeks were red. "Come and see," he said.

There was a pretty little fir tree leaning by the office door.

Sam ran past it and into the office. "Come on," he said. "Come on."

He led them around the reception desk and into the old dining room. The Formica tables were pushed against the walls. The chairs were stacked beside them. And Eustache Boisclair was on his hands and knees fiddling with the stove—an old propane affair that hadn't been run for five years.

They never got it going.

But they had one of the great all-time Christmas dinners ever.

Everyone chipped in.

Tommy fetched wood from the woodlot behind the office.

Stephanie split the wood and built a fire in the dining room fireplace.

Morley set up the dining room.

Sam stuck to Eustache like a shadow.

And Dave cooked the turkey.

He deep-fried it in corn oil in the motel's backyard. He used a stockpot from the kitchen for the turkey and an industrial burner from Eustache's shop to heat up the oil. Three minutes a pound. His first turkey boil.

Just before he lowered it into the oil, Dave asked Eustache, "What are we going to eat with it?"

Eustache looked at Sam and shrugged. *"J'ai de quoi,"* he said.

By the time they were ready to eat, the Formica tables Morley had pushed together were laden with food, miraculously produced from next to nothing. Eustache had unearthed a jar of Marie-Claire's long-forgotten preserves and, in the absence of cranberries, Morley had fashioned a wild blueberry sauce.

They made a stuffing out of bread, bacon and beernuts.

There was a turnip they boiled and seasoned with orange soda. There was a big bowl of Cheezies. And, of course, the turkey, sitting on a platter at the head of the table, golden and crackling and strangely delicious.

They drank strong tea and Eustache's homemade spruce beer.

For dessert, they passed around a plate of toffee that Tommy had boiled up using hundreds of little sugar packages.

At midnight everyone was still up. The trucker from Pisiquit had joined them. His name was Yvon and he spoke about as much English as Eustache. But they had moved well beyond language. Yvon had his feet up on the fireplace, playing a harmonica. Stephanie and Tommy were snuggled on the couch, their arms around each other, listening.

Out in the parking lot, Sam was sitting in the cab of Yvon's truck, talking on his CB, a glass of Eustache's homemade spruce beer resting on the dash.

And Eustache was sitting at the table with Dave and Morley, picking at the turkey, smiling.

At midnight Stephanie sat down beside her father.

"You look sad," she said.

"I was thinking about your grandmother," said Dave. "I feel like we let her down."

Stephanie nodded.

"You wanted to make her happy," said Stephanie.

"That's right," said Dave. "And instead I made her sad."

Eustache Boisclair walked by them and smiled at Stephanie. *"Eh bien,"* he said.

"We made *him* happy," said Stephanie.

Dave shrugged. "It doesn't count," he said.

They sat quietly for a moment. And then Stephanie stood up. She said, "It *should* count. He was sad before we got here."

"I guess you're right," said Dave.

Before he could say anything, Stephanie leaned over and kissed her father on the cheek. She said, "I'm going to bed."

"I love you," said Dave.

They made it to Cape Breton the day after Boxing Day.

Margaret, Dave's mother, greeted them at the door with cookies. They stayed four days. It was great fun. Like a *second* Christmas.

There was a steady stream of visitors through the house—neighbours and family. It was as if they had to see them with their own eyes, these hearty travellers.

"Yes," Dave overheard Margaret saying to one of his cousins. "They *drove*. Through the worst blizzard in twenty years. Not one other car made it. I told them to turn back, but David wouldn't hear of it."

On their last night, while they were sitting watching the fire, Dave looked at Stephanie and said, "I wonder what Monsieur Boisclair is doing tonight."

They were planning to stop by the motel on the way home, but it was late and they kept going.

"We'll write," said Dave.

And they will. Sam will send a postcard of the CN Tower, written in French, as soon as they get home. But Dave won't write until June. Not until the sorry summer afternoon he opens the picnic cooler and finds what remains of the flattened rodent.

Sam

Sam Speaks

My name is Sam. I mean, that is what I'm called in this book. It is not my real name, but I am not aloud to write my real name here . . . I am eleven years old. Maybe by the time you are reading this I could be twelve. I could even be a lot older. If you have found this book years into the future I could be in high school already or even in coledge. When I grow up I want to be an astronot or if not an astronot a cold water diver or a chef. It's possible that this is already far into the future and I am already in space while you are reading this. If that is true you could contact me on IPQ and tell me that you are reading this which I wrote when I was eleven years old. I would tell you what my adress is but my dad won't let me. It has probaly changed anyway.

I wasn't sure what I was suppost to write. Except I think it is suppost to be funny. I went to the library and asked Mrs. Atkinson for a book on writing funny stuff. But she didn't have anything and I'm not aloud to tell her why I needed it because no one is suppost to know that this book is about our family. Which is mest up because people already know. For instance my friend Murray knows. Because he is in the book—except in the book they call him Murphy. So he knows and I think his parents know and I know the people next door who are really the Tushinghams but are called Turlingtons in the book know too. I think lots of people know so I don't know what the big deal is about not telling people any more. But I couldn't tell Mrs. Atkinson. Not that it would have mattered because there were no books about writing funny stuff anyway.

When there were no books in the library, I went on the net and put in humour and I found a joke page. These are the three best jokes. I hope you like them.

What do cats call mice on skateboards?
Meals on Wheels.

What does the richest person in the world make for dinner every night?
Reservations.

Why did the man stare at the can of orange juice?
Because it said "concentrate."

My father said I should write about our family. I started to research our family history. My father was born in Cape Breton. On the radio they make it sound like he was born in Big Narrows but that's not true. He moved there when he was two. I asked why they don't say where he was born and he said they told him it was too complicated and it was simpler this way. Most of the rest of the stuff they say is true. So I don't know what the deal is.

My granfather was in the war and my great-granfather was a pilot in the war before that one and after the war he flew a plane under London Bridge. Or that's what my granmother told me and she should know because my great-granfather was her father. But I don't know what the point of putting that in this book is because it doesn't have anything to do with these stories. Except that it is pretty cool having a great-granfather who flew a plane under London Bridge and I think that would make a cooler story then the one about me sending away for stuff which just makes me feel imbaressed.

Anyway I soon stopped the family research which was getting complicated anyway because once you start with relatives, where do you stop???!!! And then I got really worried about what to say and I started to bite my nails again which I stopped *doing in grade five because my mother gave me $10 to stop each week I did and then you get used to not doing it anymore. When I noticed I started again I had a hard time falling to sleep at night because I would lie in bed and I would start to wonder what I should write and then I would start thinking about my nails, and its hard not to bite your nails once you start thinking about them, especially in bed at night. You should try it.*

Finally I asked my mother and she said I should just be myself and say hello.

I don't know what is funny about that.

But anyway, the doorbell just rang and I think it's Murray. I have to go

Hello. Goodbye.

p.s. I haven't read any of the stories in this book. And I don't lisen to the show on the radio. I think the music sucks.

Field Trip

THE FIRST WEEK after the Christmas vacation, Sam brought a note home from school. The grade fives and sixes were going on a field trip—they were going to spend an afternoon at the art gallery, at the Matisse exhibit. Sam needed someone to sign his permission form.

Now, getting a field trip permission slip signed is a lot trickier than it sounds. Kids don't do this sort of thing without careful thought. First, about whom they are going to take it to. And second, when they are going to present it.

Sam took the note to his mother. He waited until she was on the phone.

You just don't want to give anyone a chance to ask questions.

Sam didn't take the note to his father because he knew there was a good chance his father would want to go on the trip. And by the time you get to grade five, having your father on a field trip is the last thing you want.

Unfortunately for Sam, Dave's job has always afforded him enough flexibility to be available for this sort of thing. For two years Dave ran the pizza lunch at Sam's school, which was actually a great thing for Sam. When you are in grade two you get a lot of status when your friends believe your dad delivers pizza for a living.

"Why couldn't you get a job like that?" said Sam's friend Ben to his father one night. "What do *lawyers* ever do?"

Because of his availability, Dave has had more experience than many of his male friends in squiring kids around. When he gets together with other fathers, Dave feels confident of his parenting abilities. It's when he compares himself to the moms of the neighbourhood that he feels inadequate. But he doesn't let these feelings control him. He keeps putting himself out there—as much for his own sense of self as for the good of the kids. He's done birthday parties and sleepovers. He's coached baseball and hockey. And he's done field trips.

Field trips have never been his strong suit.

Dave got to go on only one school trip when he was a boy. Grade five. It was one of the greatest disappointments of his young life. Every other grade five before and after Dave's class at Big Narrows Elementary School in Big Narrows, Cape Breton, was taken to Doris Ekersley's Brick Apron Bakery on Main Street for *their* field trip. And not just to the front of the bakery where you went to buy stuff. They went right into the back where they baked things.

The grade fives went there every year. And when they came back to school, they brought back horrifying stories about the back of the bakery. Stories that would curdle your blood. Especially if you happened to be in grade two. The grade twos would listen to the stories at recess, and many of them would start to weep because they knew that one year, *they* would have to go to the back of Doris Ekersley's Brick Apron Bakery themselves. And when they went there, they would meet Chopsy, the one-eyed baker.

Chopsy, who never shaved, chewed foul-smelling cigar butts, breathed fish breath on you and stared at you with his one bulging, infected, yellow eye.

Everyone knew the story of Chopsy. Chopsy had been a cook during the war. And the soldiers in Chopsy's unit were fearless because they were so well fed. They would do anything, as long as they knew they could get back for supper every night, because Chopsy was the greatest chef in the entire army. Then one day Chopsy's unit was cut off from its supply lines. The men were trapped in a small town by the enemy. And as the days went by, the generals came to Chopsy and said, "We are doomed unless you can do something." They were running out of food.

Anyone else would have given up.

But not Chopsy.

Each night, Chopsy sneaked into this town, wherever they were—it was, like, in Poland or Saskatchewan or somewhere like that—and Chopsy would hunt for rats in the sewers. Every morning before dawn he would return with a bagful of writhing rodents. Because they were short on ammo he had to use his carving knife to kill the vermin (which is how he got his nickname). He cooked those rats with such skill that the men had no idea what they were eating. (It was, after all, their first time in Europe.) Chopsy told them it was quail. And they all survived. But, tragically, Chopsy went crazy, which was why he was living in Big Narrows.

The most horrible thing, however, was that he had developed a taste for rats. He raised them in a secret room in the back of the bakery. And the rats ate children. And that's why they had the tours—because Chopsy needed children to feed to the rats.

There were traps for kids back there. There were sinister vats of whipped cream that attracted boys. Boys wandered into that bakery and were never seen again. They just vanished. And it didn't take a genius to figure out what had happened to them. Chopsy.

Parents wouldn't talk about this, of course. No use asking your parents about Chopsy. Parents didn't want to worry their kids. But everyone knew that's what happened to Chan Gillespie. The grown-ups said she had gone to boarding school in New Brunswick. But Joey Talarico's older brother, Michael, found one of Chan Gillespie's hairs in a chocolate eclair, and he kept it in a jar in his locker. For five cents he would open his locker and show the hair to you. And for a dime he would let you hold the jar.

Dave and his friend Billy Mitchell had been looking forward to their trip to the bakery since grade three. They had a plan.

They were going to take Dave's younger sister, Annie, with them. Annie was in kindergarten. They figured if Chopsy came after them they would offer him Annie in their place. Dave actually favoured handing Annie over right at the start of the tour and getting it over with—that way they could enjoy the rest of the day.

Billy and Dave knew there was a kettle of melted chocolate in the back of the bakery. The second part of their plan involved getting some of that chocolate. When they got to the chocolate vat, Billy was going to create a diversion, and while everyone was looking at Billy, Dave was going to take his empty Cub canteen (which he would have been wearing around his shoulder, and which he would have been pretending to drink from all afternoon) and fill it full of melted chocolate.

Dave and Billy were going to drink the chocolate after the tour.

Straight.

And then they were going to dump Billy's marble collection into the machine that mixed the cake dough—to see if they could get real marble cake.

But they didn't go to the bakery the year Dave finally made it to grade five.

They went to the sardine plant.

The sardine plant is no longer operating in Big Narrows. It was closed in 1961 after a Norwegian sardine expert came to town and told them they had to change the way they were packing the sardines. They always put the sardines into the cans in two rows, with their tails resting at either end and their snouts meeting at the middle. The guy from Norway came to town to tell them they should put the tails in the middle and the snouts at the ends. He said from time to time tails had been flopping over the edges of the cans when they put the lids on, and they weren't getting good seals, and there had been some problems. This could be avoided if they'd put the tails in the middle and the noses at the ends.

The women in the Big Narrows plant took this as a personal insult.

"We've been packing sardines this way for twenty-two years," said Norma Cavanaugh when she heard about the proposal. "And I ain't changing."

"No way tails is coming out," said Nance McDougall.

The plant closed soon after. Before it closed they had begun to pack them tail-in, but it was too late.

Anyway, Dave and Billy had to go to the sardine plant the year they were in grade five, and Dave still can't open a tin of sardines without checking for marbles.

And that was it for field trips. Dave didn't go on another school trip for thirty years—until Sam was in grade two (which was before Sam had figured out who he should take his notices to when they needed to be signed).

They went to the zoo. Dave was given a group of . . . well, that was the problem. By the time they got to the hippo paddock, Dave couldn't remember how many kids he was supposed to have in his group. He knew the number six was part of the equation, but he couldn't remember if it was Sam plus five made six, or if it was six plus Sam made seven.

Which wasn't such a big deal right then but would be at the end of the day. Numbers weren't important at the hippo paddock because one of the six (or seven)—one of Dave's kids, at any rate, a kid called Mark Portnoy—had somehow scaled the concrete wall surrounding the paddock and was marching back and forth along the top of the wall screaming, "Come and get me!"

And one of the hippos, an animal about the size of a bus, seemed to be thinking it over.

Dave got Mark Portnoy off the wall, which was harder than it sounds. And he said, "Is everyone here?" And everyone said, "Yes," and he counted them: one, two, three, four, five, six . . . seven.

"Hey," he said to the kid in the Montreal Canadiens hockey sweater who was walking away from the group. "What's *your* name?"

"That's George," said Mark Portnoy. "He's in my Hebrew class."

And Dave said, "Okay, George. Let's go."

George looked at Mark, and Mark said, "Come on."

And Dave, whose patience was growing thin, said, "I don't want to hear another word out of anyone."

"Come on," said Mark Portnoy.

How was Dave to know that Hebrew school was all George and Mark had in common?

How was Dave to know that George was at the zoo with his mother?

How was Dave to know that when he said, "Okay, George. Let's go," George's mother was standing not ten yards away with her back turned to them, tying George's younger brother's shoelace?

How was Dave to know that when she turned around and found George, her son, had vanished, George's mother would lodge a frantic report with zoo officials and spend the next three tearful hours waiting in the administrative building? A wait that wasn't helped by the witness who swore he saw a kid climbing into the hippo compound.

Unless someone told him, how was Dave to know any of this?

All he knew was that at two o'clock, when they got to the bus, George said, "My mom is going to be mad if I get on the bus."

Dave looked at him and snapped, "I am going to be madder if you don't."

George started to cry, and Mark Portnoy said, "Come on."

George looked at Mark, and then he looked at Dave. He shook his head and said, "You're going to be sorry." Then he got onto the bus with his head hanging down.

It was only when they got back to the school, and all the parents had come and picked up their children, and the only three people left in the schoolyard were Dave and the school principal and George—who was standing between them, weeping—that the enormity of what had happened landed on Dave.

That night at supper, Sam said the zoo trip was great but it was hard to decide if the best part was when

Oscar threw up in the bus or when Mark Portnoy ate the bar of soap and started blowing bubbles.

"What about George?" said Dave grimly.

"George was great," said Sam. "George was great too."

"Did you see any animals?" asked Morley.

"Not really," said Sam.

Dave eventually got wind of the trip to the Matisse exhibit.

"You know why I have always liked Matisse?" said Dave at supper.

Sam shook his head

"Because," said Dave, putting down his fork, "a collector once asked Matisse how long it took to paint some incredibly expensive piece that consisted of just a few breezy lines, and do you know what Matisse said? He said, 'It took a lifetime.'"

"I don't get it," said Sam.

"You will," said Dave.

They were still looking for parents to go on the trip to the art gallery.

"It's your big chance to redeem yourself," said Morley.

So Dave signed up to go.

So did his neighbourhood nemesis . . . Mary Turlington. Mary and Bert Turlington live two doors down from Dave and Morley. Mary is an accountant, and she and Dave rubbed each other the wrong way the moment they met.

It was something about Mary's politics, something about the way she dressed, the condescending way she talked about Dave's record store that bugged Dave.

It was the way Dave seemed to glide through life without trying, that he didn't dress like a grown-up, that he made his living playing records, for heaven's sake—that was it, he played, he didn't work, that's what irked Mary.

As soon as Dave saw her standing at the back of the classroom on the day of the trip, all of his confidence evaporated.

Mary was holding a clipboard. And a neat pile of name tags—one for each child in her group.

"Hello, David," she said when she saw him.

They were always polite. They were neighbours.

"Hi," said Dave. "Where do I get the tags?"

"I brought them from home," said Mary archly.

There were five boys, including Sam, in Dave's group. "Five," said Dave, smiling confidently at Sam's teacher as they were getting ready.

"Five," he repeated earnestly to himself.

One for each finger.

When no one was looking he took out a ballpoint pen and wrote the number five in ink on the back of his wrist.

He looked across the room. Mary Turlington had her group sitting in a circle. She was filling out the name tags.

Five.

Five would be easy.

As it turned out, one of Dave's five was late for school that Tuesday.

"They just phoned," said Sam's teacher. "They're on their way."

"Go," said Dave. "You go. We'll catch up. We'll meet you at the gallery."

They were travelling by subway.

"Be careful," whispered Dave to Grace Weed as she led her group out of the classroom. "There is a guy in the basement of the museum who is crazy."

"What?" said Grace, not sure if Dave was serious or not.

"His name is Chopsy," said Dave. "I'd watch the kids very carefully if I were you. The guy is crazy as a loon."

By the time they got to the subway, Dave's boys—they all seemed nice enough—were wound up like cheap tin toys. Dave felt like a sheepdog. Keeping them together required his full attention.

Two of them had tried to slip into a corner store to buy candy.

"No candy," said Dave.

At the first intersection, three went one way and two the other.

Again at the next.

Then they wanted pizza.

"No pizza," said Dave. "No pizza now. No pizza later," said Dave. "We're going to a gallery. We are going to see art. We are not going for pizza."

Dave felt as if he were a piece in a giant game of snakes and ladders.

He'd win the game, as long as he kept everyone in sight, as long as he returned with the same number he'd left with.

"Five," he said to himself again.

Eventually he chivvied his boys onto the subway platform.

By the time the train arrived he had them more or less circled.

The doors of the subway car opened.

"Wait," said Dave, holding them back a second. "Okay . . . now."

The boys went, but Dave didn't go. Dave held back, counting the bodies as they got on the train.

One, two, three . . . four boys. Where was five? Dave looked around. There was five. Five was tying up his shoe.

"Come on," said Dave, looking nervously at the train.

"Coming," said number five, who hop-slid onto the subway doing his sneaker up at the same time.

Dave sighed . . . *all present and accounted for, sir.* He took one last look up and down the empty platform and then he turned to get on the train himself—just in time to watch the door slide shut in his face. Leaving Dave on the platform and his five boys on the train, which was pulling out of the station.

The boys all looked at Dave quizzically through the window.

"Wait-at-the-next-station," he shouted, all in a rush.

The last thing he saw of them, the boys were shrugging and pointing at their ears.

It took four minutes for the next train to arrive. Four minutes during which Dave accepted Christ Jesus as his personal saviour.

"Please, Jesus," he said, "make them get off at the next station and wait."

When the train finally arrived, Dave leapt aboard and continued praying.

He wasn't worried that the kids would fall to any harm. They were, after all, ten years old. There were, after all, five of them. It was just that they might get hopelessly lost. And if they got separated—he didn't even want to think of that.

"Please, Jesus," he said again, "make them wait for me."

It is only a minute-and-a-half ride between stations.

Halfway there, Dave's train passed a train coming from the opposite direction. Dave pressed his face to the car window. In the dark, blurred half-light of the subway, he saw what he didn't want to see: Sam and his buddies pressed against the window heading back to the station Dave had just left. They were jumping up and down and waving at him. Laughing and pounding the glass.

Dave raised his hand in a half-hearted wave. Sam did the same.

"Why, Lord?" he muttered.

Now Dave didn't know *what* to do. Should he go back again like the boys had? Were they waiting on the platform for him to appear? Or should he stay put? Someone had to stay put. What would they be thinking? Who knows how a ten-year-old thinks—especially when there are five of them?

Dave decided to wait.

He waited for three trains. Nothing happened.

Now he *knew* the boys were waiting for him. And he knew that *they* knew *he* was waiting for *them*. Dave felt as if his head was going to explode. It was a nightmare. He waited for two more trains, then he said, "Damn it, Jesus," and ran up the stairs and over to the other side of the tracks, heading back to the station where everything had started.

The boys weren't there.

They had either gone back to school or gone on to the gallery.

Now Dave felt trapped. He didn't want to alert the school if the kids hadn't. On the other hand, if the boys were waiting for him at school, and he didn't phone, what would the parents, the principal, the school secretary think?

He decided to make a precautionary call.

When the school secretary answered, he said, "Hi, it's Dave. I'm just checking in. Just making sure everything is all right."

"Everything is okay," said the secretary. She sounded doubtful.

"Good," said Dave. "Everything is okay here too."

"That was pretty strange," said the secretary when she'd hung up.

Dave was certain his boys weren't at the gallery. Dave was now certain the whole thing on the subway platform with the untied shoe had been a ruse—a carefully constructed plot designed to give him the slip. He felt like a fool. They all wanted pizza. That's what they wanted. They were probably in some internet cafe right now munching on pizza and downloading unthinkable smut.

He checked the three internet cafes he knew near the school. He came up empty.

Then he hit the pizza joints, with the same result.

He phoned the school secretary again.

"Hi," he said. "It's me, Dave."

"Dave who?" she said.

"Nothing," he said and hung up.

And because he had no better idea, he got back on the subway and headed for the gallery. He vowed as he went that Sam wouldn't eat pizza again as long as he lived.

When he got there he walked around the block looking for a local pizzeria. There were none. With a heavy heart, he walked through the large front door of the gallery. He checked out the cafeteria. Nothing.

He went to the gift shop. At first the gift shop looked empty too. Dave was about to leave when he suddenly spotted Mark Portnoy—the perennial trouble-maker—alone in the corner. He had his back to Dave. He was holding something in his hands. Dave moved over an aisle to get a better view. As soon as he did, Dave realized what Mark Portnoy was up to. The boy was about to slip whatever he was holding into his backpack.

Dave knew he was going to apprehend the boy. He had a split second to decide whether he should do it before or after the theft. He didn't have time to mull over the repercussions of the two options. Operating on instinct, he gave the boy a break.

"What do you have there, Mark?" he said, stepping around the corner of the aisle.

"I was just looking at it," said Mark.

He was holding a little book. Dave took it from him. *Great Masterpieces of the Western World Daily Affirmation Book.*

They went up to the gallery office together and found a hysterical Mary Turlington.

"He was in the gift shop," said Dave.

"Thank you so much," said Mary. "I just saw your group working on their sheets on the second floor. I wondered where you were. How did you know we needed help?"

"Oh," said Dave, "you know. A father's intuition."

He found Sam and the other four boys in his group sitting in a circle in front of a painting of a woman in a pair of red gypsy pants and no top. They were so busy with the sheet they were filling out that they didn't notice him until he sat down.

Sam looked at him and smiled.

"What took you?" he said.

"Oh," said Dave, "you know . . ."

A chance to redeem himself, Morley had said.

Yeah. Right.

His redemption, such as it was, had come from his

ten-year-old son, and from five boys who had the good sense and maturity, when faced with confusion, to head for the gallery and begin their school assignment.

He was the one who had missed the subway. *He* was the one who had panicked.

Dave heard footsteps and looked, at the same time as Sam, to see Mary Turlington heading towards them.

Sam looked back at his dad and noticed his face drop.

"I was thinking," said Sam, a sly look crossing his face, "maybe on our way back to school we could stop for pizza."

All five boys were staring at him now.

Dave stared at them in disbelief.

"I was just thinking," said Sam, ". . . just in case anyone asks," and he glanced at Mary Turlington, "that, you know, everyone in this group would have much happier memories of the morning if they were remembering things on a full stomach."

The boys started to nod. All of them.

Dave opened his mouth.

He was about to object.

He thought better of it.

He reached for his wallet.

No Tax on Truffles

Morley took Sam to the dentist for a checkup at the end of the first week of school. A busy Thursday afternoon. They blew into the dentist's office five minutes late. Morley had been running late all day. She looked quizzically at Vicki, the receptionist, and pointed towards the doctor's office. Vicki—who was, as usual, on the telephone—shook her head, tucked the receiver under her shoulder and held up ten and then five more fingers. Then she shrugged: *What do you expect?*

Morley headed for the pile of magazines on the table by the door. She flipped past two issues of *Dental Surgery,* a *Chatelaine* and a dog-eared copy of *People,* but she stopped, with a smile of perverted pleasure, when she came to the August edition of *Healthy Guns.* She didn't realize her mistake until she was halfway across the room. *Gums.* Not *Guns.* She returned sheepishly to the pile and traded the *Healthy Gums* for the *People,* then dropped into her regular chair beside the chest of children's toys. She always sat in this chair—so she would be close to Sam.

She flipped open the magazine and settled into a profile of an author who had interviewed people about their dreams about members of the Royal Family. Morley was halfway through a dream involving the

Queen Mother and a pack of feral corgis. "It happened in a Spanish sort of town," explained the British soccer player to whom the dream had been granted. "Sort of like the running of the bulls. Except instead of bulls there were giant feral corgis. And the only one running was the Queen Mum. She was running like hell. And all these Spaniards lining the streets were cheering her on. I *think* they were cheering her. I guess they could have been cheering the dogs."

Morley was considering the implications of this dream when she realized that Sam was not beside her. Or by the aquarium either. Sam had settled into a chair on the other side of the waiting room. He was swinging his legs back and forth as he rummaged through the magazines. Morley watched him choose a magazine and drop the rest back on the table. She squinted at the cover across the waiting room: *Epicure*.

Could be worse, she thought. He could have chosen *Healthy Gums*.

Morley put her own magazine down for a moment and watched her son. She watched him the way any mother would watch her eleven-year-old boy if he had turned his back on a tub of toys for the first time. She looked at him with a mixture of regret and great affection. Eleven years old—and growing up so fast. He had just begun his last year in junior school. A week of grade six under his belt and suddenly he was too sophisticated for the toy box.

Sam hadn't let Morley or Dave walk to school with him all week. On Wednesday morning, Morley couldn't stand it any more. After he left she waited for five minutes and then walked to school by herself. For old times' sake. She met a bunch of neighbourhood moms on the corner and stopped and talked.

On her way home she passed a group of girls from grade seven. With their platform shoes and their make-up, their pierced ears and their halter tops, they all looked about thirty-five years old. Grade six was hard enough. How was Sam going to survive next year when he was in the same class as these Amazon women?

The following Monday, the Monday after the dentist, Morley stayed home. The theatre is closed on Mondays. *Monday wash day. Everybody happy? Well, I should say.* Morley has a cleaning lady who comes on Monday, a woman from El Salvador. When she's there, Morley does laundry, changes beds and pays bills. Monday afternoons she goes to yoga.

On the Monday morning after the first week of school, Morley was in Sam's bedroom changing Sam's bed. When she put her hand down between the mattress and the bed frame to tuck in his blanket, it brushed against something she wasn't expecting. Something that should not have been down there. Something smooth and slippery. Something that felt like a thick, glossy magazine. She pulled her hand out of there so fast she scraped her knuckles.

She stepped back from the bed and closed her eyes. She looked up towards the ceiling. *I don't know where I stand on this, Lord.* Then she sighed and opened her eyes and ran her hand through her hair. Maybe it was time for Dave to have a man-to-man talk with his son. Or maybe—*Please, Lord?*—maybe this was one of those things you were supposed to ignore. Maybe if she ignored this shiny thing, it would go away.

But she wasn't going to ignore it, she knew that. She couldn't ignore it. And before she knew it, she was back beside the bed, reaching down into that dark, tight, secret place between the bed frame and the mattress and pulling the magazine out. It *was* a magazine. She held it up and looked at the cover in trepidation.

It was the July edition of *Epicure*. It was the gourmet magazine Sam had been reading at the dentist's.

Because Morley didn't mention this to anyone—not to Sam and not to Dave—because she decided to let nature take its own course, because she put the magazine back where she had found it and didn't mention it to anyone, Dave found himself flying solo two days later, Wednesday, when Sam unexpectedly arrived at the Vinyl Cafe after school. This is not something Sam ever does. Hardly ever. So Dave suspected something was up. But Sam did not say what it was. He walked self-consciously up and down the aisles. He looked, half-heartedly, at some records. He stared at the customers for a while. And then, after twenty minutes, he said, "I'll see you later," and left as abruptly as he had arrived.

The purpose of the visit didn't become clear until after dinner, when Sam came downstairs and found Dave lying on the couch, reading.

"I need to talk to you," he said. And then he looked around and added, "Alone."

Dave struggled up onto an elbow, looked around the room and nodded.

Sam said, "I'm a little embarrassed about this."

Dave rested his book in his lap. *Unknown Legends of Rock and Roll,* by his friend Richie Unterberger. He was reading Richie's account of Syd Barrett, one of rock's most fascinating cult figures.

Barrett was the founder of Pink Floyd and the spark behind their first, brilliant album. He was gone from the group by the time Dave worked with Pink Floyd. The songwriter, lead guitar player and lead singer unravelled over a three-month period in 1967. Addled and laid almost comatose by massive ingestion of LSD, Barrett would stand onstage for entire concerts playing one note on his guitar, or maybe no notes at all.

The mythic founder of one of rock's biggest-ever groups has lived, Richie wrote, as a virtual recluse in his hometown of Cambridge, England, rumoured to be hideously overweight and almost blind due to complications from diabetes. He recorded two treasured, but erratic, solo albums in 1970. Since then he has virtually disappeared off the face of the earth. He hasn't responded to offers from record companies—offers of hundreds of thousands of pounds to record anything, even *fragments* of songs in his living room, even spoken lyrics. He is the James Dean of rock and roll. The brilliant artist who never fulfilled his potential.

That he, unlike Dean, is still alive—or breathing, anyway—has helped create a powerful mystique that grows by the year.

Upstairs, over the Vinyl Cafe, Dave has a roomful of rock memorabilia. The jewel in the crown is the cassette tape of six songs Barrett wrote and demoed that were deemed too whimsical for that first Pink Floyd album, *The Piper at the Gates of Dawn*. As far as Dave knows, it's the only copy of those songs that exists. Dave got the tape from producer Joe Boyd for safekeeping twenty-seven years ago. He has played it exactly three times. If he wanted to sell it he could get—well, who knows? He could name his price. But he doesn't believe it is his to sell. Boyd gave it to him so it wouldn't get lost.

"Okay," said Dave, moving his finger, which had been marking his place on the page, and turning his book over on the arm of his chair, giving his son his full attention. "I think we're alone."

"I saw a magazine," said Sam. He was fidgeting. He wouldn't look his father in the eye. "I noticed a few things that I'm interested in."

"Uh-huh," said Dave. It seemed like the safest reply.

"What is a musky aroma of motherly bosom?" blurted Sam.

"Uh-oh," said Dave under his breath, Syd Barrett driven completely from his mind.

"What?" asked Sam.

"Just which magazine have you been reading?" asked Dave.

"It is a magazine about . . . it's . . . uh . . . it's about . . . That's one of the things I'm embarrassed about," said Sam.

Now, Lord, thought Dave. *Take me now.*

"It's about eating," said Sam. "It's a food magazine."

"Huh?" said Dave.

"And I read this article about truffles. And it said that a truffle tastes like . . . it says it's one of the most wonderful tastes in the world."

"Thank you, Lord," said Dave.

"And I don't know what a truffle is," said Sam.

"Yes," said Dave.

"What is a truffle?" said Sam.

"Wellllll," said Dave. "I'm not sure I understand *everything* there is to know about truffles. When I was a boy we didn't . . . it's not the sort of thing a boy would talk about with his dad."

Sam was frowning.

"Not that there is anything wrong with truffles," added Dave quickly. "A truffle is a beautiful thing. A truffle is a very special thing. You usually share truffles with someone who is very special to you. When I met your mom, for instance . . . not right away . . . but after I had known her for a while . . . I got *her* a truffle. Actually, to tell the truth, I gave her a box of them. Truffles. And I had never done that for any other girl in my life. Which shows you how special your mom was. And I knew that . . . and so did she."

"But what are they?" asked Sam.

"I'm getting to that," said Dave. "A truffle is like a chocolate."

"But what *is* it?" said Sam.

"I'm telling you what it is," said Dave. "It's a little chocolate . . . like the kind we get at Christmas . . . except they are very expensive and very delicious."

"What does that have to do with the fragrance of a mother's bosom?" asked Sam.

"I'm not sure," said Dave.

"Because I was thinking," said Sam. "After I read about them, I saw a sign at Harmon's that says they're coming."

"They're coming," said Dave.

"Truffles," said Sam. "From France. They're putting them on a plane on Friday. They'll be here Saturday. And I wanted to get one. It says they are the most delicious taste in the world."

"Well, there's nothing wrong with that," said Dave.

"Good," said Sam. "Because I already did it. You have to order in advance. I just wasn't sure if it was . . . like, if I was allowed. I thought maybe you had to be older. Or something."

"Well, most people do wait till they're older to try their first truffle," said Dave. "But I don't see a problem. How are you going to pay for your truffle?"

"With my allowance," said Sam.

"Good," said Dave.

"Good," said Sam.

And then Sam stood up. He was halfway out of the room when he stopped and turned. "I'm glad we had this talk, Dad. I feel a lot better. I feel sort of older."

"Me too," said Dave.

Sam gets five dollars a week allowance. He has never spent a cent of it. He has a bank account, and every time he gets money he puts the money in the bank. He puts his allowance in the bank, and his Christmas money and the money his grandmother sends him on his birthday. It all goes in the bank.

So when Dave told Morley that Sam had gone to the bank and withdrawn twenty-five dollars to pay for truffles from Harmon's, they were both delighted. Delighted that he was finally *spending* some of his money. That was the point, wasn't it? You learned to save, and when you'd saved for a while you bought something you wanted. It didn't matter what it was. It mattered that you learned the process of deferred gratification.

Truffles were a little odd, perhaps. But it didn't matter. It was the process that mattered. Sam had over eight hundred dollars in the bank. It made Dave and Morley uncomfortable. So they were delighted. And as they lay in bed that night, Dave said, "I wonder how many truffles you get for twenty-five dollars? I hope it's more than one."

Thursday at supper, Sam said, "Two more days."

Friday at breakfast he said, "My truffles come tomorrow."

Saturday morning he was up and out the door at nine. "I'm going to get my truffles," he said.

Harmon's is one of those specialty food stores that you visit when you want to indulge yourself. You might go on an auspicious Saturday morning and buy maybe a baguette and some sharp cheddar cheese. Or a small container of black olive paste. Harmon's is compact, elegant, friendly and ridiculously expensive. And each time you go, you wish you had enough money to do all your shopping there. Everything at Harmon's looks better than the stuff they have in your regular grocery store. The carrots at Harmon's look as though they were manufactured in a sterile hydroponic factory in Sweden and have never come in contact with . . . well, earth, for one. Human hands, for another. The potatoes are round and clean and polite. And they have things on the shelves at Harmon's that you have never seen before in your life—tiny red berries that look as though they would be extra sour and really good for your urinary tract; miniature squash and zucchini that seem to have been grown especially for dollhouses; giant cherries the size of tangerines; green beans the length of your arm. And coffee that smells so good it would be a shame to drink it.

And, of course, truffles.

The sign by the cash register said, "Truffles from France. One of the most ecstatic, enchanting edible experiences you'll have in your life. Order now for Saturday delivery."

And here is Sam, coming through the door in his sneakers and jeans and T-shirt. He has locked his bike to the "No Parking" sign out front. Sam is standing in front of the deli counter, where Mr. Harmon is fiddling with a ceramic bowl of grilled mixed peppers. Mr. Harmon, in his white shirt with the sleeves rolled up and his green apron. Mr. Harmon is arranging yellow and green and red peppers that he has grilled gently and mixed with garlic and onions and olives and salt and pepper. The peppers are floating in the ceramic bowl in the finest Italian virgin olive oil.

Sam is standing quietly in front of the counter, watching, waiting to be noticed.

When Mr. Harmon sees him, he leaves the peppers alone and smiles.

Sam says, "Did they come?"

Mr. Harmon nods. "They came this morning. Direct from Orly. A box of jewels."

"Jewels," says Sam, his mouth beginning to water.

"Better than jewels," says Mr. Harmon, leaning forward over the counter and lowering his voice. "Magical powers have been attributed to these things."

Then he says, "Come. You can see for yourself." And he points to the large walk-in cooler at the back of the store.

Sam licked his lips.

He followed Mr. Harmon through the store, past the mysterious fruits and the fresh sticks of bread and the jars of jams and the bottles of caviar. He followed

Mr. Harmon to the back of the store to the walk-in cooler. He waited while Mr. Harmon pulled the big silver door open and stepped back, like a hotel doorman, motioning him in.

As Sam slipped past Mr. Harmon and through the door, he thought to himself, *I will never forget this moment as long as I live*. It was like walking into one of the great pyramids of Egypt.

It took a moment for Sam's eyes to adjust to the cool, dim light. He had a momentary twinge of anxiety when Mr. Harmon stepped into the cooler and pulled the door closed behind him. He shivered and wondered what would happen if they couldn't get the door open again. Then he heard Mr. Harmon calling to him.

"They're over here," said Mr. Harmon.

As Sam stepped around a huge crock of olives and ducked under a large ham hanging from the ceiling, he forgot all about the closed door. *He was walking in a refrigerator*. It was as if he had been made miniature. Like he was walking around in the fridge at home.

He felt light-headed as he watched Mr. Harmon lift a wooden box from a high shelf. The box was the size of the television set in his parents' bedroom. It was covered with a piece of cloth. Mr. Harmon put the box down and removed the cloth. It was full of rice. Mr. Harmon picked up a wooden spoon off the shelf and began to dig in the rice. After a moment he lifted the spoon out of the box and held out a dirty, roundish, brown lump. He was beaming.

"The black diamond of Provence," he said.

He bent over and smelled the dirty lump, and then he pushed the spoon towards Sam and nodded.

Sam looked puzzled.

"Go ahead," said Mr. Harmon. "Smell. It's like a distant field of pineapples."

Sam leaned forward and breathed in. He wrinkled his nose. He wasn't sure what to say.

He looked up at Mr. Harmon. Mr. Harmon was smiling at him.

"What is it?" said Sam finally.

"It's your truffle," said Mr. Harmon, taking a step back.

"But it looks like a . . . a . . . fungus," said Sam.

"It *is* a fungus," said Mr. Harmon.

"But I thought it was made out of chocolate," said Sam.

"Chocolate?" said Mr Harmon. "Where have you been getting your information? The schoolyard? The street corner?"

"My dad," said Sam.

Another man, a more sensitive man, a man less obsessed with food, might have offered to refund Sam's money. The idea never occurred to Mr. Harmon. Not because of avarice. He could easily have sold the truffle two or three times over. And not out of a meanness of spirit. Quite the contrary. Mr. Harmon believed that in Sam he had met his *kindred* spirit. He believed he was doing the boy a favour. Mr. Harmon was completely out of touch with what children *like* to eat.

In his heart of hearts, Mr. Harmon believed that Sam would love the truffle. Needed the truffle.

"Pasta," he whispered, as they stepped out of the freezer. "Slice it as thin as you can. Slice it as thin as paper. Arrange the slices on a dish of pasta . . . and the flavour . . ." His hand flew up to his mouth as he searched for the words. "It's something that cannot be explained. It must be experienced. Ambrosia."

Sam followed Mr. Harmon to the cash register. He reached into his pocket and carefully counted out the money he had withdrawn from the bank: $28.75. He handed it to Mr. Harmon.

"This is too much," said Mr. Harmon. "It is only $25."

"The tax," said Sam, who had worked everything out to the penny.

"No tax," said Mr. Harmon, handing the $3.75 back to Sam. "No tax on truffles."

Sam stood on the sidewalk beside his bike, clutching the brown paper bag Mr. Harmon had handed to him. He was confused. This was not anything like he had imagined. He had imagined he was going to pedal home with a large box of chocolate. Twenty-five dollars' worth of chocolate. He had imagined it would be like Hallowe'en. He had imagined there would be so much chocolate he might have a hard time carrying it on his bike. Which is why he had worn his backpack.

He stood on the sidewalk unsure what he should do next. He had imagined taking the chocolate home, setting it on the kitchen table and allowing everyone, each person in his family—his mother and his father, even his sister—one chocolate each. He felt alone and small and miserable. He felt like crying. He didn't want to cry on the sidewalk in front of Harmon's.

He took off his backpack and dropped the paper bag inside. He got on his bike and pedalled off down the sidewalk, weaving around a man with a dog and past a woman pushing a stroller.

Most of all, he didn't want to look stupid. Especially in front of his parents.

Three blocks later, instead of turning right on the street that would take him home, Sam stood up on his pedals and wheeled left. Five minutes later he was at the IGA standing in front of the pasta display, frowning at the dizzying packages of different-shaped noodles.

He had forty-seven cents left when he walked out of the store. Before he went home, he went to the bank and returned it to his account.

Sam cooked supper that night for the first time ever.

"I don't need any help," he said. "I'll call you when it's ready."

He set the table himself. Everyone got a paper towel as a napkin and a serving of Coca-Cola poured from a glass bottle. Sam believed that it tasted best out of glass bottles.

"Dinner's ready," he said.

They all came into the kitchen.

When they were sitting at their places, Sam carried one covered dish carefully across the kitchen to the table, his bottom lip sucked tightly into his mouth.

He set the dish in front of his mother.

Morley shook her head. "The chef serves," she said.

He moved the dish to the place in front of his own chair and sat down.

Dave said, "What have you cooked us?"

Sam took the cover off the dish.

Stephanie said, "Kraft Dinner."

Sam said, "Kraft Dinner with truffles."

Morley sucked in her breath and looked at Dave, her hand on her mouth. And then she looked quickly over at Stephanie, who hadn't said another thing. And now it was Morley who wanted to cry.

She was watching her son spooning the sticky orange pasta onto the plate his sister was holding patiently in front of him.

Morley knew the next few years would bring challenge and frustration for both her and her son. But, sometimes—often enough, she hoped—there would be moments like these.

All she wanted was to be there. All she wanted was a seat at the table so she could watch the changes unfold.

She realized he was smiling at her.

She picked up her plate and passed it to him. "These are the truffles," he was saying. "They bring out the flavour in the cheese. But you have to try them. It's hard to describe."

Gifted

THE SCHOOL YEAR had hardly begun and Sam, still ten years old (but so close to eleven you could call him that—he did)—Sam, still ten, but *almost* eleven, had already had two major crises. Sam's best friend, Ben, moved over the summer—to Texas.

Before Ben left, he and Sam worked out a plan that would have allowed Ben to stay in Canada. It involved Ben sleeping on a futon in Sam's cupboard.

"He won't be any trouble," said Sam to his mother. "Ben is very quiet. He hardly eats at all. We could do our homework together. We won't talk at night."

But Ben's family left in July, and Ben went with them.

On the first day of school, Sam found himself entering grade six without a best friend. Without a friend in the world, it seemed. Or in his class, at least (which, for the best part of every day, *was* Sam's world).

On the first morning of school, Sam dragged into his new homeroom and chose a seat in an inconspicuous part of the room—not too close to the front and not too close to the back. A seat where he hoped no one would notice him.

As he sat down and looked around the room, Sam felt a dark cloud settle upon him. Anyone who had a remote chance of being a new best friend was in the other grade six. In Mr. Jackson's grade six.

In *this* grade six there was twelve-year-old Greg Hamara, who had already done grade six last year. Greg Hamara, who looked like he should be in high school with his low-slung, baggy jeans, his underwear showing at his waist, his belligerent scowl.

In this grade six there was Bucky Zaharis, whose father drove a BMW. Bucky, who was bigger even than Greg Hamara. In grade five Bucky used to make kids show him their lunchboxes so he could help himself to whatever caught his eye.

And in this grade six there was Ian Morrison, who had bumped into Sam deliberately on his way into class.

Worst of all, there was Mrs. Estabrooks.

The new teacher.

Mrs. Estabrooks was not understanding Sam at all.

On that very first day of school, the very first morning of school, Mrs. Estabrooks gave Sam a detention—for no good reason. For nothing.

He was sitting in his inconspicuous seat minding his own business when Greg Hamara chucked an eraser at Bucky Zaharis. The eraser missed Bucky and bounced off the blackboard. Sam laughed. He wasn't the only one who laughed. But he was the only one laughing when Mrs. Estabrooks turned around. He was the only one who got a detention.

"But I didn't do anything," he said.

Sam had never, ever, in seven years of school, had a detention.

He got his second one before the first week was over. He hadn't done his math homework, due on Friday morning, and Mrs. Estabrooks made him stay behind at the end of the day to do it.

"I didn't know we had math homework," said Sam.

"That's because you were too busy fooling with erasers," said Mrs. Estabrooks.

Sam hated Mrs. Estabrooks.

She made him stay while she corrected his work, and then she told him he was a bright boy. She told him she wasn't going to let him slide away.

"You aren't going to slide away," she said.

"Watch me," muttered Sam under his breath as he left, his backpack bouncing off the door frame.

"I hate school," he said at dinner.

On Thursday of the second week, Sam came home at lunch, and, for the first time in his life, no one was waiting for him. He was used to finding either his father or his mother at home, always. Sam stood in the hall and called but there was no answer. Instead there was a note on the kitchen counter beside a jar of peanut butter and a loaf of bread

He had never made his own lunch before.

He felt grown-up.

He opened the jar of peanut butter. It was brand new, the surface smooth and glistening. He sunk his finger in, right up to the second knuckle, bent it, pulled it out and brought it to his mouth.

Arthur, the dog, sitting at his feet, began to whine.

Sam got another fingerful and held it high in the air above the dog.

Arthur began to twitch, his tail thrashing, his rear end bouncing against the counter.

Sam shook his head and said, "Bad dog," and licked the second lump of peanut butter deliberately off his finger.

Arthur looked so crestfallen that Sam scooped out an even larger fingerful, reached down and smeared it on the floor, like he was finger-painting.

"Here, Arthur," he said. Then he dropped to the floor and watched Arthur lick the peanut butter up.

When he was finished, Arthur looked at Sam and cocked his head. Sam took another lump of peanut butter, a lump the size of a golf ball, and stuck it to the wall about four feet off the ground. He sat and watched Arthur jump and snap.

When Arthur finally dislodged the lump of peanut butter, he carried it in his mouth into the living room and dropped it on the rug.

Sam made himself a sandwich. Honey, mayonnaise, ketchup, peanut butter. He poured himself a glass of milk and stirred chocolate powder into it. He carried the glass of milk and the sandwich to the kitchen table and sat down.

There was a pile of mail lying on the table: a few bills, a *Canadian Geographic* magazine and, on the top of the pile, a large envelope with a clear plastic window. Sam flipped the big envelope over. He read the big red letters printed on the back. They said, "Is your child gifted?"

Sam frowned.

This was something he had never wondered about himself.

Ray Aboud was gifted.

Ray was the only gifted person Sam knew. Ray was in grade four with Sam. Ray was always getting in trouble. He used to push people, and he never did his homework. He was very funny in class.

One day Ray was whisked off during gym. The next week, Ray announced that he had gone for tests and the tests showed he was gifted. And now Ray took a bus to a school for gifted kids.

Sam had never thought about what might go on at the gifted school.

As he stared at the envelope with the red letters, it occurred to him that, whatever it was, it wouldn't involve Mrs. Estabrooks or any of the kids in his stupid class.

He turned the letter over. It wasn't addressed to any member of his family.

Sam opened the envelope.

There was a brochure with pictures of children his age reading books. There was another sealed envelope attached to the back of the brochure. He stared at it carefully.

"Find out if your child is gifted. Give him or her this simple test."

He heard someone coming in the front door.

Sam shoved the test and the brochure in his backpack.

Sam did the test that night, sitting at the desk in his bedroom. His door was closed, his legs were swinging earnestly under his chair and his math homework was spread out beside him in case someone came in.

There were ten questions.

He already knew the answers to three of them.

If you were in a square house, with four walls and four windows, and if you were looking south no matter which window you looked out of, and you looked out one of the windows and you saw a bear, what colour would the bear be?

Sam was smiling as he wrote the answer with his specially sharpened pencil.

White. The bear was white.

The house was at the North Pole.

The next day, after school, he went to the bank and stood in line for twenty-two anxious minutes. He was afraid that his mother might come in and ask what he was doing. When it was finally his turn, he shoved the return envelope with his completed test at the teller and he said, "If I wanted to mail this, how much would I need?"

The teller stared at the envelope and then leaned forward and whispered, "This isn't a post office. It's a bank."

Sam said, "I know. But how much money would I need? To buy a stamp?"

"It's to the States," said the teller. "I don't know."

The teller went away, and Sam stood there, not sure what to do, not sure if the teller was finished with him or not.

Sam looked at the people behind him in line. The man at the front was frowning at him. Sam looked down at his shoes, and then he looked at the teller, who was talking to someone else. Sam thought he'd better go before he got in trouble.

As he started to head out, the teller returned and beckoned him back. He said, "Sixty-five cents. Sixty-five cents to the States."

Sam pushed his bank book at the teller. He had $832 in his account. He chewed his lip.

"Can I have forty-eight cents?" he asked.

He had seventeen cents in his pocket.

The teller handed Sam the coins.

Sam said, "I have never done this before. Do you know where I can buy stamps?"

He checked the mail every day at lunch. Each day he flipped through the pile of envelopes on the kitchen table with his heart pounding. It took three excruciating weeks.

On a Thursday, three weeks after he had mailed his test, he came home and found what he was waiting for—a large envelope with his name on it. It came from the Bright Star Learning Institute in Boulder, Colorado. He opened it in his room. With his door shut.

Dear Sir,

Thank you for your recent inquiry. We at the Bright Star Learning Institute believe nothing is more important to the fabric of society than the academic success of our children. One of our educational consultants has scored your child's results.

Sam's heart was pounding.

We are delighted to inform you that his score makes him eligible for our enriched study program for gifted students.

Sam sighed heavily. He began to nod slowly. He wasn't surprised. But he *was* relieved.

As a successful applicant at the grade six level, we have enrolled your child in our monthly program for accelerated study. Each month your child will receive a workbook designed to challenge and advance his learning.

Sam smiled. This was just what he needed.

We will invoice you a low monthly charge of $6.99 plus shipping and handling. You may cancel at any time.

Sam looked at his bank book lying on his desk. He could afford $6.99 a month. This was, after all, an investment in his future. A surefire ticket away from Mrs. Estabrooks and her class of losers. After a few months of the program, when he was really accelerated, Sam would get the school to give him the same test Ray Aboud had taken.

That night, as he lay in bed, Sam imagined what gifted school would be like. They wouldn't waste time on things like math and social studies. That was for sure. Gifted students like him wouldn't need that. There would probably be trips . . . Sam imagined getting on a gifted bus to go places like the circus. There would be washrooms on the bus. And video screens.

Mrs. Estabrooks would regret the day she was mean to him.

Ben's parents would rue the day they moved away.

The first installment of Sam's self-improvement program arrived two weeks later. It was a thick workbook—156 pages thick. To finish it in twenty-eight days, and read the instructions, Sam would have to complete six pages every night.

That night, after supper, Sam shut his bedroom door and opened the book at "Module One." It was a math module.

He felt exhilarated as he picked up his pencil. He felt special. He felt at the top of his game. He felt . . . gifted.

He stared at the pencil and got up and went downstairs and sharpened it. He came back upstairs and sat down. Then he got up again. He went downstairs again.

"Someone chewed the top of this pencil," he said. "I want an unchewed one."

It took him an hour and a half to complete the six pages.

He was exhausted when he finished. But he was pleased with himself.

He went downstairs and said, "I've finished my homework. I am going to bed now."

Dave and Morley looked at each other, puzzled but delighted.

Before he turned off his light, Sam picked up an essay that had arrived in his package from Colorado. It was about gifted people like him.

He learned that just because you had difficulty in one area didn't mean you weren't gifted in another. He read about Albert Einstein, who, for instance, had faced his own fair share of difficulties, his brilliance notwithstanding. And who was not without certain . . . eccentricities. Sam learned that Albert Einstein hated shoes. Albert Einstein used to wear sandals without socks, or, if he could get away with it, no shoes at all.

Thursday night was Scouts. Morley was late coming home, so they ate after Scouts. That meant Sam didn't have time for his workbook.

On Friday, when Morley said, "We've rented a movie. We're going to order Chinese food," Sam shook his head and said, "I don't have time for a movie. I have homework."

He went to his room and in two hours he got eight pages of his workbook done.

When he got up on Saturday morning Sam did four more pages. He was still four pages behind.

He was exhausted. But he could feel himself getting smarter.

The next Monday was the day Morley got a call from the secretary at Sam's school.

"We were hoping you could bring him a pair of shoes. He didn't wear shoes today."

"I hate shoes," said Sam, when Morley arrived at school.

"Well you have to wear them, sweetheart," said Morley.

"What about socks?" said Sam. "Do I have to wear socks? I hate socks."

That night, Sam stared into the bathroom mirror and decided he didn't look gifted enough. Albert Einstein had a big moustache, wavy hair and deep-set, dark eyes. Albert Einstein wore glasses. Albert Einstein issued theories.

Sam found a pair of scissors and cut random hunks from his hair.

When he was finished, he had a pleasing, hedgehog sort of look.

When Morley saw him she tried to be calm. She said, "What happened to your hair?"

Sam said, "I have a theory about that."

Sam tried to stay awake as late as he could. He lay in his bed with his eyes stretched open. First thing every morning he peered at himself in the bathroom mirror. He wanted to see if the lines under his eyes were darkening.

Then he bought himself a pair of glasses. He bought them at the drugstore after school. Clear plastic rims, like Albert Einstein's. They were the weakest they had: point-five magnification.

He took them to school the following week and put them on with some ceremony when math began.

"My eyes are very weak," he told Mrs. Estabrooks. "The eye doctor thinks I strained them when I was very young. He said I read too many big words before my eyes were ready for big words. My parents didn't know any better."

Things were going better with Mrs. Estabrooks. Sam was getting his homework done. There had been no more detentions. Nothing, however, had changed with the other kids in his class.

He spent his recesses alone. He didn't play soccer or tag. Sometimes he stayed at his desk and read.

When he went outside he would walk rapidly around the schoolyard with a preoccupied frown—as if he were going somewhere. He would weave around the playground as if he were on an errand.

"A strange boy," said the gym teacher, Mr. Lovell, one morning.

"Lonely," said Mrs. Estabrooks.

By the end of the month, when the second workbook arrived, Sam still had eighteen pages left in the old one.

He read the letter to parents with a sinking heart. "Do not let your child fall behind. It is imperative they keep up."

The letter gave a list of strategies to motivate recalcitrant children.

Sam looked up *recalcitrant* in the dictionary.

He made up a new schedule. If he followed it, he would be caught up in two weeks. He folded the schedule and hid it under his mattress.

He didn't go to Scouts that Thursday.

"Too much homework," he said.

"I think I should speak to your teacher," said Morley.

"Don't do that," said Sam. "Don't do that."

Mrs. Estabrooks told him he couldn't stay at his desk at recess.

"You have to go out with the others," she said.

She found him the next day sitting alone under a tree in the corner of the playing field. He had his shoes and socks off.

"I am reading Charles *Die-kens,*" he told her when she sat down beside him.

"Ahh," said Mrs. Estabrooks. "Which one?"

"Hard Times," said Sam.

"Ahh," said Mrs. Estabrooks, nodding sympathetically. "That's a good one. I have always liked Dickens."

Sam nodded.

"You look tired," said Mrs. Estabrooks.

"Really?" said Sam, brightening. "Thank you."

He looked at Mrs. Estabrooks.

"Would you mind if I took my shoes off in class?" he asked. "I seem to work much better in bare feet. When I have shoes on, I seem to be recalcitrant."

Then he yawned.

Greg Hamara and Bucky Zaharis cornered him the next day.

"Hey, Einstein," said Greg. "Want to play tag?"

Sam kept walking.

Bucky Zaharis slapped him on the back. "You're it," he said.

Sam didn't want to have anything to do with any of these kids. He didn't want to be noticed. But he had made himself so noticeable he was becoming an object of ridicule. He was too exhausted to figure out what to do. He wanted to cry.

Murphy arrived at the beginning of the next week. Murphy, from Winnipeg. A small boy for his age who sealed his fate on his first morning in school by striking out three times in a row during a gym class baseball game—with men on base each time.

The next day at recess Sam settled into his spot under his tree at the far end of the playground and began to take off his shoes and socks. When he looked up, there was Murphy peering at him over his glasses.

Sam said, "What?"

Murphy said, "How come you're not playing ball?"

Sam said, "Because I am gifted."

Murphy said, "How do you know?"

Sam said, "Because I was tested."

Murphy said, "I'm gifted too."

Sam said, "Have you taken the test?"

Murphy said, "No."

Sam said, "Then how do you know you're gifted?"

Murphy said, "I can just feel it."

Sam said, "I have a test."

Murphy came home with Sam that day after school. Sam had an extra test that came with the first workbook.

"It says it's for siblings but I don't think it matters," said Sam.

Murphy nodded.

"It costs sixty-five cents for a stamp to the States," said Sam.

Murphy said, "I know."

Sam said, "Do you want to play on the computer?"

Murphy came over again the next afternoon. And again the next one. And then two afternoons the following week.

Sam went to Murphy's house. Twice.

Murphy was making it more and more difficult for Sam to keep up with his workbook. Every night he fell a few more pages behind. When he received the third workbook he was barely a quarter of the way through the second. He was trying so hard, but he was falling further and further behind. He worried that he was getting recalcitrant.

When Murphy got his letter from the Bright Star Learning Institute, he called Sam right away.

"Same as you," he said. "Same letter. Same score. Same everything."

"We need to talk," said Sam. "Bring the letter."

They met in the schoolyard. It was five o'clock. The only other person around was a man hitting tennis balls against the school wall.

They went around the corner to the tree where Sam had been sitting the recess he met Murphy. He didn't sit there much any more. Usually at recess he and Murphy played, or sometimes they just walked around talking.

When they got to the tree, Sam took out his letter and took Murphy's from him. He reached into his pocket and got out a package of matches he had sneaked from home.

Murphy said, "What are you doing?"

Sam lit a match and said, "We are burning these."

Murphy thought he was joking. His jaw dropped when Sam put the match to the first letter.

"What are you doing?" he said again.

"I know what I am doing," said Sam. As the letter flared under the greying sky, he waved it away from his body and let it go, fluttering orange and black bits onto the grass.

"It's better this way," said Sam, inhaling the sweet smoke in the late afternoon.

"It's better no one knows," he said.

"The other kids," said Sam.

"Oh," said Murphy.

"And the teachers and everyone. If they know, they'll send us away, to another school. And I like it here."

"Yeah," said Murphy. "Me too."

Planet Boy

Morley can pinpoint the exact minute when Sam received his first phone call from a girl: Tuesday, October 14, 6:48 p.m.

She was getting ready for book club . . . that's why she knows it was a Tuesday. And she was cutting it close—watching the clock. It could have been 6:47 or it could have been 6:49, but it wasn't 6:50. She was in the car at 6:50—she remembers the clock on the dash. It was 6:50, and that meant she could make it if she was lucky with the lights.

And before that, before 6:50, just as she was about to leave the house, Morley remembers the telephone ringing, remembers hesitating by the back door, conflicted, thinking first that she should get out of there fast, in case it was for her. Then thinking that she should stick around for the same reason—maybe someone was calling because they needed a ride. She remembers standing by the door not knowing whether she should stay or go, as clearly as if it happened yesterday.

"Sam," she said. "Can you get that?"

She remembers watching her son intently, her eyebrows raised. He hadn't answered the phone yet and already she was asking with her eyebrows, *Who is it?*

She remembers Sam picking up the receiver.

She remembers all this so clearly she could testify about every moment with a clear conscience, so help her God.

Sam said, "Hello?" and she stared at him with her eyebrows up. He stared back at her. And that's when she felt it. *Before* he turned away from her. *Before* he started talking in the monosyllables that she was so used to hearing from him herself. *Before* any of that, Morley felt the barometric pressure in the room drop dramatically and she knew, she knew right away. It was as if they were in a plane and the window beside her had blown out—there was a *whoosh.* It was the sound of Sam's childhood being sucked out of the room.

He said, "Yes." He said, "I don't know." He said, "Maybe." He said, "Yes," again. Then he said, "Okay," and hung up without saying goodbye.

Morley said, "Who was that?"

"No one," said Sam, and he walked out of the kitchen, leaving Morley alone by the back door. It was 6:50 on the nose when she got to the car.

It happened again a few weeks later, and then again. And then it began to happen a lot: girls—girls calling her little boy.

It took a while before Morley realized that Sam wasn't getting it. The girls got it. The girls were out there on the far side of the fence, firmly in adolescence. They were reaching over the fence, trying to tug her little boy over it. But Sam, bless his little heart, wasn't getting it at all. He saw the fence, all right. Morley was sure he knew the fence was there (he had seen the film at school every year since grade four). But he was still only interested in throwing things at it, or running a stick along the pickets. The idea of scaling the fence and dropping down onto the other side hadn't even occurred to him. The idea that something was going on over there that he might find interesting had never entered his mind.

And then one Thursday night after supper, Sam said, "There's a dance tomorrow night—at school."

And there it was again—the *whoosh,* the air rushing out of the plane of childhood. Morley felt her stomach drop. The plane was coming down too fast. She'd known this was going to happen one day. But not so soon. She didn't want the flight to end. Not yet.

The dance was supposed to start at seven o'clock.

Dave said, "I'll drive you."

Sam said, "I'm going with Murphy."

Sam's best friend, Murphy. Murphy, the smallest kid in his class, who knows more about movies than any other human being that Dave has ever met. "The Murph," who taught Sam to sleep on his side.

"I figured this out at camp," he explained earnestly the first night he ever slept over. "They had really crappy beds."

He was lying on the top bunk in Sam's bedroom, and Sam immediately began worrying that maybe *they* had really crappy beds too.

"If I lay on my back the mattress curled up on either side of my head. Have you ever seen *King Rat*?"

Sam shook his head. "No," he said, he hadn't. This was before they'd figured out that Sam hadn't seen *any* of the movies Murphy had seen.

"It doesn't matter," said Murphy.

Then he said, "The air you breathe out is heavier than oxygen."

"So?" said Sam.

"If you sleep on your back," said Murphy, "and the mattress is curled up, all the bad air builds up around your head and you can suffocate."

Sam was looking to see if *his* mattress was curled. He couldn't tell, but he didn't think so.

"I was lucky," said Murphy. "I kept waking up just in time. I'd wake up and wave my hand across my face and clear the bad air. That's when I figured out if I slept on my side with my face on the edge of the mattress the bad air would fall over the edge."

"What about the guy on the lower bunk?" said Sam, looking around.

"I *hated* the guy on the lower bunk," said Murphy.

Then, after a moment of silence, Murphy added, "Don't worry, I'm lying on my back."

Sam lay there for a while. "Are you okay?" he said finally.

But there was no answer. Just the slow, rhythmic breathing of Murphy asleep.

"Murph?" said Sam into the darkness.

"Are you asleep?" said Sam again as he rolled over

onto his side, his face carefully lined up with the edge of his mattress, his hands tucked by his chin. Just to be safe.

"I'll drive you both to the dance," said Dave.

"To the corner," said Sam. "Not to the front door."

"Just to the corner," said Dave.

"We have to leave at 6:45 so we won't be late," said Sam.

"On the nose," said Dave.

And so it was that on Friday night, Sam and Murphy, both of them wearing their favourite clothes, arrived at the school dance at seven o'clock on the nose. As Dave drove away, they were standing at the entrance to the gym, side by side—standing there as if they were standing in front of the gates of Heaven. They looked small and confused.

"How come no one else is here?" said Sam.

"Are you sure no one else is here?" said Murphy.

Murphy had taken off his glasses in the car. Without them Murphy was virtually blind. To Sam, the gym looked dark and foreboding, unfamiliar and empty. To Murphy, the gym looked like a blotch of mysterious colours, like a dark impressionistic painting.

"Are you sure this is the gym?" he asked.

It was the gym all right, but it wasn't the gym they knew from gym class. There was a stage at the far end and two huge columns of speakers on either side. There was crepe paper. There was an enormous mirrored ball hanging from the ceiling. And a spotlight. In front of the spotlight there was a revolving disc with a green section, a red section and a yellow section, so the light in the room kept changing.

Murphy squinted. "What's the matter with the lights?" he asked.

"We're too early," said Sam. "Let's go to the corner and come back."

Murphy reached for Sam's elbow. They headed down the gym ramp towards the boys' locker room like two old tailors.

"I thought it started at seven," said Murphy.

They walked to the corner. They went into Snyder's. Murphy bought licorice Nibs and a Vanilla Coke. Sam didn't buy anything. He had exactly $5.25 in his wallet. Five dollars to get into the dance and a quarter in case he needed it for the phone.

When he finished the Nibs, Murphy bought chips. They walked around the block while they shared the chips. Then they walked around again.

They went to Lawlor's and Murphy bought a stick of deodorant. They went into the washroom at Snyder's and opened the deodorant. It was the first time either of them had tried it.

"How do you do this?" said Murphy.

"You put it on where you sweat," said Sam.

Murphy rubbed the bar of deodorant across his forehead and along the back of his neck.

They went back to school. This time they weren't the only ones there.

The first person Sam saw was Andrea Young, their math teacher. Ms. Young is six feet, one inch tall.

Behind her back, her colleagues refer to Ms. Young as *Her Hugeness*. The students in Sam's class call her *Andrea the Giant.*

Ms. Young was standing by the gym door talking to a girl Sam didn't know. Ms. Young was wearing a dark-blue shirt and a crocheted vest and the shortest skirt Sam had ever seen. Sam took one look at Ms. Young's thick thighs and looked away quickly. Her thighs made him nervous. His forehead felt hot and sticky. Perspiration was beading at the back of his neck. He wished he had put on deodorant.

There was something vaguely familiar about the girl Ms. Young was talking to. Sam felt he knew her from somewhere. He watched as the girl touched her lips self-consciously. He thought, *That girl reminds me of Alison Metcalfe*.

Except she was taller than Alison Metcalfe. And her hair was fluffy and Alison's hair wasn't like that. And Alison didn't wear lipstick or earrings. And there was something wrong with this girl's eyes—her eyelashes looked black and spiky.

"Hi, Sam," said the girl.

"Hello . . . Alison?" mumbled Sam.

He suddenly felt that this dance was not a place where he belonged. There were things happening in the gym that he felt he shouldn't be exposed to: girls dancing together in groups, boys circling the periphery of the dance floor like skittish schools of fish, the flashing lights and the music—even his father didn't play music this loud.

Murphy had to yell right into his ear to make himself heard.

"Who was that?" yelled Murphy.

But Sam didn't answer. Sam was staring at Mr. O'Neill. Mr. O'Neill taught them social studies. Mr. O'Neill, who normally wore corduroy pants, a plaid shirt and a woven tie, was leaning against the gym wall. Tonight, Mr. O'Neill was wearing black pants, a black turtleneck and a black leather jacket. His hair was shiny and greased back.

Murphy, who was still squinting at Alison, said, "Who *was* that?"

And still Sam didn't answer. Sam was frozen. The whole thing was too much for him. The music was too loud. The girls too tall. The gym too dark. And the teachers were too weird. Sam felt overwhelmed.

Murphy said, "I am going to ask Emily to dance."

Murphy let go of Sam's arm and Sam watched him walk across the gym. Sam saw Murphy skirt a group of girls standing by the equipment room and realized belatedly what was about to happen.

In his myopic state, Murphy was about to make a terrible blunder.

He was heading towards Patrick Kemble, not Emily Traversy. It was an honest mistake. Patrick wore his hair long and on this night, especially for the dance, Patrick was wearing it in a ponytail—just like Emily. Sam started to move but he was only halfway across the room when he saw Murphy tap Patrick on the shoulder with a flourish, saw Murphy lean forward and whisper something in Patrick's ear. He watched Patrick take a step backwards, watched Patrick wind up, and then Sam was grabbing Murphy and pulling him away as Patrick's fist sailed through the air.

"Come on," said Sam to Murphy.

"He was just joking," Sam yelled over his shoulder to Patrick.

Just at this moment—as Sam was dragging Murphy out of the gym and Patrick Kemble was pointing at them as they went, saying something vaguely menacing to a group of boys hanging around the stage—a girl wearing big hoop earrings, a midriff T-shirt and low-cut jeans was standing on the front stoop of Sam's house. Just as Sam and Murphy disappeared down the ramp that leads out of the gym and into the boys' locker room, the girl, who had been waiting with her hands on her hips for her mother (who had driven her there) to leave, opened her purse and took out a stick of lip gloss—cherry. She ran it over her lips, checked that her mother had really gone, then reached up and rang the bell.

"Hello," said Dave, who answered the door.

"Hello," said the girl. "I'm Emma. Where's Sam? I'm his date."

There are moments in a man's life when something happens that is so unexpected—so beyond the realm of what he has considered might happen—that he must give himself over to the moment and not try to impose his will upon it. Because, under the circumstances, it is likely he will have no will—or none, at any rate, that would serve much purpose.

"Hello, Emma," said Dave, knowing as he spoke the next three words that he was, for all intents and purposes, abandoning his own free will. "Hello, Emma," he said. "I'm Sam's dad."

And that's how it came to pass that, as Sam and Murphy were slipping into the science room, seeking sanctuary from the posse that was seeking them, Dave, with one last forlorn look at the television (he had been watching a bootlegged video of a 1968 Monkees concert shot in Czechoslovakia), was backing his car down the driveway, driving Emma to the dance—trying to make small talk with a girl who wasn't the least bit interested in small talk. Or him.

"He said he would go to the dance with me," said Emma, sitting beside him but staring ahead. "What a loser. I should have asked Aiden."

Dave didn't know what to say to that. He had been completely rocked back on his heels by this child. His only intent was to get her to the dance, and when he got her there, to find his son and instruct him in a few of the rudimentary courtesies of dating.

"That light was yellow," said Emma. "Who taught you how to drive?"

"Sorry," muttered Dave.

"Honestly," said Emma. "Men."

Meanwhile, Sam and Murphy, who had sneaked into the science room and were crouched behind the demonstration table at the front, trying to be as quiet and inconspicuous as two boys on the lam can be, were suddenly aware that they were not the only ones there.

"We're not alone," whispered Murphy.

Sam nodded. "Ssshhhh," he said. "I know. Wait here."

Sam waited himself. Waited and waited until he felt it was safe. Then, ever so slowly, he raised himself up to the height of the tabletop so he could see. He peered into the gloom, across the room, to where Ms. Young and Mr. O'Neill were locked in a passionate embrace.

"Ohmigod," said Sam, dropping back behind the table.

"What?" said Murphy. "What?"

"Ohmigod," whimpered Sam again.

Dave, at that moment, was not fifty yards away, standing at the gym door beside Emma, looking around with the anxious distraction of an animal whose instinct for danger has been alerted.

"What do mean you're leaving?" Emma was saying, her hands on her hips. "You can't leave. I told my mother you would look after me."

Dave shuffled awkwardly, wondering what could possibly come next.

What came next was Sam and Murphy pelting down the hallway. They galloped by so fast that Dave was sure they hadn't noticed him or Emma. Sam and

Murphy—and hot on their heels a pack of other boys Dave didn't know, had never seen before.

Dave, who had arrived at the dance irritated with his son, planning to give him a piece of his mind, misunderstood what was going on. He thought to himself, *They are playing tag*.

He thought this with great fondness because he was remembering the dances he went to at the Community Hall when he was a young boy in Cape Breton. The hall was a two-storey, wood-frame building, with big windows, two ping-pong tables and a wide balcony along the front that overlooked the lake. At the beginning and end of every summer, a band would come from Sydney or Glace Bay for a teen dance. Dave remembered how they pushed the ping-pong tables against the walls and flipped them over so they became big green benches. Remembered the excitement one August when a group arrived from Antigonish in black pants and matching lime-green shirts—the floor packed with girls in wide skirts and ankle socks, boys with their hair slicked down, sucking on SenSens. That was the night Donald McCurdy had taken him to the relative privacy of the men's washroom and taught him how to do the twist.

Mostly he remembered the nights he was too shy to dance. Remembered avoiding the crush of warm bodies, he and his pals running around the edge of the dance floor, along the balcony, across the front lawn, believing they were impressing the girls with how fast they could run, how quickly they could duck and weave.

He once asked Morley about this. "When you were

a kid," he asked, "and you went to a dance, what were you thinking about? What were you hoping would happen?"

"I used to think that the boy of my dreams would appear and ask me to dance and it would be like dancing with a prince," she said. "But as soon as you got to the dance you learned pretty quickly that there were no princes. And that the boys who were there were the same boys from school, and they only liked the slow dances. And when you finally figured that out, it would be time for a slow dance and you would see someone like Jason McDermott walking across the gym.

"Jason sat beside me in math," she said. "And I would start to pray that he wasn't walking towards me. And of course I knew he was, and there was nothing I could do about it. I couldn't say no because, you know, I didn't want to hurt his feelings."

"That was me," said Dave.

"What?" said Morley.

"I was Jason McDermott," said Dave. "I spent years walking across the room while the girls I was walking towards were praying I'd stay put. Or not."

"Or not?" said Morley.

"Or mostly," said Dave, "I didn't cross at all."

And that's why Dave was delighted when Sam ran past him—playing tag. That's why Dave was happy his son was ducking and weaving instead of dancing. Even if it *was* totally inappropriate.

Somehow his son had agreed to come to this dance with a girl who was now, for all intents and purposes,

Dave's date. And he had done this, apparently, without any understanding of what he had done. If Sam was capable of that level of misunderstanding, what were the chances he would have had a successful date? What were the chances he would have navigated the night with grace?

Dave looked down at Emma. She was standing there with her arms crossed. Dave was having enough trouble with her himself.

The moment Dave saw Sam running by, he realized that his son was lost on Planet Boy. He had come to the school intending to give his son a lecture. To teach him a thing or two about girls. He decided to leave him where he was.

And before anything happened to change his mind, there was Emma.

"I'm thirsty," she was saying. "I want a Coke."

The dance ended at eleven. At five past eleven, Emma met Dave where they had agreed to meet—on the bench in front of the principal's office. There were three new girls with her.

"I told them you would drive them too," said Emma.

Dave didn't get home until eleven-thirty. Morley was still up.

"Where are the boys?" she said. "Aren't the boys with you?"

"I thought Murphy's dad was picking them up," said Dave.

"He couldn't find them," said Morley. "He called. I told him not to worry. I said they must have gone with you."

When Dave got back to the school the lights in the gymnasium were still on.

The DJ had left, and most of the mess had been tidied up. The stage had been put away, and the speakers were gone. The only person left was the school janitor, alone at the far end of the gym, mopping the floor. He was wearing earphones. He didn't hear Dave and Dave didn't disturb him.

Dave wasn't really worried about Sam and Murphy. There were two of them. They were good boys. They would look after each other.

As he walked through the school, he started to think about the year he was in grade six. Somehow he drifted to his geography notebook, to a picture of a codfish his mother had helped him draw.

He was so lost in the memory that he almost missed the boys.

They were in the kindergarten.

Dave walked right by it, noticing at some level of his consciousness that the lights were on and thinking that was odd. He stopped and turned, opened the door quietly and peeked in.

There they were, the two of them. They were squatting on the floor. Murphy had his hair in his eyes. Sam was in his faded red Spider-Man sweatshirt. Most of the boys Dave had seen at the dance had been wearing oversized sports jerseys. Sam's sweatshirt was at least a size too small.

Everything finds its level. Sam and Murphy were playing with the Lego.

They didn't notice Dave, so he leaned on the door frame and watched for a moment.

He drank in the wonder of boys.

Big blocks and fire engines. Toy trains and television. Bikes and balls.

They had a tower of Lego as high as he had ever seen.

Dave had his hands in his coat pockets. He was fiddling with something and he didn't know what it was. He pulled it out. It was Emma's cherry-flavoured lip balm—she had given it to him to hold when she started to dance. He pulled the top off and ran it over his lips. It wasn't bad.

One day these guys would get to try it. But not yet.

He could have been angry with them. He could have come on heavy. He could have said, *What do you think you are doing?*

But they looked so happy, what was the point?

Instead he wandered in.

"Hey," he said softly. "The dance is over." Then he squatted down on his heels. "What are you building, anyway?"

"It's a tower," said Murphy, looking at it blearily. "I think," he added.

"It's a pretty tall tower," said Dave. "Can I help?"

AFTERWORD

When I started writing *The Vinyl Cafe* show in 1994, it wasn't my plan to write only about Dave and Morley's family. In the show's pilot—which we recorded in 1989 and which sat on a shelf at the CBC for five years collecting dust—*I* was the record store owner. The conceit was that I would never actually *open* the record store, I would just talk about it a lot—wondering aloud how the store might develop and how I might, for instance, file a record I was about to play.

The idea of recording a live show in a theatre with musicians didn't occur to us until the third season. The way we saw it, the show would happen entirely in a CBC studio, and in our imaginations I would be busy with this make-believe record store.

Well, five years passed before we got to record our first show. And, truth be told, I didn't think much about *The Vinyl Cafe* during those five years. I wrote the book called *Welcome Home,* worked with Peter Gzowski on *Morningside* and continued to teach at Ryerson University. *The Vinyl Cafe* was gathering dust in my imagination, as well as on that shelf at the CBC.

From time to time I would run into Dave Amer, who produced the pilot, and one of us would mention it. *We should really do that show,* one of us would say. And we meant it. But we meant it the way you mean it when you meet someone on the street who has drifted out of your life and you say, *We should really have lunch.* You would *like* it to happen, you *want* it to happen, but in your heart you know it is just as likely *not* to happen.

It was Dave Amer who eventually got Beth Haddon to listen to our demo. Beth held some sort of position of authority at the CBC in those days, and when she heard the demo she commissioned the first thirteen shows (an act of bureaucratic bravery I will never be able to properly repay).

When I heard we were actually going to have to produce something, I thought it was high time I listened to that pilot. Which I did—for the first time ever. And I didn't like it. I thought it sounded coy, and the lie about my being a record store owner (even if only a potential one) made me uncomfortable. I decided that it didn't work. Or if it did, it didn't work for me. That's when I decided I would write about my friend Dave.

At first, I planned to keep his family out of it. Actually, I didn't think about his family at all. Not, that is, until the tenth episode of that first season when I told the story about the skunk living under Dave's porch. Only then, and only because I was now writing about Dave's home, did I realize I could no longer ignore his wife and kids.

I decided I should give them fictitious names.

Sam and Stephanie were easy.

It was Dave's wife I had difficulty naming. Interestingly, her name is the only one people ask me about. People are always asking me how Morley got her name.

Well, at first she wasn't going to be Morley. At first she was going to be Elizabeth. Here's what happened.

It began, as I say, with the skunk story. That story about the skunk in Dave's backyard is actually a true story. But it didn't happen to Dave and Morley. I borrowed that story from another friend of mine. Wholesale thievery, in fact. I lifted the entire ballet with that skunk, in all its glory, from my friend and grafted it onto Dave's life.

The story belonged to a friend whose name, coincidentally, is . . . Dave. *David,* actually. We were having lunch together when David told me the story of how a skunk had moved in under his porch. It was such a great story that I started taking notes. It was *his* story that became the spine of the story called "Skunk" in the book *Stories from the Vinyl Cafe*.

Because it was (my friend) David's story that had called (record store) Dave's *family* into being, I thought, by way of thanking him, I would name (record store) Dave's wife after (my friend) David's wife, who is also a friend of mine. Her name is Elizabeth. And Elizabeth it would have been, except I ran into a roadblock. When I arrived at the CBC studio with the story all written, Dave Amer, by now the producer of *The Vinyl Cafe,* said I couldn't use the name Elizabeth on the radio.

"Why not?" I asked.

"Because," he explained, "everyone thinks *I* am Dave of the record store, and *my* ex-wife's name is Elizabeth, and if you use the name Elizabeth no one is ever going to believe that I'm not Dave."

"But you *are* Dave," I said.

"But I'm not *that* Dave," Dave replied.

We were, at this point, all ready to record the show. We were in the studio and the clock was ticking, and I tried to explain how I had chosen the name Elizabeth because I wanted to say a private thank-you to my other friend David—whose name, incidentally, is David Morley.

"We are not using Elizabeth," said Dave Amer for the second time.

Well, we hemmed and hawed for about fifteen minutes, and I finally said I would phone David Morley and he could tell me his wife Elizabeth's second name or her birth name or her mother's name or something. Anything.

"We will use whatever he has," I said.

So I phoned, and of course there was no answer. I say *of course* because no one *ever* answers the phone when we need them to on *The Vinyl Cafe*.

And that is when Dave Amer, the show's producer, said, "Well, if her name is Elizabeth *Morley,* why don't we call her Morley?"

"Okay," I said.

And that is how Morley got her made-up name.

But, as I said, that was in the tenth episode, and I certainly didn't imagine her and the kids ever becoming front and centre the way they have. If I had, I might have spent more time wondering about their names, and I'm glad I didn't because their names seem perfect to me today. I can't imagine Morley being anything other than Morley. She feels like a Morley. She *is* Morley.

If you look at the first collection of stories *(Stories from the Vinyl Cafe),* you can see how much things have changed. There are eighteen stories in that book and only nine of them are about Dave and Morley. The other nine are about people who, for the most part, we haven't heard from since.

I have no explanation as to why Dave and Morley have taken over the way they have. It is not the sort of thing I think about. Or care to. It is just the way it worked out.

It wasn't my intention to write the biography of these people. The stories in this book are supposed to be fiction. But, of course, there is a lot of truth here.

Take Alf Murphy, for instance, the man whom Dave meets in the graveyard outside of Nairn in the story "Walking Man." The fact is that Dave didn't meet Alf Murphy during his marathon walk through northern Ontario when he was trying to quit smoking. Everything else in the story is more or less the way it happened, but not the bit about Alf. I was the one who met him—maybe twenty years ago, and not while walking through northern Ontario. It was in the small Ontario town of Elora. I was out for a Sunday drive and I ended up walking through a graveyard, and that's where I met him. Although his name wasn't Alf Murphy. That is made up. His real name is long forgotten.

Everything else about the encounter, except for the bit about Elvis Presley, is true. Alf did show me his wife's tombstone. And he did ask me to take a picture of him standing beside *his* grave so he could send it to his sister. In the story I say the sister lived in Saskatchewan. To be totally honest I can't remember where she lived. That's the way it tends to work. Often it's the mundane things you end up inventing. The fiction, as it were, often ends up in the everyday details.

To tell the truth, what is actually true and what is not true is never entirely clear, even to me, because during the process of writing the stories down I do what everyone does when they are telling a good story. I revise. I add and subtract.

It is ultimately the story that you are working for. You want to improve it as you go along, and that is a process that has nothing to do with what did or didn't actually happen.

It has been an interesting voyage, these past ten years, sailing this sea of fiction.

When I talk to groups of people I can be sure that one question will inevitably come up: *Where do the ideas come from?* I think this is because there is always someone in every audience who suspects that the life of a writer might not be a bad one, and if they could only figure out where ideas come from, they could give it a crack themselves—the assumption being that the ideas are the hardest part.

Of course the truth is this: the ideas are the easiest part.

You learn that pretty quickly the first time you sit down with a good idea and try to spin it out into a story. You find out that the idea is easy; it is breathing life into the idea that is hard.

But that doesn't answer the question. Well, here is the answer. Sometimes, as with the skunk story, the ideas come from my friends. Sometimes they come from my experience. Sometimes they come from something someone tells me or something I have read. And sometimes they come from my imagination. Sometimes the stories belong to me, sometimes to others, and I give these stories to Dave and Morley and Sam and Stephanie. But sometimes—and these are the best times of all—the ideas come from the lives of Dave and Morley and Sam and Stephanie, whom I now know so well, and whose lives and ways of looking at the world have become, much to my surprise, so central to my work.

And because they are so central to my work, I invited them to speak for themselves in this book. Which made me realize that, although this book is presented as a work of fiction, sometimes the truth is important, so I wanted to use these final pages to come clean about a few things.

As she says, Stephanie *wasn't* hysterical on the edge of the highway that late-December afternoon when the family ran over whatever it was they ran over on their way to Cape Breton. In the interests of honesty I must confess that that part of the story isn't true. They did hit some small thing on the road, but I embellished what happened. I was really writing about something else. That part of the story belongs to me. I was writing about a time many years ago when *I* was behind the wheel and *I* hit a raccoon. I wrote about it once before in "Pig," which is the first story in *Stories from the Vinyl Cafe*. That time, I wrote that Dave was driving the car. But it wasn't Dave. It was me. And unlike Stephanie (in the story in this book), I didn't stop. And I didn't get hysterical. And I didn't insist on burying it. I guess those are all things I feel I should have done, or wished I had done. Whatever. I kept driving. It has bothered me ever since. Obviously.

And it's just a small point, but the part about *Black like Me* at the end of the story called "Book Club," I made that up too. I don't even know if Morley has read *Black like Me,* although I imagine she has read *To Kill a Mockingbird*. I put in the stuff about *Black like Me* because I read it when I was a teenager, and I still own the same paperback copy with the black-and-white photograph on the cover, and it is a book I still think about, and I was hoping, by mentioning it, I might encourage someone to pick it up.

While I am at it, it wasn't Morley who drove off with the cake on top of the car, that was me. And it wasn't a cake; it was a briefcase. And although all that babysitting confusion really happened to Dave, I did once spike a baby bottle with corn syrup—in fact, I think that's what gave Dave the idea.

But about that duck and the hotel room. This is the last time I am going to say it. That *wasn't* me.

July 17, 2003
Pictou, Nova Scotia